THE STASI
GAME

East Yorkshire-born David Young began his East German-set crime series on a creative writing MA at London's City University when *Stasi Child* – his debut – won the course prize. The novel went on to win the 2016 CWA Historical Dagger, and both it and the 2017 follow-up, *Stasi Wolf*, were longlisted for the Theakston Old Peculier Crime Novel of the Year. His novels have been sold in eleven territories round the world. Before becoming a full-time author, David was a senior journalist with the BBC's international radio and TV newsrooms for more than 25 years. He divides his time – and his writing – between Twickenham in the UK and the Cyclades islands in Greece.

Also by David Young

Stasi Child
Stasi Wolf
Stasi State [previously A Darker State]
Stasi 77
Stasi Winter

THE STASI
GAME
DAVID YOUNG

ZAFFRE

First published in the UK in 2020 by
ZAFFRE
An imprint of Bonnier Books UK
80–81 Wimpole St, London W1G 9RE
Owned by Bonnier Books
Sveavägen 56, Stockholm, Sweden

A CIP catalogue record for this book is
available from the British Library.

ISBN: 978–1–83877–252–9

Also available as an ebook

1 3 5 7 9 10 8 6 4 2

Typeset by IDSUK (Data Connection) Ltd
Printed and bound in Great Britain by Clays Ltd, Elcograf S.p.A.

Zaffre is an imprint of Bonnier Books UK
www.bonnierbooks.co.uk

A huge thank you to all my readers in the UK and beyond.
This book is dedicated to you all.

Introduction

This novel is set in communist East Germany, the German Democratic Republic (*Deutsche Demokratische Republik*, or DDR) in 1982, at a time when the first cracks were starting to appear in the Soviet bloc – thanks to the Solidarity movement in Poland. In December 1981, the Polish prime minister, General Wojciech Jaruzelski, had begun a crackdown against the movement, declaring martial law.

Nevertheless, there was no real inkling at the time that East Germany itself would within nine years cease to exist, and that the hated Berlin Wall – or Anti-Fascist Protection Rampart as it was known in the DDR – would be torn down even sooner.

East Germany has come to be identified with its feared Ministry for State Security (*MfS*), more commonly known as the Stasi, a contraction of its official German name. It was one of the most extensive security networks in the world, where friends reported on friends, neighbours on neighbours and even family members or lovers on each other.

But there was more to East Germany than the Stasi, many things that are still mourned by its former citizens. The sense of community, excellent childcare facilities, and one of the highest standards of living in the Eastern Bloc. What always rankled though, even for those who didn't fall foul of the Stasi, was the lack of freedom – particularly freedom to travel to the west (unless, of course, you were a pensioner).

Criminal investigations were generally the preserve of the People's Police (*Volkspolizei*) and in particular its CID division (the *Kriminalpolizei* – *Kripo* or *K* for short), but those with significant political overtones could be taken over by the Stasi. Former detectives who served with the People's Police have always insisted to me that they operated like regular policemen, 'just like at your Scotland Yard', and had little or nothing to do with the Stasi (even though many People's Police officers were unofficial Stasi informants). But many DDR citizens regarded the *Volkspolizei* and the Stasi as being little different at their core – both were organs of the state.

For the sake of authenticity, I've retained the German ranks for the police, which followed military lines. My main character, Karin Müller, has in this book been reduced in rank to *Hauptmann*, or captain. For other ranks and an explanation of occasional German words in the text, please see the Glossary at the back of the book.

As things stand, this is likely to be the last story of the series. It's a separate case, and so can be read and enjoyed without having read the previous books in the series.

DY, July 2020

Prologue

Bastei, Bezirk Dresden, East Germany
March 1982

She decided to approach the rendezvous point from the high sandstone plateau above the Elbe Valley, instead of climbing up from the spa town of Rathen – the usual route. It felt more like a dull November day than the start of spring, an incessant drizzle falling through the mist, with visibility reduced to a hundred metres or so. She knew the magnificent vista of the Elbe was there somewhere, snaking past Rathen itself and the other spa towns on its banks, but for now it was hidden by the greyness. The only shapes in that grey screen were those of trees, looming like featureless giants – as though they had come to watch what transpired.

Hauptmann Karin Müller hunched down into her People's Police overcoat, trying to protect herself as well as she could. The only sounds were her own footsteps on the track and the doleful drips of water from the tree canopy. She felt a frisson of fear, but then she always did when she was meeting agents of this particular Ministry of the Republic.

The Ministry for State Security.

The Stasi.

One of the most feared secret services in the world. And probably one of the most effective.

As a captain with the People's Police crime division, she and the Stasi men should be on the same side, fighting to defend the socialist Republic of Workers and Peasants. The smaller half of Germany. The half where making more money than your neighbour wasn't the be all and end all of life. But too often she found that the organisation's covert, underhand methods went right against the grain of regular police work. If the Stasi wasn't her actual opponent, why did it so often seem to be? Was it something in her own character, her own way of doing things? Had she become a rebel almost involuntarily, even though she worked for an organ of the state? If so, her position was even more precarious than she'd realised.

All of a sudden, emerging from the gloom, were shapes other than trees. What looked like a restaurant, a union holiday home perhaps, the trappings of the Republic's tourist infrastructure. They still appeared to be closed for winter. The only sounds remained constant: the drum beat of her own police boots, and the accompanying percussion of water drips – this time from the concrete buildings.

She checked her map, open at its page inside a cellophane wrapper to keep out the damp. According to this, just a few metres to go. Yet still she could see little through the mist.

Then – in an instant, as she reached the edge of the high plateau – the veil lifted. Here, the view was other-worldly, heart-stopping. She imagined this might be what it would be like to suddenly land on another planet. More gnarled, giant figures, but here hewn and weathered by nature from rock rather than grown from seed. Far below, the snaking waters of the Elbe. Between the two – the valley and plateau – swirled up columns of mist, dancing to their own silent tune and adding to the ethereal feel.

She saw him then. The man she was supposed to meet. Stasi *Oberstleutnant* Klaus Jäger. Jäger the Hunter. Yet when he'd contacted her asking for this meeting, his voice had held an unusual haunted tone, almost that of a frightened man. Like her, in the past few years he'd had to suffer the ignominy of a demotion of rank. But he was still a powerful man. Though at this moment it looked as though nature could overpower him in an instant, silhouetted as he was on the crenelated viaduct, spanning the sheer drop to the Elbe Valley below.

It took Müller a few minutes to reach him, winding down a circuitous path. Then she began the walk across the bridge itself. She knew it was him from his familiar haircut – the one that looked like that newsreader on the BRD's nightly bulletin. A few years ago, in the early 1970s, that cut of shoulder-length, sandy-brown hair had been the height of fashion. Now it was distinctly passé, as – perhaps – was Jäger himself.

Only when she got nearer, and the man turned – no doubt hearing her footsteps echoing against the valley walls below – did she realise something was wrong. Very wrong.

This wasn't Jäger. Just someone dressed exactly like him, probably wearing a wig from the Stasi's disguise box. Instinctively, she began to reach to her shoulder holster.

'Freeze!' shouted the man, drawing his own handgun. A Makarov. She was close enough to recognise it. So even though it wasn't Jäger, he almost certainly *was* a Stasi agent. 'Put your hands above your head, Comrade Müller.'

She did as she was told, but at the same time glanced round to see if there was an escape route, back along the way she'd just come.

There wasn't. Another man was blocking the other end of the bridge. And he too held a raised gun.

But this was someone she *did* recognise. The English businessman from the Interhotel in Dresden. Only clearly, he wasn't a businessman at all.

Finally, the penny dropped.

She'd just walked into a trap.

She was in its jaws – both sides determined to stop her solving this case.

But there remained one important question to which she didn't know the answer.

Was she the bait?

Or the prey?

1

Dresden, East Germany
February 1982

Dawn had cracked, the sun edging above the skyline, suffusing the scene with a fierce orange glow. Those citizens who had already roused themselves to start their early shifts, those who were old enough to remember that day thirty-seven years earlier, they would be shivering. Not from the winter cold, but from a terrible knotted fear deep in their souls provoked by that amber sky, something they would live with for the rest of their lives.

The firestorm. When it seemed like the whole city was ablaze.

The silhouetted skyline still had its half-destroyed Baroque ruins, buildings erected when the kings here pranced around on gilded horses, marrying off their sons and daughters so they could seize control not just of Saxony, but of swathes of neighbouring Poland too. When the city's glories were said to match those of Paris, Vienna, and Venice.

Then the Anglo-American bombers came, wreaking a terrible vengeance not just on Nazi Germany, but on all Germans, even those who'd already lost everything, driven from their homes further east by the relentless, ruthless advance of the liberating forces of the Red Army. Even on those who'd already come to see what Hitler really was – a megalomaniac bent on taking his country down with him.

They didn't need to descend to Hell. The fires of hell rained down on them instead, turning the cellars where they sheltered into furnaces, sending a vicious superheated wind snaking through the underground tunnels, through the streets, consuming everything in its path, except a few rumps of stone façade.

The city would bear its terrible scars for ever more.

By the time *Hauptmann* Karin Müller reached the scene, the fiery orange had mellowed into a wan gold, and daylight was nearly upon them. She was fascinated by another grotesque silhouette right in front of her eyes. Not that of Dresden's skyline; this was an arm, waving helplessly, but statically, like a snapshot of a drowning man at sea. Yet the sea his body was encased in was solid, and it was patently obvious he was beyond rescue.

Three workmen, supervised by uniformed People's Police officers, were attempting to break up the ground around the outstretched arm with hydraulic jackhammers. You could see their bodies shaking as they tried to keep the machines on target, and the vibrations and hammering set Müller's teeth on edge.

'You're sure it's more than just the arm?' she asked the uniformed captain nearest the entombed body part. There was a note of pathetic hope in her question, as though someone might have simply planted a severed limb there, though the thought of that was bad enough.

The officer knelt down and brushed some of the loosened concrete aside. She could now see locks of dark hair, matted with the newly dried concrete of the building site. Beneath them, the dome of a skull.

'I'm sure, Comrade *Hauptmann*,' the man replied, looking up at her with a thin smile. 'The builders had already managed to break away some of the new concrete around the arm. That's why they called us.'

'Have you secured the scene, Comrade?' asked Müller.

The captain gestured with his eyes. Müller followed his glance and could see a couple of *Vopos* marking out the perimeter of the incident site with red and white police tape. Beyond that, in the shadows of one of the half-finished apartment blocks of the Neu-Gorbitz district of Dresden, there was a group of what Müller at first took to be onlookers. They were dressed more casually than the detectives, with leather jackets *de rigueur* rather than winter overcoats. They could have been shift workers interrupting the walk to their factories to gawp. The giveaway was their studied, theatrical indifference. They *wanted* to appear like factory workers, but Müller knew they were not. She felt that familiar tingle in the back of the neck as her body hairs stood on end. They were almost certainly agents of the Ministry for State Security.

Concrete Man – and from what had been uncovered of the body so far it did indeed appear to be male – seemed to have attracted wider interest than simply that of her branch of the People's Police, the *Kriminalpolizei* or *Kripo*.

She was distracted, and strangely relieved, by another arrival – or rather, another two arrivals. Her forensic officer,

Kriminaltechniker Jonas Schmidt, heralded as always by the pungent smell of his *wurst*-breath, panted out as though he was in pain, and her deputy, *Oberleutnant* Werner Tilsner.

All three had been in disgrace for nigh on a couple of years now, but the one concession from their boss, *Oberst* Reiniger, after a case in which they'd shouldered the blame for the escape of a couple of *Republikflüchtlinge*, was that they could stay together as a team. Rather than the grand title they had before – the 'Serious Crime Department' – they were now simply a floating murder squad, sent wherever, and whenever, particular regions of the Republic were understaffed.

She watched Tilsner hold his hands over his ears and grimace, trying to shut out the machine-gun hammer of the pneumatic drills. His face was pale – perhaps the sound was too close a reminder of actual automatic weapons, the memories of what she knew he'd witnessed and taken part in as a teenager during the war.

'You've already clocked our spectators, I expect,' Tilsner shouted into her ear above the din.

She glanced towards the group of what they both assumed were Stasi officers, and nodded. Although for Tilsner, given his own close association with the *MfS*, perhaps it was less an assumption and more him recognising his colleagues from 'the Firm'.

'What shall I be getting on with, Comrade *Hauptmann*?' asked Schmidt, the words uttered in a slightly staccato fashion, like the ubiquitous noise of the hammer drills. He was still out of breath from rushing to the site. 'I don't want to be treading on the toes of the local team.'

'Don't worry about that, Jonas. I'll talk to them. To start with, get as many photographs from as many angles as you can. We need to try to establish whether he slipped into the new concrete by accident, which seems unlikely, or whether it was something more sinister.'

The uniformed captain overseeing the extraction of the body from the concrete base must have heard the exchange during a pause in drilling, because now he was beckoning her over.

'There's your answer, Comrade *Hauptmann*,' he said, pointing at the skull of Concrete Man, which had now been exposed even further. Müller knelt amongst the dust and rubble to get a closer look. The uniformed officer waved his finger from side to side, a few millimetres above the man's cranium. The hair there was not just matted by dried cement, but by something dark and congealed that looked a little like burnt oil. Both police officers knew what it really was – dried blood. 'He's suffered some sort of blow to the back of the head. And in that position, it doesn't look like it was just some drunk falling over legless. It looks like someone's attacked him, from behind.'

Müller raised her eyes from the victim's skull, towards the group of leather-jackets chatting and laughing by the entrance to the neighbouring newly erected concrete high-rise. What this site would also become in a few weeks' time, once Concrete Man had been extracted from his cement grave. One of the Stasi men caught her eye, smirked and shrugged.

The manner in which the victim had met his end was probably no surprise to that little group. The fact that they had gathered here so soon – apparently to oversee the police operation – indicated they already knew not just of the man's demise, but probably how it came to pass too. In fact, it wouldn't be a surprise to Müller if one of their number had directly, or indirectly, delivered the final blow.

2

Oberhof, Bezirk Suhl, East Germany
January 1982

Snowdrifts several metres high, and bitter cold – Müller had experienced all this before some three years earlier on Rügen, during the case that had seen her demoted. But this time, despite the freezing weather, her heart was suffused with a warm glow as she watched Johannes and Jannika ski in front of her with neat parallel turns. They'd been staying with their adoptive grandmother, Rosamund, partly because of Müller's new role as firefighting murder squad leader – called off to different parts of the Republic at a moment's notice. But the main reason was a sadder one: Helga's unexpected stroke. The twin's natural great-grandmother – who they still called Oma and who was young enough to pass for their real gran – had been their main carer for several years in Berlin while different criminal cases took Müller herself away from the capital. Now that arrangement was at an end, and Rosamund had stepped up to help, for which Müller was eternally grateful, given their sometimes frosty relationship. Helga had returned to her own flat in Leipzig to be amongst friends. The outward effects of the stroke were now barely visible, but she still confused words, and had much less energy than before.

Energy was something the twins –especially Johannes – had in abundance. Heart in mouth, Müller watched as her son ducked into a *schuss*, ski poles raised at his sides, and headed for one of the smaller jumps formed from snow at the side of the piste. He was going too fast, surely? But he took the jump like an expert, then slid to a halt, his skis perfectly parallel. Not yet six years old, but already looking like a future expert. Not to be outdone, Jannika followed, though Müller's daughter put in a few more turns before she ducked down and arrowed her skis straight ahead towards the mound of snow. She'd taken the jump slightly slower, but Müller noticed the trademark push just before the top of the mound, so that actually her daughter was airborne for longer. Like her brother she landed perfectly, then slid to a halt, as though it was nothing out of the ordinary for a child under six. Müller didn't want to be outdone. She started from even higher than Johannes had done, racing down in her crouch, reminding herself of when she'd jumped for real as a schoolgirl – before her fear of heights had kicked in. That, and the fact that there were no official ski jump competitions for women, had shattered her dreams of becoming a winter sports star. She took the jump well, but on landing nearly lost her balance.

'You need more practise, Mutti!' shouted Johannes. 'We're better than you now,' he added, cheekily.

Müller felt a flush of embarrassment. She'd been shown up by her five-year-old twins.

When they got back to the kitchen of the Bergpension Hanneli, her adoptive family's small bed and breakfast hotel, there was a stranger sitting at the kitchen table alongside her adoptive mother.

'Did you have a good ski?' asked Rosamund, the woman who Müller had believed was her natural parent until just a few years earlier.

'It was great, Oma,' said Jannika, before Müller herself could say anything. 'Johannes and I both did the jump, but Mutti nearly fell over when she tried.'

Rosamund looked at Müller in apparent surprise, and the man sitting next to her laughed. Müller felt strangely defensive.

'I'm out of practice.'

'You certainly are if you nearly fell over on the Fallbachhang. It's not exactly Mount Everest.' She turned to the man next to her. He was middle-aged, with the leathery, weathered tan of a ski instructor. 'Have you met Herr Mayer before, Karin? He's the ski trainer for the younger children at the Internat – the sports boarding school, here in Oberhof.'

The man got up from his chair and stretched his hand towards Müller. She tried to match his firm grip and smiled. 'Pleased to meet you.'

'I'm delighted to meet you, too, Frau Müller.'

Frau Müller. It had an odd ring. Very few people called her that. At work, it was just 'Karin' or 'boss' from Tilsner, and

'Comrade *Hauptmann*' from Schmidt. The irony of calling his female colleague 'head man' always seemed to be lost on her forensic scientist in his desire to be completely formal and correct.

'Wolfgang already knows the twins,' said Rosamund. 'Where are your manners, Johannes and Jannika?'

Jannika smiled sweetly at the man. 'Good afternoon, Herr Mayer.'

Mayer returned her greeting with a bow. 'Good afternoon, Fräulein Müller.'

Johannes, for his part, played the grown man, extending his hand.

'Herr Mayer.'

'*Herr* Müller. Lovely to see you again. Did you and your sister put into practice any of the tips I gave you?'

'For the jumps? Yes. We did them really well. Didn't we, Mutti?'

'Very well,' said Müller. She couldn't really disagree, given her own performance had been so woeful.

The five of them sat round the table, then Rosamund got up and busied herself at the stove. 'Will you have another coffee, Wolfgang?'

Herr Mayer and Müller both opted for coffees, while the twins whined that they wanted hot chocolate. As Rosamund Müller prepared the drinks, she began to explain the reason for Herr Mayer's visit.

'He thinks both the twins have potential in winter sports, so he wants to take them under his wing and train them.'

'That's correct,' added the man. 'But would it be better to have this conversation out of the hearing of the little ones?'

Rosamund nodded. 'Jannika, Johannes. Can you go into the playroom, please? The adults need to talk.'

'About us?' asked Jannika.

'Never mind, you nosey little miss,' said Rosamund, tapping the girl's nose lightly with her finger. 'Just run along and play.' Johannes had already escaped to the playroom, needing no excuse or encouragement, and his sister was now quick to join him.

Once the children were safely out of earshot, and the three of them had their coffees, Müller began to question the man, and her adoptive mother, about what their proposal entailed.

'It's just an idea I had after talking with Wolfgang,' said Rosamund. 'I was obviously happy to look after the twins for as long as I possibly could after Helga's health problems. But I suppose I didn't realise that, really, she wouldn't be getting better. And you're not in a position to give them the support they need because of your work, not to mention the fact that you're away from Berlin so much.'

Müller found herself bristling at the implied criticism.

'So we think we may have found a solution to help both you and me,' continued her adoptive mother.

'That's right,' added the man. 'You were probably surprised how good they were on their skis just now.'

'Well I was certainly impressed,' said Müller. Then she smiled. 'I'm not sure about surprised. It's probably in the genes. But yes, considering their age, they seem to be very good.'

'Not just very good,' replied Mayer. 'I believe they are exceptional talents. With the right nurturing, who knows what they could achieve when they're teenagers and adults. Which is where I come in.'

'How so?' asked Müller.

'I want to offer them special scholarship training places at the school.'

'The school?'

'Kinder and Jugendsportschule Rosa-Luxemburg – here in Oberhof.'

'Aren't they a little young?' Müller was wary. They might love skiing now, but what if they came to hate it, as she had in the end with ski-jumping? As for mapping out their life at less than six years old, it seemed ludicrous.

'They love their skiing, though, you've got to admit that,' said Rosamund. 'Since they've been living with me, it's all they ever want to do. And this provides a solution.'

'A solution?'

'Your mother—'

'*Adoptive* mother.' Müller wasn't sure why she corrected the man. Perhaps he'd just rubbed her up the wrong way. Rosamund and he seemed to have hatched some plan, and were only now inviting Müller – who was the twins' mother, after all – to give her thoughts on the matter. She saw that Rosamund looked hurt, laid her hand on hers, and mouthed a 'sorry'.

'Well, yes . . .' stumbled the man. 'Anyway, I think Frau Müller – fit and active though she is, of course – has been finding things all too much.'

'Is that true, Mutti? You've never mentioned it to me.'

'Well, I didn't like to bother you, dear. And I know you've had enough on your plate, what with Helga, and the work... complications.' She meant Müller's demotion from *Major* to *Hauptmann* and the incumbent dismantling of the Serious Crimes Department. But she was too polite to spell it out. It appeared she'd also been too polite to alert her daughter that it was all getting too much. 'But they're both so full of energy. It wouldn't be so bad if Sara could help, but she's got her hands full with her own little ones, and to be honest, I feel bad I can't help out there.' Sara was Müller's adoptive sister – Rosamund's natural daughter. Married to the local butcher, Roland, with a toddler and baby girl.

'Anyway.' Herr Mayer cleared his throat. 'The whys and wherefores aren't that important. What is important is that the Republic has been trying to identify future sports stars as early as possible. Jannika and Johannes were recommended through their kindergarten ski instructor. The long and short of it is, we'd like to offer them a place at the school. As you can imagine, such places are extremely coveted.'

'It's a great honour,' gushed Rosamund, looking slightly flushed.

'But I thought it was a boarding school?' said Müller. 'Do you have day pupils?'

'Ah, no, sorry. You misunderstand. You're quite right, it *is* a boarding school.'

'Well, that's ridiculous,' said Müller, aware she was shouting. She lowered her voice, not wanting the children to hear. 'They're just kindergarten kids.'

'Well, yes,' said Herr Mayer. 'This is specifically a new programme for gifted youngsters. It's a great honour.'

Müller looked at Rosamund in horror. Did she really want her grandchildren to be sent away to school, aged barely six?

'They'd still be able to come home most weekends, darling,' soothed the older woman.

Müller thought back to the last time she'd seen Oberhof children taken away against their will. Back when she was just five years old, and her childhood friend – another Johannes – and his family had had their guesthouse confiscated and been sent away from the town as part of a forced nationalisation programme by the socialist authorities. The trouble was, in her heart she knew her Johannes and his sister would probably be thrilled by the idea.

'Thank you for your kind offer, Herr Mayer,' said Müller, finally. 'My inclination is to say no . . .' She heard Rosamund about to interject. 'But first I want to talk it over with my mother, and then I'll let you know my decision.'

'Of course, Frau Müller,' the man said, rising to his feet. He gave a slight bow towards her adoptive mother, who blushed like a schoolgirl in return.

'Thank you so much for coming round specially, Wolfgang,' said Rosamund. 'As Karin says, we will give it serious thought and let you know. Won't we, Karin?'

Müller nodded. But she knew she had a sour expression on her face. This was something she really didn't want.

On the drive back to Dresden, Müller found herself regularly having to wipe the moisture away from her eyes. It was hard enough leaving the children behind now, knowing they were safely with Rosamund and her adoptive family, knowing they were being cared for. How much harder would it be if she agreed to Herr Mayer's plan to hot-house them at the sports boarding school? The thought was almost too much to bear. And yet . . . And yet here she was, driving more than 250 kilometres away from them. Leaving them behind again for the sake of her work. What sort of a mother was she?

When she finally arrived back at the police apartment she shared with Tilsner and Schmidt, she was exhausted and depressed. Thankfully, Schmidt had gone out to meet with his own family visiting from Berlin.

'You look completely done in,' said Tilsner. 'I thought it was supposed to be a weekend's rest back in the bosom of the family.'

'I don't want to talk about it,' countered Müller. How had she allowed her life to become such a mess?

'Is there anything I can do?' asked her deputy.

She looked at him. Into his ice-blue eyes. The ones she'd found so attractive when they'd both been so much younger, starting out with her as the new head of the Mitte Murder Commission, in the centre of the Hauptstadt, and he as her number two. That first time they'd ended up in bed together after downing too much vodka in the bar in Dircksenstraße. The night that had preceded the start of the graveyard girl case. Life here in Dresden – their latest emergency posting, covering staff shortages in the local *Kriminalpolizei* – had been so much more mundane. Nary a murder worth speaking of, but an endless round of missing people – who often turned out to be *Republikflüchtlinge*, or would-be escapers from the Republic – suspicious deaths which weren't that suspicious, and a few domestics that had escalated too far, usually thanks to citizens' prodigious consumption of various forms of alcohol.

'There is something you can do, yes,' she said.

She grabbed him by his belt buckle and dragged him to her bedroom. He wasn't exactly unwilling. She just wanted to use him. Use him to hammer away the hurt of leaving her children behind. He seemed happy enough to play the role. Lovemaking? No, that was too high a concept for this.

This was just sex. Sex used as an emotional anaesthetic.

3

ARNIE

Bad Schandau, Germany
Summer 1938

I've never really understood my father. He's always been a bit stand-offish with me. In fact, I sometimes wonder if I might have been adopted. The worst times are meal times. There is so much silence and formality, shouting at me if I hold my knife or fork in the wrong way, or – even more unforgiveable – if I talk with my mouth full.

Sometimes, at home, I'll go round to my friend's parents' house and knock on their door, asking if Cliff's at home even when I know he isn't, just so they'll invite me in for a cup of tea or a squash or something. Cliff's mum's Scottish and a real gossip so it's a chance to catch up on what all the neighbours are up to. She seems to know everything. She's fun. His dad's very friendly too. It's somewhere I can relax without getting told off all the time, or worse than that, getting slippered. But you should hear what my father says about Cliff's dad behind his back. He's always saying things like 'he's never made anything of himself' just because he's a salesman for Reckitts, whereas my father runs the family building firm.

My mum's OK. She doesn't like Father doing that anyway, the slippering that is (and it flipping hurts, I can tell you), but she won't stand up to him when he's in one of his moods. I think she's a bit in awe of him – either that or frightened of him – or a bit of both.

I'm not saying my father's a monster. He's not. I suppose it's just because he had a very formal upbringing too. I mean, my grandpa is even more frightening. Always quoting these odd phrases from Shakespeare at every turn. To me, it's silly language and means nothing, but you can tell he thinks he's very clever and it's all terribly profound. When I was a young boy he'd always be pressing this penknife blade against my thumb or finger, rasping at me: 'What's this, boy? It's a *blunt* knife, that's what it is.' I never really understood the point of that. Was I supposed to be frightened? And why the odd emphasis on the word *blunt*? I think he's a bit mental. Him and Father are always arguing, usually about the business.

Look, I know there are boys worse off than me. I know I don't have a bad life. 'You're lucky you don't live in one of those slums,' my father will say when we're driving past Hessle Road. He's right, of course. There's talk of sending me off to boarding school soon. I don't want to go. However bad it is at home, I don't want that.

So why am I thinking about this when we're on the family holiday? It's because of the atmosphere in this train compartment.

Mum just wanted to go to Scarborough to be near to Nana, who's in Brid, just down the coast. But for some reason, Father insisted we were going to Germany. The ferry was quite fun. They even gave me some pocket money to buy sweets from the shop, and allowed me to go off on my own. I was standing at the railings, minding my own business, letting the spray hit my face, when one of the ship's officers asked what I was doing there on my own. He said it was no place for a young boy, asked me my cabin number and then escorted me back there. When Father finally answered the door, he looked really angry and red in the face. He and Mum were only half dressed, as though they'd been having a sleep.

That earned me another slippering. Mum was angry too and this time didn't try to stop him. I thought I might get away with it on holiday, but he brought the slipper with him specially! God, my arse stung. It's been bloody uncomfortable sitting on these train seats as station after station passes by. We seem to be going to the furthest point in Germany possible.

It wouldn't matter if Father wasn't so strong. But that's why we're going to this place. He likes climbing rocks, so his forearms are huge. Mum says me and him are chalk and cheese. I'm more interested in all the trains and things, and the different cars they have over here.

The only time Father and I seem to get on OK is when he's explaining history or politics to me. I'm interested in that sort of thing, and he is too. He was trying to explain to me what's happening in Germany now. Someone called Hitler's in charge. Not everyone's sure that's a good thing. Dad says there's good discipline here in Germany. *They don't suffer fools gladly.* That's his favourite phrase. I'm a bit scared though. I've never really understood why he didn't fight in the Great War, like lots of my friends' dads did. But I don't blame him. The Great War sounded like a terrible time. And Germany started it. The Germans seem like bad people to me. I don't know why we're paying good money to visit their country. Well, I do really. It's so he can attempt to climb something called 'The Devil's Tower'. He's been going on and on about it, as though I should be interested. He keeps on showing me photos – how the valley side of this bit of rock has never been climbed unaided before, and he's going to do it. I can tell Mum thinks he's mad, and is a bit frightened by it all. To me, it all looks pointless. Why would someone want to risk their life to get to the top of a piece of rock that looks like a man's willy?

Just outside our hotel, though, there is something that interests me. It looks like a giant skeleton on stilts, wearing a strange foreign pointy hat. A bit like the pictures of the Tin Man in that American book some distant relative got for me one Christmas.

'What is it, Mum?' I ask after we get out of the taxi which collects us from the station.

She looks it up in her guide book.

'It's just a cliff lift. Like the ones in Scarborough.'

'Wow! It looks more exciting than that. Can we go up it?'

Mum looks over at Dad. 'Perhaps later. It's been a long journey. Your mother and I want to have a bath first, and then we'll go for a walk and something to eat. You need a bath too, Arnold.'

The hotel looks posher than the bed and breakfasts in Scarborough. My mother and father's room has a balcony looking over the big river, the Elbe. I open the doors and stand outside, taking in the view. What looks like the village green one way, the river the other. Then I'm hoiked away by my father. The owner wants to show us my room too. We climb another two flights of stairs.

'Will he be all right so far away from us?' my mum asks.

'He'll be fine. He's a growing lad. Too big to share his parents' room now.'

I'm hoping I'll get a balcony too, but I'm disappointed to see my small single room is in the attic. Mother and Father tell the owner the room is fine – I think so anyway, Father is speaking in German so I don't really understand. I want to say *No, it's not fine, it's small, poky and too hot*. Mum looks worried.

'Will you be all right here on your own, Arnold?'

Dad ruffles my hair. 'Of course he will. It's exciting, isn't it, Arnold? I'd have loved to have had a room of my own at your age.'

I give a feeble smile and nod.

'Yes, thanks. It's nice,' I lie.

The owner's showing us something across the landing. It's the bathroom. At least there *is* a bath, though goodness knows how you use it. I don't even know what the German for 'cold' and 'hot' is, and I'm too embarrassed to ask.

Then I'm shooed back to my bedroom. Mother and Father want some 'quiet time' for a couple of hours.

'We're all tired after the journey,' says Father. I want to say *I'm not*, and that I want to go out and explore the cliff lift, but even I know there are times when children have to just shut up. 'We'll come and get you at half past three, Arnold, and we can go out for a walk before finding a café.'

'That'll be nice, Arnold, won't it?' says Mum, trying to chivvy me along. She probably saw I was on the point of crying. She tries to give me a hug but Dad pulls her away and they're off clattering down the steep stairs, as though they can't get rid of me quick enough.

I slump down on the bed face up, wipe my eyes, and stare at the ceiling. There's an awful sinking feeling in the pit of my stomach – that lurch when you're ill, just before you're going to be sick. I'm not going to be sick, but I've realised all my hopes for this holiday, all the build-up to it in my head, it's all going to be dashed. I'm going to hate it all, I know I am.

I must have dozed off because when there's a knock on the door I wake with a start, confused at first. That sometimes happens when I stay the night at Nana's. When I wake I can't understand why I'm not in my own bed. There's another knock – louder, more impatient. I look at my watch – the one Nana gave me – thinking I'm late to meet with my parents. But it's only one o'clock: only half an hour has passed since we arrived.

Then a voice, shouting through the door. A girl's voice, in broken, guttural, fierce English.

'Hallo. Muttilein says I must come to see you. She says I have to show you the village.'

Who's Muttilein? What a strange name. Maybe she's got the wrong room by mistake. Then she knocks again – so loudly, I think she's going to break the door or hurt herself. I jump up off the bed, and open the door.

She looks me up and down, a curious smile on her face.

'Hallo,' she says. 'You are Arnold. I am Lotti. Lotti Rolf. My parents own the hotel. They say you are to come out and look at the village with me.'

It's not a question. It's like an order. I look at my watch again, just to check I haven't made a mistake. It's still only one o'clock, as it was a few seconds ago. Two and a half hours before I have to meet with Mother and Father for 'the walk'.

'Just a moment. I've got to get my shoes and pullover on.' I sit on the bed, expecting her to wait outside, but she comes into the room and leans on the small washbasin, looking at me.

'What?' I ask.

'You are quite handsome,' she says.

I feel my face burning, and don't know how to reply. I've never met anyone so forward. Instead, I stare downwards, concentrating on lacing my shoes.

Then I grab my jumper. When, finally, I look up at her, she's smirking at me.

4

The autopsy on Concrete Man was being held in the Carl Gustaf Carus Medical Academy in Johannstadt, to the east of the centre of the Altstadt and what had once been its most iconic landmark, the ruined Frauenkirche. Müller and her small team travelled there in the pool Wartburg. It was a Tourist, or estate version, unmarked, but with plenty of space in the rear for forensic officer Jonas Schmidt's cameras and equipment – not that he'd need them here. His role at the post-mortem would be simply that of an observer.

'Stalinist architecture,' said Tilsner, as they drew up to the building and he parked the car. 'It looks a bit like something out of Eisenhüttenstadt.'

Müller nodded. She knew the comment was made in appreciation, not deprecation. It made a change from the other buildings in the neighbourhood – monotonous blocks of *Plattenbauten* – the favoured building method nowadays. They were prevalent here, and where the body had been discovered, in Gorbitz.

Müller wondered how much actual demolition had been needed to clear the way for the new blocks. Perhaps it had all been done for the builders by the bombers in 1945? The identikit apartments were much sought-after by citizens, but this building was more of a statement piece: its façade almost neoclassical, like the grand apartment blocks where Müller used to live in Karl-Marx-Allee, a privilege since withdrawn.

'Correct, Comrade *Oberleutnant*,' said Schmidt. 'It's just over a quarter of a century old – 1954, if I'm not mistaken.'

As they climbed out of the car, Müller glanced over each shoulder quickly – a reflex response to make sure they weren't being followed. Whenever the thought of the Stasi came into her head that was what she did involuntarily, as surely as night followed day. There was nobody obvious on their tail. Perhaps there would be a welcoming party inside the actual autopsy room. Müller had half expected the case to have already been taken out of their hands by the Ministry for State Security, given their presence when the body was being disentombed. So far, though, it appeared that they were being allowed to continue their investigation uninterrupted, embryonic though it was.

They were met at reception by a nervous-looking junior medic, and then ushered along a warren of corridors, down a flight of stairs into the basement, and then along more corridors. Müller steeled herself mentally before they entered the actual autopsy room. She'd never seen a body that had been encased in new concrete before – she wasn't sure what to expect.

One thing Müller had learned as the head of a murder squad was that any pre-judged mental image of what a pathologist was going to look like was usually wrong. Nevertheless, Dr Berndt Giesler looked even more left-field than anyone she'd ever envisaged. His jet-black hair, greased or gelled back in a full-bodied quiff, looked like something a 1950s American pop star might sport, and although he wore spectacles, their square black rims were fashionable rather than functional. She was struck by the lack of magnification, positive or negative, through the lenses – almost as though they were made of non-refractive glass. In other words, he was simply wearing them for effect.

On the mortuary slab in front of him lay the corpse, and Müller was surprised to see it looked much like other naked bodies she'd seen in similar circumstances.

'He's cleaned up quite well, don't you think?' said the doctor, taking his forensic glove off and extending his hand for Müller to shake. 'Berndt Giesler. I'm the senior forensic pathologist here. You must be Karin Müller?' He rose an eyebrow archly. They each already knew who the other was – they'd done their homework. The man's informality would have jarred with other police captains. No mention of rank, no 'Comrade this' or 'Comrade that', but Müller found it refreshing.

She shook his hand and introduced Tilsner and Schmidt, careful to give the latter his full Comrade *Kriminaltechniker* title. Schmidt was probably the most junior of the gathering, but appreciated all the little formalities. 'Is it all right if they both sit in too, Dr Giesler?'

'Call me Berndt,' said the man. 'Everyone here does. We can't stand stuffiness here. We just get on with our jobs to the best of our abilities. And yes, of course they're welcome to stay.'

'So,' said Müller, 'what can you tell us so far?'

'Well, I can tell you the victim was male.'

There was a harrumph from Tilsner. 'I think we managed to work that one out for ourselves.'

Giesler didn't seem to take offence, and just chuckled. 'You'd be surprised at some of the ones we get on here. It's not always obvious straight away – especially if they've been crushed, or in a fire.'

Müller found herself grimacing and fighting to hold her breath even more strongly than she'd been doing since they entered the mortuary room.

'Anyway,' he continued, 'male, late fifties or early sixties I'd say. Reasonably well-nourished . . .' Müller saw Tilsner raise his eyebrows towards Schmidt. It was their little joke when they reached this part of a pathologist's speech – Tilsner perhaps implying that 'well-nourished' would be an understatement should his corpulent forensic officer colleague ever have the mis-fortune to find himself on the slab. 'No obvious sign of injury—'

Müller frowned. 'But I thought—'

'Aah, patience, my esteemed People's Police Comrade. No obvious sign of injury *except* –' Giesler paused and gave a slightly devilish smile – 'for a rather obvious blow to the back of the head, caused by a blunt object wielded with considerable force. All of which I think you already knew, because it was all fairly obvious. In fact, the People's Police captain at the scene—'

'*Hauptmann* Schriver,' prompted Tilsner.

'That's the one. Well, he gave me all that information before I'd had to so much as lift a finger or scalpel. So I suppose what

you good people want to know is what else I can tell you, eh?'
The pathologist started poking at the cranium of the body now,
parting the still slightly matted hair, then lifting the neck. Rigor
mortis had clearly already dissipated. Müller did a quick calculation in her head – so the victim must have been killed at least
forty-eight hours previously. That seemed too long. She'd need
to check.

'Here is the wound caused by the blunt object,' said Giesler.

'Enough force to be lethal?' asked Müller.

The pathologist shrugged, and then waved his arms about in
a slightly theatrical fashion. 'Well, yes and no. Enough force to
kill, probably. Did it kill him? Probably not, at least not directly.
See here?' Dr Giesler was pointing to some cement-like smudges
around the wound. The three Berlin detectives craned their
heads forward to see, almost bumping into each other in the
process. 'Very interesting. They're cement or concrete-covered
finger imprints, surrounded by bruising. That's consistent with
what else I found.'

'Which is?' asked Müller.

'Classic signs of asphyxiation. Petechiae in the facial tissue
and eyes, once I'd cleaned them as well as I could, which as you
can imagine, was a devil of a job. And various points of oedema,
swelling in the bodily tissues.'

Schmidt took the opportunity to summarise. 'So, Comrade
Doctor, you're saying the victim was hit – from behind we think –
with a heavy blunt object, but that actually the cause of death was
drowning. In newly laid concrete. And that someone very forcibly
pushed his head down so he couldn't escape.'

'That's about the size of it, I'm afraid. Distinctly unpleasant way to go. And it would appear that he was still conscious when all this happened.'

Müller watched Tilsner tilt his head as a puzzled look appeared on his face. 'Why do you say that?' he asked.

'Simply the description about how one of his arms seemed to be petrified into a wave. I suspect that is what he was doing, or trying to do: wave, one-handedly. Attempting to attract someone's attention in his last seconds.'

There was silence as the four of them mulled over the implications.

Müller was the first to break it.

'Do you have any idea what he was hit with?'

''Fraid not. Occasionally in similar circumstances – well, actually . . .' he said, *sotto voce*, ' . . . I've never dealt with a drowning in concrete before – but in similar instances of trauma to the head, there might be traces of wood or metal or rust or even skin fragments which could give us a clue. But I'm afraid I've no idea. There is one interesting thing, though, which is unusual.'

'The timings?' asked Müller.

'Yes. Bravo, Captain! How did you know that?'

'The way you handled the victim's head. Rigor mortis has already dissipated.'

'Exactly. Yet the body was found this morning, and we all would assume – given that this happened in a high-traffic residential area – that the death must have happened last night. But no. It must have been at least twenty-four hours earlier. What are we now? Wednesday lunchtime? I would say death occurred at the latest on Monday evening, possibly a little earlier. Something doesn't add up, does it?'

Tilsner still looked puzzled. 'Why do you say that?'

'Think about it. High-traffic area, a building site even. Yet the police aren't called until around thirty-six hours after this death happened. But his arm was there in broad daylight, for a whole day, frozen in a petrified wave, although at that stage he was well beyond help. What does that tell you?'

'That the body was discovered earlier?' said Müller.

'Exactly,' said the pathologist.

'And that the People's Police weren't informed?' added Tilsner.

'Yes. So, I wonder which of our Republic's wonderful state institutions *was* informed? Or perhaps, even, knew already? I believe I can hazard a guess, can't you, *Hauptmann* Müller? Sorry, I should say *Comrade* Müller. How very remiss of me.'

The sarcasm dripping from the man's words was not that uncommon these days. Ever since martial law had been imposed in Poland the previous December in an attempt to crush the Solidarity movement it seemed as though citizens had started sniffing a whiff of change, and were more prepared to speak their mind.

Dr Giesler hadn't actually uttered the words, but there was no subtlety in what he was implying.

The crime scene had already been discovered and covered up, then 'rediscovered' a day later by the police.

But those first at the scene had almost certainly been members of the Ministry for State Security.

The Stasi.

They were in it up to their necks and beyond, just as Concrete Man had been.

5

The three Berlin officers arranged to meet *Hauptmann* Schriver in the HO restaurant Am Zwinger back in the Altstadt. The restaurant was on Ernst Thälmann Straße, opposite the Zwinger itself – the Baroque orangery, gardens and ornate buildings constructed during the reign of Augustus the Strong. Old-style imperialism and functional, modernist socialist architecture sitting as uncomfortable neighbours on the street named after Germany's former communist leader. Thälmann had been executed on Hitler's order in Buchenwald in 1944. Virtually every other street in the Republic seemed to be named after him – it was a favourite game of Müller and the twins on long car journeys: whoever counted the most Ernst Thälmann streets or buildings was declared the winner.

Just before they parked the car, Tilsner voiced his plans for the Dresden uniform captain.

'If it's a Stasi set-up, and Schriver's involved, we need to shake him up a bit. I don't like being messed about like this.'

Müller rolled her eyes, and glanced at the western watch glistening on her deputy's wrist. It had always been beyond the means of a lowly *Unterleutnant* – Tilsner's rank when the timepiece had first appeared. Immediately it had raised Müller's suspicions, suspicions that had later been confirmed. Tilsner had, at some stage, been an unofficial informer for the Stasi. To hear him moaning now about being 'messed about' by them smacked at the very least of hypocrisy. Of course, it could be something worse. Tilsner might know very well what was going on, might have already been given the inside track by his contacts at the Ministry for State Security. He could just be playing her and Schmidt. Müller hoped not. She hoped his loyalty to her trumped that – even though there had been plenty of times when he'd more than stretched her patience.

'Let's just play it gently with Schriver,' she warned. 'We'll do better with him on our side than by making an enemy of him.'

Inside the square, modern building – nicknamed by Dresden-ers the 'eating cube' – their chosen meeting spot was the 'rustic Radeberger beer cellar': a faux reproduction of the real thing, complete with waitresses in dirndls. To Müller it all had too much of a West German, even semi-Nazi atmosphere. You could quite imagine Hitler, Göring and their cronies being at home here, with the Bavarian-style wood carvings and furni-ture, and animal heads and horns adorning the walls. The venue had been arranged by Tilsner. When their drinks were served, the waitress's dress almost lost its battle to contain her décolle-tage, and Müller shook her head as she watched the men's eyes – even Schmidt's – glaze over.

Tilsner slapped his thighs, as though he were in lederhosen, to grab Schriver's attention.

'So, Magnus,' he said, 'let's not talk around the hot porridge. The pathologist has unfortunately raised a little problem with our Concrete Man.'

Schriver took a long gulp of his beer before saying anything. 'What exactly?' he asked, finally.

'It seems as though he was in the concrete for longer than we thought.'

There was a bemused look on Schriver's face.

'How's he come to that conclusion? We attended the scene as soon as we were alerted to it.'

'Who alerted you?' asked Müller.

Schriver made a play of looking it up in his notebook. 'It was an anonymous phone call.'

'That figures,' said Tilsner.

Schriver slammed his beer down, his face creased in confusion. 'Sorry. What exactly are you implying?'

Müller decided to take control before things got out of hand. '*Oberleutnant* Tilsner is not casting any aspersions on your work, Magnus. Far from it. We all need to work together as a team to try to solve this one. That's why we called this meeting. To make sure the *K*, we detectives, work in harmony with your uniform team. But it seems the victim was attacked a full day earlier than we thought.'

'At *least* a day,' emphasised Tilsner.

'And?' asked Schriver, still apparently none the wiser.

'And someone's been trying to pull the wool over our eyes.'

'What *Oberleutnant* Tilsner's trying to say is that if the body was there, half buried in the concrete of a busy building site, someone would have seen it earlier.'

'It's possible, I suppose,' said Schriver.

'No,' insisted Müller. 'It's *impossible* it wouldn't have been seen. So either the pathologist is mistaken – which I doubt very much – or it was hidden, or it was reported to someone else.'

'Or,' said Tilsner, with a hint of menace in his voice, 'it *was* reported to the police in the usual way, but someone at People's Police HQ decided someone else should hear about it first.'

'Meaning?' challenged Schriver. Müller could see – even in the half-light of the beer cellar – that his face was flushed with anger.

'It's not a personal accusation,' said Müller. 'It's not even an accusation against your team. But we all know every police district has its official and unofficial liaison officers working with the Ministry for State Security. Our suspicion is, if the incident was reported in the normal fashion, that the Stasi was tipped off first.'

'That's a very serious accusation,' replied Schriver. 'If – and I stress *if* – there is any truth to it, then perhaps whoever did this had good reason. Perhaps they knew the case had political overtones and therefore it was, quite correctly, the preserve of the Ministry for State Security.'

Schmidt, who up until now had been silent, cleared his throat. 'With respect to all of you, rather than debating the whys and wherefores of how and when the crime was reported, shouldn't our focus be on solving it? Isn't that why we're having this meeting?'

Tilsner was about to shout Schmidt down, but Müller held up her hand.

'Jonas is quite correct, of course. But as part of that, one important focus is finding who this anonymous tip-off came from. And whether anyone witnessed an argument, fight, or anything similar from anytime from Monday through to when the body was discovered by your officers, Magnus.'

Schriver took a deep breath, as though he wanted to give Müller and Tilsner a piece of his mind, but was counting to ten first.

'OK, so what you're talking about is block-by-block inquiries in Gorbitz, where the blocks have already been occupied, and close questioning of the construction workers where apartments are still being built. That's easy enough, although it will take a lot of manpower. I'll get on it right away. But just to make myself clear – my team is happy and willing to co-operate with you as far as is practical. I see that as our duty to the Republic. What I don't appreciate is the implication that one of my officers might have been trying to undermine the investigation even before it's started. It might be all right to go slinging round accusations like that in Berlin, but that's not the way we do things round here.'

6

ARNIE

Bad Schandau, Germany
Summer 1938

I wonder about disturbing my parents to let them know where I'm going – it feels wrong somehow just to sneak off. I voice my worries to Lotti. She looks at me with pity.

'Why do you need to tell them anything? They're probably busy . . . you know . . .' She crosses her fingers, one over the other. I don't think she's wishing for luck.

So I sneak quietly past their room, trying to keep up with my new German friend.

When we're outside the hotel, she asks me what I want to do.

'I'd love to go up the cliff lift, but I haven't got any money.'

'The cliff lift?' she repeats back to me, clearly not understanding what I mean.

I pull her after me, walking quite quickly, past what looks like the village green with the brook running through it. 'This way.'

When we turn the corner, suddenly her face lights up as I point at it.

'Ah. I was not understanding. The *Personenaufzug*. Yes, OK. We go up there. It will be fun.'

'But I haven't got any foreign money.'

She looks at me uncomprehendingly. I try to remember what the German currency is called.

'Reichsmarks,' I say. 'I don't have any.'

'No problem,' she laughs. 'The lift operator knows me from the Young Girls' League. We will be able to go for free.'

I don't really know what this Young Girls' League is, but I don't want to appear stupid in front of her, so I keep my mouth shut. Mother and Father will be so jealous when they find out I've been up the tower without them. Perhaps I'd better not tell them.

When we get to the lift, something slightly odd happens. Lotti and the lift operator both raise their right arms to each other, keeping the arm straight and at an angle, and shout 'Heil Hitler!' The woman glowers at me when I don't join in.

Lotti digs me in the ribs and hisses in my ear. 'You must do the same greeting, Arnold. Especially if we want a free ride. Frau Holzmann expects it – she's a very loyal party member.'

I'm not really sure what to do, but if the woman is going to take us up for free it seems only fair to do what she wants. It can't do any harm, surely? So I copy what they've just done, although my pronunciation is rubbish, and I'm not sure I'm holding my hand or arm correctly. But Frau Holzmann 'Heil Hitler's me back and smiles. It seems I've passed the test.

As the lift climbs, I feel as though my stomach is falling out. The view is amazing from the lift cage when I do look out, but most of the time I'm looking at the floor of the cage itself instead, willing myself not to be sick. Perhaps this wasn't such a good idea. Lotti smiles at me and squeezes my hand.

'We can walk back down, if you don't like the height,' she says, when we finally reach the top. 'It takes longer, but . . .'

'Oh no. I'm not scared. It's just the journey from England was such a long one, I'm feeling a bit ill.'

She moves out of the lift and onto the viewing platform. I steel myself and follow. From here, the view is even better. The wide Elbe river stretching to left and right, with Bad Schandau itself far below, and – on the opposite bank – the railway we arrived on. Father said if we'd have stayed on the train, we'd have ended up in Czechoslovakia within a few miles.

'Beautiful, yes?' she says. She gathers me close to her and then points out a table-top peak in the distance. 'The Lilienstein. It is the sign of this area – Saxon Switzerland.'

'But we're not in Switzerland, are we?'

'Of course not, silly. It's just the area's nickname because it's a bit like the Alps.'

'Well, it's certainly a great view.' I don't feel so nervous about the height standing up here on the static platform – it was just the moving lift giving me trouble. But my heart is still beating fast from being so close to Lotti.

'Do you have a girlfriend, Arnold?'

What sort of question is that? I'm only twelve. The Germans seem so forward. Whatever they're thinking, they just say it. I can feel myself blushing and getting hot.

'N-n-no. N-n-not yet. Mother and Father say I'm not old enough. There's one girl at home I like.' It's my Friend Cliff's older sister. Of course, she doesn't know I like her. Not unless the stammer and red face which always erupt whenever I'm near her are a giveaway. A bit like now with Lotti. Although until now, I hadn't really thought of Lotti like that. She isn't beautiful, more . . . I don't know how to put it, really. More *earthy*. She seems very knowing.

She squeezes my hand. 'Would you like to be my boyfriend, then?'

This seems stupidly fast. I don't really know the girl, have spent about fifteen minutes maximum with her, and now she's asking me to be her boyfriend. But although she isn't beautiful, there is something in her eyes, her blonde hair, her emerging shape beneath her thin summer jumper, that's well, *sexy* I suppose the word is. Suddenly, to my shame, I feel my body reacting down below as she strokes my hand with her fingers.

'Yes,' I find myself saying, not really understanding why. 'Yes, I would.'

No sooner are the words out of my mouth, than she leans in for a kiss.

7

Dresden
February 1982

On exiting the Am Zwinger, Müller found a welcoming party for her, Schmidt and Tilsner. She couldn't be sure, but the man looked very similar to one of those she'd taken to be agents overlooking the crime scene.

'Are you off back to Gorbitz, Comrade *Hauptmann*?' asked the man. 'We're heading up that way. Why don't we give you a lift?' He was holding open the rear door of a black Volvo saloon.

'That's kind of you,' replied Müller. 'But there's no need. We've got a People's Police pool car at our disposal. And we'll need it at the scene. Also, you may know who I am, but I've no idea who you are.'

The man took his ID from his pocket and flashed it at Müller. The familiar insignia of a muscular arm holding a rifle, with a depiction of the Republic's flag flying from its bayonet. '*Major* Rüdiger Bahlow, Ministry for State Security. It's nothing to worry about.' The man's smile – on a youthful, carefree face – seemed genuine enough. But Müller knew better than to trust the Stasi. 'I simply want to discuss whose patch is which, and make sure we don't step on each other's toes, as it were. If you need your car, your deputy can bring it, can't he? Along with your forensic officer.'

Müller turned to Tilsner. He just shrugged, as though to say that she would have to talk to the Stasi at some stage – so it might as well be now.

'I'll see you two up there,' she said to her team, climbing into the back of the Volvo. Bahlow shut the door after her. It closed with a muffled thud: the classic sign of a luxury western car. There was no need to slam it shut, as with the Wartburg.

There was another man in the driver's seat.

'This is *Hauptmann* Gottschald.' The driver, thickset and ruddy-faced – from what Müller could see of his face – didn't turn to acknowledge her, and instead simply started the car and drove off. 'He's a Sorb,' said Bahlow, as though that explained everything. 'Don't worry if he seems grumpy. That's what they're like.'

The Stasi major flicked open a pack of cigarettes, lit one with a silver-cased lighter, and then offered the unlit filter end to Müller. She declined, but not before noting the brand: 'West', a new marque she'd seen advertised on western TV when she'd been at her adoptive mother's in Oberhof, something she couldn't watch here in Dresden. The whole city – thanks to its low-lying position in the Elbe Valley, surrounded by hills – was in a shadow area for transmissions from the west. Hence its nickname, Valley of the Clueless.

The look was picked up by Bahlow, who'd now passed the cigarette on to his deputy, while lighting another for himself. 'Sorry, not very patriotic smoking a western brand, I know. A relative on the other side sent them to me. Willy here and I rather like them, but please don't snitch on us to our bosses.'

Müller gave a thin smile.

'Anyway, let's get down to business,' he said, turning in his seat to face her again. 'As I said, nothing to worry about, although Berlin informs us that you're used to liaising with the *MfS* on your cases. Klaus Jäger has been your main contact, I believe?'

'That's correct.' Müller felt surprisingly calm. Bahlow gave off an air of a younger Jäger. Before the older man had lost some of his zest and youthful vigour, and before Müller had discovered the secret from the war years that – to some extent – had neutered him. A melange of menace and bonhomie. Like the good cop, bad cop role incorporated into a single persona.

'So you're aware how we operate, and why sometimes we have to get involved in cases?'

Müller nodded.

'At other times, we simply have a watching brief. I would say at the moment, from what I know, this is one of those cases. However, should things turn more – what shall we say? – more delicate, more political in nature, then we will have to immediately take control and you will need to hand all your information over to us.'

Müller jerked forward as the car made an emergency stop. She felt her stomach lurch upwards, as though her lunch might be regurgitated. Then they were underway again. Bahlow's deputy shouted angrily and waved his fist at a motorcyclist who'd cut him up.

'Does that seem fair?' asked Bahlow, seemingly unruffled by the near miss.

'It's nothing unusual,' said Müller. Was it *fair*? No, of course not. She would much rather see cases through to their conclusion. That was all any police officer would want.

Bahlow smiled. 'Great. That was it really, from our side. Do you have any questions?'

'Yes,' said Müller, running her fingers through her shoulder-length blonde hair. For the first time, now she'd tipped over into what might be described as the latter end of her mid-thirties, she'd started to dye it. Her looks were fading – it was a woman's curse – something men didn't seem to have to worry about for another ten years or so. 'Yes, I have plenty of questions.'

'Shoot,' said Bahlow, as though he was in a slick American cop show, rather than working underhand for an organisation which, to Müller's eyes, was little more than a pale copy of the Soviet KGB.

'Do you know who the victim is?'

'No.'

'Why he was killed?'

'No.' Bahlow's face was deadpan. He'd be a dab hand at poker.

'How he was killed?'

'No, other than that he seems to have been buried alive in concrete. But presumably *you* know, as you've just been to see the pathologist. I'll be having a chat with him later.'

'What about *when* he was killed?'

Müller let the question hang in the air. Bahlow seemed in no hurry to answer this one, and let a small smile play on his face. The purr of the Volvo's engine – so much smoother than the two-stroke Wartburg – filled the silence.

'All right. You've got me there. Our helpful pathologist Dr Giesler isn't much of a friend of my esteemed organisation. I can't think why. No doubt he's already been making insinuations.'

Müller returned his smile. For a Stasi man, he didn't seem entirely awful, although Müller could have done without this 'friendly chat' before the investigation had even got underway. His teeth shone in the afternoon sun a little like – Müller imagined – some of the sparkling jewels of the kings of Saxony, temporarily housed in the Albertinium in the old city centre. Their normal home, the *Grünes Gewölbe*, the Green Vault, hadn't yet been restored after the terror bombing at the end of the war. 'I found Dr Giesler extremely co-operative. It was refreshing.' She liked having one up on a Ministry for State Security agent, no matter that it was an insignificant victory. 'And yes, he highlighted the discrepancy – there seems to be a missing day at least, perhaps longer.'

'We had to do a small pre-investigation first. To make sure the case was indeed one for the *Kripo*, rather than us.'

'And what satisfied you on that count?'

Bahlow didn't answer. Gottschald had braked to a halt, and the view from the window – rows and rows of *Plattenbauten*, some built, some half built – told her they'd reached their destination. The crime scene, or at least, the scene where the body had been discovered. She saw Tilsner and Schmidt getting out of the Wartburg ahead of them.

'Aha,' exclaimed Bahlow. 'Your deputy's reputation precedes him – not only does he play it fast and loose in investigations, he does in cars too. Impressive that he managed to beat us in one of the Republic's models.' He got out of the car, and held the rear door open for Müller. Then he banged the roof of the Volvo. 'Perhaps the Swedes can still learn something from us.'

Müller shrugged. She wasn't going to get into a conversation about boys' toys. However, she wasn't prepared to let the implied slight against Tilsner pass without comment. '*Oberleutnant* Tilsner is an excellent and loyal officer.'

'He is indeed, he is indeed,' Bahlow said aloud. Then he leaned in to whisper into her ear, with the same menacing tone she'd heard so many times from Jäger. 'For you *and* us, as I'm sure you're aware.'

Despite Bahlow's not so friendly warnings, Müller felt slightly more at ease now everything was out in the open. She didn't have to worry about a viewing party of leather-jacketed men: they were still there, she knew, just less obviously in the open. They'd be on their own, sitting in cars round corners, pretending to read the newspaper. Or hidden away in delivery vans, or behind the tarpaulins of trucks, posing as the builders themselves. Clicking away with their hidden cameras. Checking that Müller and her small team of detectives and *Hauptmann*

Schriver and his larger team of uniformed People's Police didn't start discovering things the Stasi didn't want them to discover.

'What was all that about?' asked Tilsner.

'You can probably guess, can't you? A combination of a *friendly* warning and a setting out of whose patch is whose – and why we shouldn't stray into their concerns.'

'Did you get anything out of him?'

'What do you think? He's cut from the same cloth as Jäger.'

Tilsner laughed as he glanced back to the two men in the Volvo. 'Looks like a younger version of him too. He's probably a secret love child.'

They found Schriver's team, and then divided up the blocks between them for apartment-by-apartment questioning. A few years earlier, in a similar collection of *Wohnkomplexe* – in Halle-Neustadt – they'd been warned off house-to-house inquiries by the local Stasi, as though crime wasn't something that could be acknowledged in the Republic. Now, there appeared to be more of a sense of reality. After all, *Polizeiruf 110*, the Republic's TV crime show, was one of its most voraciously watched. Lenin might have expected crime to wither away without classes to suppress, but his citizens' appetite for crime, albeit of the fictional kind, seemed insatiable.

Müller and Tilsner took the nearest occupied block, while delegating Schmidt to do a centimetre-by-centimetre re-check of the crime scene for forensic clues: cigarette butts, footprints, fingerprints and tyre tracks. Though Müller had her doubts as to its worth. Anything there was to find now – after the Stasi had, in effect, pre-sifted the area – would either be something the Ministry for State Security *wanted* them to find, or had planted there themselves.

From the entrance lobby, Müller took the left side of the block, Tilsner the right. Immediately, Müller could tell the inquiry had been compromised.

'Someone's already been round, officer,' said the elderly man who answered the first door she tried. 'Wasn't he with the police? I just assumed he was. I told him all I knew.'

'Which was?'

'Nothing really. I'm a bit hard of hearing, you see.' Müller could hear a television or radio blaring away at full volume from inside the flat. 'I have to put the TV volume on its highest setting, and when I do that I can't hear much else. It's a wonder I heard you ring the bell just now.'

Müller realised further questioning of the man would be next to useless, especially as he'd already been 'got at' by Bahlow's men.

It wasn't until about the twentieth apartment she tried, one on the first floor, that Müller finally made some progress.

Her first thought when the young woman – replete with safety-pin piercing her right nostril and bright-orange spiky hair – opened the door was that she was unlikely to get much co-operation. Punks were notoriously anti-police, thanks to the amount of surveillance and hassle they encountered. But this young woman defied the mould, and was friendliness personified.

'I was just making a coffee. Would you like one? There's enough in the pot,' she asked.

'That depends. I'd love one, but I'm working. So *is* there anything you can tell me about the night in question?'

'There is indeed, officer. Quite a lot. So, the coffee?'

'That's kind of you. Milk, no sugar.'

While the young woman busied herself in the kitchen, Müller had a nose around the living room. 'Do you live here alone?' she shouted. The photograph on the bookshelf seemed to imply she didn't. The woman's arms wrapped round another – older – punk, a man who was slightly less flamboyantly dressed. As Müller turned away from the photo, the young woman was back with coffees. The pot must have already been on the stove.

'That's my husband,' the woman said. 'He's a lecturer at the university.' Müller raised her eyebrows – and the woman clearly registered the look. 'Yes, don't worry. He gets plenty of grief for his appearance, although he tones it down during the daytime. I was his student – I still *am* a student. That's why I'm here at the moment. Supposed to be revising for exams.' Her eyes flicked to the dining table, full of half-open textbooks and sheaves of notes. Then she gestured to the sofa – an orange corduroy affair: an almost exact match for her hair. 'Shall we sit here and then I can tell you everything?'

'Let's start with your full name, please,' said Müller.

The woman identified herself as Petra Abt, a graphic design student at Dresden University of Technology. Müller now understood the garish murals decorating the walls. They were probably self-painted, either by Petra or her husband. It appeared they hadn't yet had a visit from the Stasi in connection with the incident that had happened outside their block, because for most of the previous evening and night they'd been out at a punk concert. Her husband played in a band – so they'd had to go early for the set-up and soundcheck and then weren't back till late. So far, they'd escaped the rounds conducted by Bahlow's team, it appeared.

'You're the first police officer I've spoken to,' insisted the woman. Despite her appearance, there was an openness and honesty to the young woman which Müller found quite appealing. She reminded her a little of Irma Behrendt – once of Rügen, and a feature of two of Müller's high-profile cases. Now, apparently, enjoying her new life in a remote Austrian skiing valley. In Irma's case, though, the bright-red hair was natural. Petra's clearly wasn't.

'So what is it that you think you saw or heard that may be relevant?' asked Müller, taking out her notebook and readying her pen.

'Detlef and I were on the way back from his final rehearsal before the gig. We saw a man and a woman arguing near the building site, near where the body was found – well, I assume that's where it was found. Where the police tape is.'

Müller nodded. 'What time was this?'

'It must have been about 10.30 p.m. or so on Monday – not that late.'

'Was there anyone else about?'

'No. It's usually pretty quiet around here at that time. Not all the apartments are occupied yet, and as you've seen some aren't even built. Detlef was about to go and intervene because it sounded very heated. There was pushing and shoving going on. But I told him to keep out of it. It looked like a domestic row. Sometimes those can look worse than they really are. How I wish now he *had* intervened.'

'The row was violent, then?'

'I wouldn't say that exactly – pushing, shoving, shouting – that sort of thing. No actual blows being exchanged.'

'Did you hear any details of exactly *what* was said?'

'The man seemed to be repeating "*You lied to me, you lied to me.*" And the woman was saying "*You never loved me anyway.*"'

'That's why you concluded it was a lover's argument?'

'Yes, of course.'

'What about ages, appearance?'

'I honestly couldn't see a lot. They haven't finished the street lighting yet. So you have the lights at the entrances to the blocks that are finished, like ours, and not much else. We usually carry a torch to get home safely.'

'So did you shine the torch at them?'

'To be honest, it was either in Detlef's or my pocket. I was carrying his box of gear – effects pedals, leads, that sort of thing – and he had his guitar and practice amp. We had our hands full.'

Müller's heart sank. What had at first seemed a promising breakthrough was fast unravelling. 'You must have been able to make out their height, build, hair colour . . . something?' The last word was said with a certain hopelessness.

'I'd say medium build. Perhaps the woman was a little thicker-set. Medium height too – nothing out of the ordinary. Middle-aged, or late middle-aged. Fifties or sixties I'd say. Not *very* old but certainly not my age, or your age come to that.' The woman tugged at her hair nervously. 'Sorry I'm not being much help here, am I?'

'It's not your fault,' smiled Müller, trying to cover her frustration. 'Anything else?'

'I couldn't see their faces or heads properly because it was bloody freezing, to be honest, both of them had dark-coloured anoraks or coats on, with the hoods pulled up and quite tight around their faces. I could see that the man was wearing spectacles, I remember that.'

'Style?'

'Quite big, round frames – possibly wire frames?'

'Good, that's useful.' Petra smiled at the praise, pleased to have got something right. Müller couldn't remember if that description tallied with the victim or not. The age did, certainly, but had he been wearing glasses? She'd have to check with Schriver's team and the pathologist. 'What I'd like you to do now, Petra, if that's OK, is come out to the crime scene with me and show me exactly where the couple were standing. Is that OK?'

'Of course,' said the woman. 'I'm happy to do anything that might help.'

Once outside the block, Müller looked for Schmidt. When she spotted him, rifling through a litter bin, she beckoned him over.

'This citizen was the witness to an argument around the time our victim is thought to have met his death, Jonas.' Schmidt was staring at the young woman dubiously through his pebble-thick glasses. His look betrayed his thoughts – why should the People's Police give any credence to someone who dressed like that, with dyed hair, slashes in her black clothing, and a safety pin through her nose? 'I want a photo of the position she saw the couple in, please.'

'Of course, Comrade *Hauptmann*,' said the forensic scientist. 'I'll just get my cameras from the car.'

While Schmidt was gathering his equipment from the rear of the Wartburg, Müller asked Petra Abt to try to position herself where the woman had been, and to guide Müller into the place where the man had been standing.

'About like this,' said Petra.

'OK.'

Schmidt had now returned, and Müller got him to take shots from a couple of angles.

'Thank you, Petra,' said Müller. 'You've been very helpful.' The detective knew that wasn't really true – but it didn't seem as though the lack of information was really the woman's fault.

The woman shook Müller's hand in a curiously formal way, then turned to go back inside her apartment block. After a couple of paces, she stopped and looked back.

'Oh. I've remembered one thing that might be relevant.'

'What's that?' said Müller.

'The accents. The woman sounded like she was from the Dresden area. Lots of "*nee*" rather than "*nein*" – you know, the way Dresdeners say it. The man had a strange accent, though.'

'Not from Dresden, then?'

'Oh, no. Absolutely not. But more than that. His German was very precise, and correct – but there was a hint of a foreign accent. I don't think he was German at all.'

8

ARNIE

Autumn 1938

That kiss, well, it literally took my breath away. I got back to the bed and breakfast with Mother and Father none the wiser that I'd even been out. All I could think of was Lotti this and Lotti that. She just seemed so *knowing*. I barely knew what the word sex meant, and Lotti was always egging me on, trying to get me to do things I was scared of. For the rest of the holiday there was plenty of mutual fumbling, and at one stage – at the end of the valley where the tourist tram runs in Bad Schandau – she dragged me into the woods, hoiked up her skirt, and pulled my trousers open, expecting something to happen. But I was too nervous, too ignorant, to be able to take advantage. I can still feel my face burning with shame even now. I think Mother and Father eventually got wind of what was going on, and decided to cut short the holiday. Mother was disturbed by all the Nazi goings on, and Father had failed in his bid to climb the rock penis, so they were both very grumpy – lots of shouting at each other, and me when I disappeared off with Lotti.

Lotti's family weren't very happy about us going early and said we'd have to pay anyway, which started a right old ding dong. In the end, we just left very early without telling them, disappearing into the night. I think Dad just left the money for the days we'd stayed and not a *pfennig* more, and then we caught a very early train to Dresden, where Father managed to change all the return tickets for an earlier date. Every time a policeman or official came near us, Mum was frightened they were going to arrest us for bunking off from the hotel early. That just created more arguments, so the atmosphere was like ice all the way back to England.

I'd been hoping we might have the chance to spend a night in London to see the Tower and the other sights, but no – it was straight onto a train back to Hull once we reached London from Harwich.

All the time, all I could think of was Lotti. It was real love, I was sure.

As soon as I was back in my bedroom in Hull, I wrote a letter to her, but it took me a few weeks to work up the courage to actually send it. I didn't really know how much the postage cost, so I just stole three of Father's tuppenny stamps from his writing desk, stuck them all on, and then wrote '*Par Avion*' on the envelope before grabbing my bike and cycling off to the letter box.

I knew from school that air mail was a fairly new thing. Maybe even a tanner wasn't enough, even though it was more than my weekly pocket money, but I just hoped a friendly post-man might help it on its way.

I'm astonished when, less than ten days later, I receive a letter postmarked Bad Schandau, covered in greeny-grey '*Mit Luftpost*' stickers, and stamps in a similar colour showing Adolf Hitler's head.

Mother hands it to me slightly furtively in the hall of our house in Pearson Park, just before I cycle off to school. 'Don't show your father. He doesn't want to know anything more about Germany – wishes we never went there. Still less will he want to know you're carrying on a correspondence with that girl.' Then she winks. It's our secret.

I wait till the mid-morning break at school, then hide away in one of the toilet cubicles and rip the flimsy envelope open. It's so thin, it's like tissue paper.

As soon as I start reading, I realise Lotti can't have got my letter yet. This isn't in any way a reply – it's been writ-ten without her knowing I've written to her. In one way, I'm disappointed. I half wonder if my letter will ever get there. I shouldn't have been in such a hurry, and like her, I should have used a proper airmail envelope, the proper stickers and the correct value of stamps. The Germans are always so cor-rect! But at the same time, I'm quite excited. The fact that she's written to me, without knowing I've written to her, must mean she's pretty keen on me. I feel a hot flush of excitement through my body as I start to read her words.

Bad Schandau 13.10.1938

My dear Arnold,

   You will excuse my poor English.

   Are you good? Did you safely back in England arrive? You must at the soonest write. In English or German, it doesn't matter. But it is best in English because your German is not good.

   We were all sad when you and your family disappeared. My parents were angry to begin with, but I think they are all right now.

   Do you remember your holiday with good feelings? I hope so, anyway. And I hope I am still your girlfriend, like you say when we took the tram on the Kirnitzschtalbahn. You mean it when you said you love me, I hope it too.

   What are they saying about Hitler in England? We hear they bad things say, but really you must understand that He is by all German people supported and loved. I am glad that your Prime Minister Chamberlain has understood why Germans in the Sudetenland must be part of bigger Germany.

   It was very exciting since some of the soldiers in their vehicles through Bad Schandau came. We lined the streets to wave them. One of the big Sudeten towns, Tetschen, is not far from here. We have some German relations there. They tell us they much safer now they are part of the glorious Reich.

   School is tried to very boring but we have a lot to do. We toys and frocks for poor children have been making. I hope some will go to the Sudetenland because we hear they by the Czechoslovaks, have not been well treated. Hopefully all will be well now.

So you must tell me all your news and about Hull. (Or should I Kingston-upon-Hull call it? I know you just said Hull. I didn't realise such a big city it was.) You can even to me write about your football team if you want. I find football very boring but my friend Hans is interested even though he says the team in your city is not good. You can me things write and I will them to him pass. He would be interested in newspaper cuttings.

I wait for your letter, Arnold!

Your loving girlfriend,

Lotti XXX

9

Stasi HQ, Normannenstraße
Berlin, Hauptstadt der DDR
February 1982

'We have a job for you, Jäger. A chance to redeem yourself, perhaps.'

Klaus Jäger surveyed the young Stasi colonel, Rainer Specht, with distaste – though he was careful not to let it show on his face. The man was leaning back in his chair in the wood-panelled room, rotating the thumbs of his clasped-together hands. The syrupy tone of voice spelled danger. Jäger had hoped to see out his days as head of the records department – where he'd been banished after his demotion following what had become known as the Arktika affair. The Stasi had almost allowed a Soviet nuclear submarine to be blown sky high by dissident *Republikflüchtlinge* some three years earlier, and Jäger – unfairly in his view – had shouldered the blame.

'Yes, Comrade *Oberst*. I am of course ready to serve the Republic in any way that is required of me.'

'We want you to go to Dresden. There's a case there that could prove difficult. And you have contacts with some of those involved.' Jäger's heart sank, and this time he failed to disguise his feelings. He knew Specht had seen the look of disappointment. The younger man, who was obviously being fast-tracked up the ranks by the high-ups, gave a smirk. 'Comrade *Armeegeneral* Mielke specifically asked that you should take charge.'

'Well then that is an honour, Comrade *Oberst*.'

'Yes. It's an apparent murder case. Our team has already, shall we say, laid some of the ground work. You'll find all you need to know in this file.' He pushed a bulging grey-green folder across the desk. 'Report to the Ministry for State Security regional headquarters in Bautzner Straße as soon as you arrive in Dresden. Your train tickets are in the folder. They'll sort a pool car out for you there.'

Jäger flicked open the folder. 'The tickets are for this afternoon. I need to pack, talk to my fam—'

'There won't be time for that, Jäger. You'd better get yourself down to the station. Don't you keep a bag ready-packed here at headquarters? You should, you know. I always do. Anyway, no time for chit-chat. As I say, *Armeegeneral* Mielke himself has selected you for this assignment.'

'And who is it there that I've worked with before?'

'From our team? No one. Although we have a contact embedded with the *Kripo*. We're not sure he's entirely trustworthy, however. Your contact at Bautzner Straße, who'll act as your deputy, is *Major* Rüdiger Bahlow. It's the *Kripo* team where you know some of the people.'

'Not—'

'Yes, indeed, Jäger. A chance to get reacquainted. A chance to put things to rights.'

Müller and Tilsner. Jäger didn't need it spelling out for him. The little upstart in front of him might be talking about a 'chance to put things to rights', but Jäger knew it was almost certainly something else.

His last chance. And he couldn't help but feel he was being set up to fail.

10

Despite being in the middle of a murder inquiry, Müller still had the future of her children preying on her mind. In the midst of a case like this, there was no way she would be able to have them with her in Dresden, despite the Republic's excellent childcare facilities. The agonising decision almost became a fait accompli when Rosamund rang her saying she'd had a fall on an icy pavement. Müller's adoptive sister, Sara, had been helping her mother out temporarily, but Rosamund made it clear that couldn't continue.

'*I'm not getting any younger, Karin, and your father's no longer around to help.*'

'Are you going to be all right, though?' asked a concerned Müller.

'*I'll be fine, I'm sure. My thigh's turned a horrible purple-yellow colour, but the doctor insists it's just bruising, nothing more. But I think we're going to have to take Herr Meyer up on his offer. It's a great opportunity for Johannes and Jannika and they'll still be in the bosom of the family each weekend. They'll love being with children of their own age.'*

Müller gritted her teeth and said nothing for a moment. Even if she had, finally, agreed to the scheme, it wasn't supposed to turn out this way. She'd imagined taking them to the school herself, with tearful hugs and kisses, before they ran off to join their new friends. Instead, the decision was being made for her, while she was hundreds of kilometres away. But it wasn't Rosamund's fault. And perhaps she was being selfish – after all, she hadn't actually provided an alternative solution. Instead, she'd chosen to dedicate herself to her job, working for the Republic – for better or for worse.

'Karin? Are you still there?'

'Yes, sorry, I was just thinking.' Müller heard herself sigh. 'You're right. It's the only alternative. The important thing is that you get better, Mutti.'

'I'm sure it will turn out for the best, Karin. And if they really don't like it after a few weeks, I promise you we can try to work something else out.'

The phone call had come in to the incident room they'd set up in Dresden *Volkspolizei* headquarters just as she and Tilsner were about to start ploughing through piles of missing persons files. Müller couldn't help but feel a sense of déjà vu. The fact that Tilsner was chain smoking – filling the office with a horrible fug in the process – didn't improve her mood. She wondered if the day would ever come when non-smokers like herself would hold sway, offices could become healthy, smoke-free zones, and smokers could be banished to their own foul-smelling rooms or – even better – forced to stand outside in the cold indulging their nasty habit. Perhaps that was too much wishful thinking.

Tilsner exhaled right into her face, as though he wanted to wind her up further. 'What exactly are we looking for?'

Müller tried to concentrate on the task in hand, rather than her apprehension about the twins' new school, and her own feelings of guilt. 'A male, in his fifties or sixties, possibly a spectacle wearer. Blue eyes, according to the pathologist, a chest scar indicating previous surgery or injury, the pathologist couldn't be certain which—'

'Why not?' asked Tilsner.

Müller rolled her eyes. It wasn't their job to go questioning the medical experts in that sort of detail. She ignored him, and waved away his cigarette smoke.

'The pathologist couldn't establish that. What he could tell us was that the second right-hand molar in the upper jaw had been replaced by a gold tooth. And that replacement tooth had seen some heavy use, so it wasn't recent dental work.'

'Does that imply he might have been a party bigwig? Is that why the Stasi is taking such an interest?'

'Possibly. But remember we've got the witness, Petra Abt, who thinks he may have been foreign.'

Tilsner sighed and slapped his hand on his fat pile of missing persons files. They'd divided them in two. 'If that's the case, going through this lot is a complete waste of time. We'd be better off searching for places where we'd be most likely to find foreigners – Interhotels, the university, that sort of thing.'

'I've already asked Schriver's team to check both of those possibilities.' Müller glared hard at her deputy. 'But let's face it, there are plenty of other possible scenarios too. He could have been one of our Soviet friends. We're near the Czech border. We could go on and on. But this –' Müller gave her own slap to the files – 'is as good as any place to start, so why don't we just get on with it?'

They ploughed through the files for a couple of hours, taking a note of any entries that bore a remote similarity to the victim. They found middle-aged men without blue eyes, middle-aged men *with* blue eyes, but who were very obviously the wrong height and weight. Even a couple of entries that matched eye colour, hair colour, height and weight – but then the reference to chest scarring and gold dental work was missing.

Nevertheless, they took a note of those two entries with a view to following them up.

Their thankless task was interrupted by Schmidt, returning from his search for forensic evidence.

'Anything to report, Jonas?' asked Müller.

'A few bits and bobs which may prove interesting that I recovered from the bin, Comrade *Hauptmann*. Of course, they may not be in any way relevant.'

'Well come on then, Mr Esteemed Forensic Scientist,' said Tilsner. 'Don't keep us in suspense.'

'All right, so first these.' Schmidt brandished a transparent plastic evidence bag, containing a pair of large-framed, wire-rimmed spectacles. They were considerably the worse for wear.

It didn't look like they'd just been dropped on a hard floor. The way the glass was shattered and frames mangled, it appeared as though someone had ground them into that floor so that they would never be of any use again.

'Hmm,' mused Müller, turning the package in her hands. 'They certainly look similar to the ones Petra Abt described. We'll have to ask her. Do you think there's any chance of lifting any fingerprints from them, Jonas?'

'From the lenses, where you'd get the best result if they hadn't been cleaned recently, no. They're too badly damaged. From one or other of the temple tips, possibly, but it's likely to only be a partial, Comrade *Hauptmann*.'

'*Temple tips?*' asked Tilsner.

Schmidt pointed to a section of the bag. 'These bits. The plastic covered ends that fit over the ears – that's their technical name. But they're not wide enough to get a full print from. And people don't tend to clean those bits very often, so you'll have print on top of print, on top of hair grease . . .'

'Lovely, Jonas,' said Müller. 'We get the picture. See what you can do, anyway. Anything else?'

'This purse. That was interesting.'

'Why?'

'Well it's still got money in it. Nearly a hundred marks, in fact. Who throws a perfectly good purse with a hundred marks in, into a bin?'

No one with any sense, thought Müller.

'Any identification in the purse?'

'No, nothing. There were two things of interest, though.'

Tilsner gave a long sigh. 'Don't drag things out, speccy boy. Just get to the point.'

Müller watched Schmidt's face colour up. She ought to admonish Tilsner for the slight, but she too rather wished Schmidt would give them everything at once.

'Well, there's a train ticket from Pirna to Dresden.'

'Where's Pirna?' asked Tilsner.

Müller shook her head in frustration. 'It's a largish town about twenty kilometres south-east of Dresden, in the Elbe Valley. The gateway to Saxon Switzerland.'

'And,' said Schmidt, 'a bus ticket from Sonnenstein to Pirna station.'

This time it was Müller's turn to question the geography. 'Sonnenstein?'

'It's a new development of *Plattenbauten* in the eastern part of Pirna – about three kilometres from the railway station, Comrade *Hauptmann*.'

'But we've nothing to connect the purse to the glasses or to the victim, have we?' said Tilsner.

'Well ... maybe,' replied Schmidt. 'The argument that was reported by Petra Abt – according to her testimony – happened at around ten thirty on Monday evening, I think. The bus ticket was from approximately 5 p.m. on Monday, and the train ticket was bought at five 5.25 p.m. and validated on the S-Bahn at five thirty-four. So that does all tie in.'

'But it could be totally unconnected,' said Tilsner.

Schmidt's face fell.

'Of course it could,' said Müller. 'But equally the tickets could belong to our victim.'

Schmidt held the bagged, flower-print purse up to the light. 'I suspect this is a woman's purse, Comrade *Hauptmann*.'

'OK. But it could belong to the woman he was arguing with,' countered Müller. '*If* the man involved in the argument was the victim.'

In her head, she continued with a series of qualifiers.

If the evidence was genuine.

If it hadn't been tampered with by Bahlow and his cronies who – after all – had got to the scene some twenty-four hours before the police.

More than that, *if* it hadn't actually been planted by the Stasi – lock, stock and barrel.

11

The February day was drawing to a close and they'd made precious little progress. Did the bus and rail tickets provide something to work on, or were they just a false lead – planted or otherwise?

Müller weighed up the few options she had, and decided they were worth following up with a visit to Pirna – taking the opposite route to the owner of the lost, or discarded, purse.

When she told Tilsner she wanted him to carry on going through the missing persons files, his face fell.

'We're not getting anywhere, and we suspect our victim may be a foreigner anyway.'

'Still, it needs doing, and I'd like you to do it, please. Also put out an alert to other police districts in the Republic with the man's description, such as it is, and see if we can find a match.'

Tilsner didn't reply, other than to issue a dissatisfied grunt, and turn back to the files.

'I'll catch up with you later once I'm back from Pirna.'

This time, from her deputy, there was just silence.

Müller exited the Dresden People's Police headquarters building on the western, Frauenkirche side for her twenty-minute walk to the train station. She could have driven, but she wanted to get a feel for the journey taken by the purse owner – if indeed she was the other party in the argument witnessed by Petra Abt.

The two buildings looked utterly incongruous next to each other. The solid modernity of the police HQ, some eight storeys high, each lower floor slightly wider than the one above so the building had a stepped appearance, like an unfinished Aztec temple. Adjacent to it, the blackened stump of the Frauenkirche – once one of the glories of a glorious city – now left as a ruinous reminder of the excesses of imperialist and fascist ideology, and those nights of Anglo-American terror bombing. To Müller it was a pitiful sight. She understood the need to remember, and to be constantly vigilant against fascists and counter-revolutionaries. But to let it rot surrounded by a car park full of Trabants and Ladas seemed plain wrong. Either demolish it and clean up the area, and build something new like the nearby Palace of Culture – the *Kulti* – with its beautiful mural, *The Way of the Red Flag*. Or rebuild it and let Dresdeners revel in its beauty once more. This halfway house solution seemed just too sad for words.

The twenty-minute S-Bahn ride was a mere nine stops' worth, mostly through Dresden's suburbs. But towards the end of the journey, a couple of stops before Pirna itself, the line closely followed the sinuous path of the Elbe river, and Müller could sit back and enjoy the view.

When she finally reached Pirna, she wondered about quizzing the station staff, but decided she'd be better employed finding the bus to Sonnenstein, and starting her inquiries there. Once she found the bus, she bought a ticket and started to quiz the driver, while trying not to distract him – as he seemed unwilling to stop, other than at designated bus stops to let passengers on and off. His punctuality was evidently more important to him than assisting the police with their inquiries.

Müller did, however, manage to extract some useful information. There were three drivers who shared the route – and they would all usually do weekday evening shifts together, with a slightly different arrangement to cover weekends. The evening shift was from approximately 4 p.m. to midnight. From the time the woman who owned the purse had bought the ticket – 4.58 p.m. on the Monday evening according to its date and time stamp – the driver was able to hone in on which of the three shift workers would have issued it.

'That would be Ulrich Taube,' the driver said as he pressed the button to close the doors, and started to drive off. He fell silent for a few moments as he concentrated on the traffic. Then he glanced at Müller quickly before concentrating once more on the road ahead. 'You might be in luck, because he's a nosy bugger. Always likes to know other people's business at the depot. So I suspect he's the same with his passengers, especially women – although it's usually the younger ones he's interested in, dirty old man. He'll probably take a shine to you if you butter him up the right way.' He again glanced away from the road momentarily to check his wrist watch. 'If you get off at the next stop but one, Doktor-Pienitz-Park, then cross to the other side of the road, you should be able to pick up his bus in a couple of minutes. You know who the good doctor was, don't you?'

'I've no idea,' admitted Müller. She wasn't sure she cared, either.

'He was one of Pirna's most famous sons, back in the nineteenth century. A psychiatrist – one of the first to actually try to heal the mentally ill, rather than just lock them up. So there you are. That's your free tour guide spiel for Pirna.'

The bus had braked to a halt again, jolting Müller forwards then back on her heels as she stood by the driver's booth. The doors whooshed open. Müller made as if to step off, before the driver intervened.

'Not this one, love. The next.' He pointed through the windscreen into the gloom of the February evening. Snow had begun to fall, and Müller could barely see as the giant wipers made a poor job of clearing the glass. 'That one there – a couple of hundred metres ahead. We'll be there in a tick.'

The snow was already starting to settle as she crossed the deserted street. There was no one else waiting at the bus stop, which thankfully had a canopy. Müller was glad she'd wrapped up warm, with her police overcoat, faux fur hat, gloves and boots. She stamped in them now, jumped up and down on the spot, and clapped her hands together – all in an attempt to keep the blood circulating in her extremities. Through the gloom of weak street lighting, which softly illuminated the slowly falling flakes of snow, she began to take in her surroundings. It looked much like a smaller version of Gorbitz, or even Halle-Neustadt – the new town so closely wrapped up in the birth of her twins, and where they'd been conceived during her ill-fated relationship with Emil. Most of the *Plattenbauten* – the rows of concrete slab apartment blocks – were identical squat cuboids of no more than five or six storeys in height. Here, though, as in Ha-Neu, the blocks were punctuated by what looked like four high-rises, towering into the snowy semi-darkness.

Her musings were interrupted by the headlights and rough diesel-engine sound of an approaching bus. Müller made sure she was visible to the driver, and it slowed to a halt.

The bus was almost empty, which for the sake of the inquiry was a godsend. If it had been the same on Monday evening, and the woman who bought the ticket had been the only passenger waiting at the stop – as Müller was – then she had half a chance of finding out something more about her.

As she climbed aboard, the driver was already launching into his patter.

'Not the night for a pretty lady like you to be out and about on her own,' he said, as she offered up some change for a ticket. The man – and the way he was lecherously looking her up and down – immediately gave her the creeps. Müller had to remind herself that she wanted to extract information from him, otherwise she might have been inclined to give him a piece of her mind. Nevertheless, he soon grew more serious when she showed him her *Kripo* ID card.

'*Hauptmann* Karin Müller, *Kriminalpolizei*. I need to ask you a few questions.'

The man looked around nervously, as though to check no one else was watching or listening. The only other passengers were a couple of pensioners, a man and woman, and they didn't seem to be paying any attention. Nevertheless, he made as though to stand and turned his engine off.

'It's all right,' said Müller. 'It's nothing serious. Carry on driving. I can ask what I want at the bus stops or when there's not much traffic.'

The man slumped back in his seat in relief, and restarted the engine. 'I was scratching my head for a moment wondering what I'd done wrong to warrant a visit from the *K*.'

'It's not you I'm interested in,' said Müller. 'It's one of your passengers from Monday evening.'

'Oh yes,' he said, cautiously, beginning to drive off.

'Can you remember who you picked up around 5 p.m. – a couple of minutes before, actually – on Monday?'

Even though Müller hadn't asked him to, the man balanced a timetable on his lap, and leafed through it to the relevant page, while steering the bus with his knees.

'Make sure you drive safely,' she warned.

'Of course, officer.' He put one hand back on the wheel, while using the thumb of his other hand to turn the pages. 'Ah, there we are. Well, it should have been from the stop you got on at or the next one, according to this. I'm trying to remember.'

'A woman, middle-age to late middle-age.'

'Ah yes!' he suddenly exclaimed. 'It was Lotti. I can picture her face now, poor thing. She got on at the same stop as you, right enough. She lives in the block that overlooks the park. I can tell you because I live in Sonnenstein too.' He suddenly sounded slightly worried. 'It's not that I've been checking up on her or anything, but she's fairly well known round here.'

'Why?' asked Müller.

'Her face. Half of it is terribly disfigured. She's from Dresden originally. Survived the firestorm, but her face . . . well, it didn't fare too well.'

'Surname?' asked Müller curtly.

'Sorry, no idea.'

'OK,' Müller said. 'Stop the bus.'

'Stop the bus? Why?'

'Just do it! And thanks,' she shouted behind her, as she jumped out.

Müller knew there was no time like the present in murder inquiries. Trails quickly ran cold. At the back of her mind she was still thinking this was too easy. There was no firm link to the victim. No firm link even to the argument witnessed by Petra Abt – which may or may not have had something to do with the victim's murder. And above all, the path she was following was like that of a bird picking up a carefully laid trail of seeds or berries. Had it all just fallen into place naturally? Unlikely. This was almost certainly something she was meant to follow – tasty morsels offered up, no doubt, by Bahlow or one of his sidekicks, designed to steer her in a particular direction. As likely as not, away from the truth rather than towards it.

She climbed back up the gentle slope that was the Varkausring, hoping her boots would keep their grip on the pavement. Then she turned left into Straße der Jugend – aiming for the block the bus driver had pointed out. Of course, she had no idea of the woman's full name but what she saw now on the ground floor of the block, in the far corner, gave her hope. A pharmacist's that still seemed to be open. It sounded as though this Lotti was well-known around here. Surely the local pharmacy would have her details? If, as the bus driver insisted, her face had been badly burned in the 1945 terror bombing, they would at least recognise her – perhaps even provide her with salves and medicines for the old burns.

Müller hunched further into her coat, and pulled the hat completely down over her ears. The gentle fall of snow had become more insistent, accompanied by a driving wind now. Almost blizzard conditions. If it kept up like this, she might struggle to get back to Dresden tonight – the trains and buses might stop running.

In the pharmacy, the pharmacist started muttering about patient confidentiality trumping everything, and that he couldn't possibly reveal the address or full name of the woman known as Lotti.

Müller decided to up the ante. Sometimes it was the only way. In front of his shocked assistants, Müller raised her voice.

'Herr Oppenheimer. I can assure you that you absolutely are required to give me the information I request. This is a murder inquiry . . .' Müller paused for a moment, savouring the gasps of the assistants. 'Should you refuse to co-operate with the police, I will not hesitate to arrest you immediately, take you to the district People's Police offices in Pirna, and lock you in a cell where you can contemplate the error of your ways. If I were to do that, your career as a pharmacist would be as good as over. It's your choice, but I know what I'd do.'

That did the trick. The man went white in the face, and then started leafing through various papers.

'You should have said it was a murder inquiry straight away,' he protested.

'You should have co-operated with the People's Police straight away,' countered Müller.

After a few minutes shuffling through a pile of papers, he found what he was looking for, and handed it to her.

'This is her latest prescription. Her address is on there.'

Müller noted it down.

'It's in this block,' continued the man, now figuratively bending over backwards to be helpful. 'Go in the main entrance, climb the steps to the third floor, then turn right along the corridor. It's the fifth or so apartment on the left.'

The block was eerily quiet. Most of the residents wouldn't have returned from work yet. As she climbed the steps, the drum beat of her footfall triggered a memory in Müller's head about the name Sonnenstein – she'd heard it somewhere before, she was sure, she just couldn't recall it from the back of her mind. As her footsteps echoed in the darkness, she began to wonder if it had been a good idea to come on her own – especially if it was some sort of set up by the Stasi. She should have brought Tilsner with her. But then she'd never trusted him as fully since all the events at Gardelegen, and the knowledge of what he'd been involved in during the war. His membership of the Hitler Youth, even though virtually all boys of a certain age had been members of the young people's wing of the Nazi Party.

As she turned the corner into the third-floor corridor, she realised thinking of the Nazis had unblocked that memory of Sonnenstein. And recalling *why* she remembered it made her shiver. It was from one of her father's anti-fascist rants. An example of the barbarity of the Nazis. That was what had happened here – somewhere near here, anyway. In Sonnenstein, before these apartments were built for the workers of the Workers and Peasants Republic, there'd originally been a sanatorium for the mentally ill here. For its time, it had been forward thinking – that must have been where the Dr Pienitz mentioned by the bus driver worked, whom the park outside was named after. But that self-same sanatorium in the Nazi era became the site of atrocities. Sonnenstein had been a Nazi euthanasia centre: known as the National Socialist Killing Institution Sonnenstein. The thought made Müller's skin crawl. She was so wrapped up in it, she almost failed to notice the snowy footprints in the unheated corridor – leading right to apartment 315, her destination.

Lotti's flat.

Someone was at home.

For some reason, perhaps some sixth sense, Müller deliberately quietened her footfall. She had an inkling something was wrong. She tried to approach as quietly as possible, but she could hear her own breathing, see the cloudlets of condensation in the cold air in front of her, and hear her heartbeat hammering in her ears.

When she reached the door to 315, and saw the splintered wood of the forced lock, she realised she was right. Someone had got here before her.

Slowly, she drew her Makarov from her shoulder holster and released the safety catch.

She pushed at the now unlocked door, opening it a millimetre at a time, hoping with every little push that it wouldn't suddenly squeak on its hinges.

When it was fully open, she advanced equally slowly into the dark interior of the apartment, holding her gun pointed in front of her in both hands, finger ready on the trigger.

She knew the layout of these flats from the countless ones she'd been in – in Ha-Neu, the Hauptstadt and now Gorbitz. They were all near identical.

She didn't need a light to guide her, but ahead – in the lounge – she could see there was one. A torch, being flashed around. The sounds of drawers opening, being rifled through.

Someone was looking for something. Something belonging to Lotti.

If this was a trail of crumbs laid by the Stasi, it had turned up trumps. But perhaps she had just struck lucky.

She entered the lounge and pointed the gun at the intruder with the flashlight.

'People's Police!' she yelled. 'Freeze! Hands above your head.'

At first the intruder seemed to obey, but then the torch moved towards her and shone directly into her face. She resisted the reflex to shield her eyes from the light.

'Drop the torch, or I'll—'

Müller didn't get a chance to complete her warning.

First, she heard the thud of something heavy crashing onto bone, then a microsecond later blinding pain on the top and back of her skull.

She had time for one quick thought. *This is what happened to our victim in Gorbitz.*

Then she was falling.

Crumpling in terrible, awful pain. Pain like she'd never felt before.

Then all was black.

12

ARNIE

Pearson Park, Hull
September 1939

We knew it was coming, of course. First the BBC news announcement that Germany had invaded Poland – that was on the Friday, I think. Then a couple of days later, on the Sunday morning, just after we'd got back from church, we all gather round the wireless, in our Sunday best. Mother and Father look really serious, although that's nothing out of the ordinary. My new baby brother, Fred, starts bawling as Mr Chamberlain begins to speak in his boring clipped voice. I think Fred was a result of that German holiday – he's an ugly bugger. Anyway, Father looks daggers at Mother, who goes out of the room to feed the baby, so it's just me and Dad left listening.

Chamberlain is going on about a 'final note' given to the Germans demanding they withdraw their troops from Poland after their 'wicked and unprovoked attack'. Of course, soon enough, the Prime Minister's voice is drowned out because Father starts talking over him, saying he shouldn't have been so weak-minded to start with.

'He's let Hitler get away with far too much for too long, Arnold. You realise that, don't you?'

He looks at me with a serious expression, as though he wants a reply. I don't know what to say. It's scary. Not just for myself, but for Lotti. I'd hoped that I'd be able to persuade Mother and Father we ought to go on another holiday to Bad Schandau – maybe Father could try to climb his beloved piece of rock again. But now I realise that won't be happening. Probably not ever. Certainly not until this bloody war is over. I can feel tears starting to well in my eyes, and don't want Father to see them, so I rush from the room and up to my bedroom. I slam the door shut, then get Lotti's most recent letter, lie on top of the bed, and read it through for perhaps the twentieth time.

Bad Schandau 21.07.1939

Dearest Arnold,

I am so sorry that you say you will to this go Scarborough for holidays this year and not again come to Saxon Switzerland. Is there something you could say to make your parents do a different decision?

So we will instead write each other.

Please tell me about Scarborough when you go. How lucky you are to have the seaside only seventy kilometres distant. The nearest seaside in Germany it is nearly five hundred kilometres! I have only ever one holiday made there. We go camping in the Baltic coast.

You say you are worried about what is happening in Europe and that your father thinks there will be a war. I do not think this and my father is agreeing with me. Hitler is only asking for what is correct. Poland is unreasonable demands making. It is obvious that Danzig is a German city.

School was boring for me too so I am pleased the holidays here are. Mutti and Vati give me a little money for helping in the guest house. We do not have English guests this year but lots of Germans. We are very busy.

Do you still our kiss remember on the platform of the Personenaufzug? I hold it close in my heart and I will kiss you again soon. I hope it, anyway.

Write me soon!

Your girlfriend,

Lotti XXX

13

By the time Tilsner had finished ploughing through all the files, he started to wonder where Müller was. Their strange relationship had become even weirder. Müller would summon him for sex at the drop of a hat, and then virtually ignore him the next second – as though she was ashamed of her own needs. Men were much simpler beasts. For Tilsner, sex was a necessity – and he'd always fancied her. Mind you, the years were starting to take their toll now – but they were on him too. It was said that men over fifty became virtually invisible. He was lucky that in his early fifties, he could pass for early forties – perhaps younger. It meant he still got the come on from waitresses in cafés – especially in the provinces, where they regarded Berliners as some sort of special exotic breed. The trick didn't work quite as well here. Dresden women seemed to have too high an opinion of themselves for Tilsner's liking.

It was his roving eye, of course, which had caused all the problems with his ex-wife, Koletta. That was all in the past now, she'd found a new man. A new man and a new life, and she'd taken their children with her. Not just to another city, but across the bloody state border. Still, he had a plan for that. One that – thanks to his childhood friend Manfred – ought to be far-advanced by now. He'd need to catch up with him soon and find out how things were going.

Tilsner slammed the last file shut. A thankless task. About four people of the right age to follow up – but none of them matched all the characteristics of Concrete Man. In any case, as he'd insisted to Müller, if that punk girl was correct and the victim was a foreigner, most likely he wouldn't appear in the Republic's missing persons files.

The story was the same in the teleprinter room. They'd sent out a bulletin to other forces to see if anyone had a likely fit for their victim. So far – as the headshake from the pretty tele-printer operator made clear – no one had responded positively.

He tracked down Schmidt in the forensic lab.

'Any sign of Müller?' he asked.

'No, Comrade *Oberleutnant*. I've not seen her since earlier this afternoon.'

Tilsner frowned and checked his watch again. 'She was chas-ing up on that bus and train ticket you found, wasn't she? Do you still have the details of them? Times, dates, starting and des-tination stops and stations?'

Schmidt moved over to a grey metal filing cabinet and pulled out a folder. Then, as Tilsner made a careful note, he listed all the information from the tickets.

Having consulted a map, Tilsner reckoned it would normally take him about half an hour – perhaps a little more – to drive the thirty kilometres or so to Pirna. But as he saw several centimetres of snow lying in the police car park, and on top of the Wartburg itself, he revised that estimate upwards. Maybe that was all it was. Müller had got stuck in the snow. Yet Tilsner could see that the streets of Dresden, although slushy, still had traffic running freely and the buses still appeared to be working. Something didn't add up.

He used his gloved hands to clear enough snow from the windscreen, side and rear windows and mirrors to be able to see, and then fired the car up and began to drive.

Tilsner's big advantage in trying to follow in Müller's footsteps was that he knew how her mind worked. He could predict the steps she would have taken to find the owner of the bus ticket and purse. They didn't have a name, and the description given by Petra Abt had been pretty useless. And that was only the woman in the argument. There was absolutely nothing to say it was the same woman who'd lost the purse. In fact, Tilsner would stake money that it wasn't. Karin had decided it had been enough to start what was in all probability a wild goose chase – his task was to try to follow the same trail.

He knew he was on the right tracks when one of the bus drivers mentioned a pretty female detective who'd been asking the same questions. Then he found the second driver – who'd given Karin the woman's first name and had pointed out the block she lived in. Now he just had to narrow down the apartment number.

All the time, his sense of foreboding grew. She clearly *hadn't* just been delayed by the snow – unless their paths had crossed without him realising, and she was now on her way back to Dresden. Some sixth sense, though, told him something was wrong. He didn't want her to meet a lonely end in this windswept, snowswept, concrete maze on the edge of Pirna. For one thing, he enjoyed working with her. Down the years, he'd grown very fond of her – even though she could be infuriating at times. Was he being disloyal in the plans he was making with Manfred to get a chance to see his own kids again? Probably. But one day she might understand. For now, it was her immediate wellbeing that was his primary concern.

Once he reached the block in question, things became more difficult. No one knew a Lotti, no one had seen a female detective matching Müller's description. But then why would they? In this snow, she'd have had her hat pulled down over her head, her coat collar up, and even if she had her police overcoat on, most of the fuckwits here wouldn't know what one looked like. This was going to be a thankless task. Knocking on every door would take ages.

Instead, in case something had gone wrong, he decided to do a quick visual check of each floor.

It was on the third floor where he struck lucky. He saw the shards of wood first, then looked up to see that the door lock on apartment 315 had been forced open. He was tempted to call out her name – but then what if she was being held captive in there? Instead, he drew his Makarov from his shoulder holster, slid off the safety catch, and carefully opened the door.

It wasn't until he was a few paces inside the apartment that the light coming through the window illuminated her body – slumped on the ground.

'Karin!' he shouted. 'Are you OK?' The question was redundant. He could see she wasn't.

He knelt down beside her, blood pounding in his head, and felt for a pulse.

Thankfully there was one. As he did so, he noticed the wound on the back of her head.

He manoeuvred her onto her side, bent one leg and one arm to make sure she was in the recovery position.

Then he got out his handheld radio and summoned an ambulance.

14

Müller panicked when she finally regained consciousness. She was in a strange bed – a hospital bed – and it brought back bad memories of a previous hospital visit, in Halle-Neustadt, which had nearly seen her and her twins losing their lives. She found herself struggling for breath, hyperventilating, and heard the monitors that were checking her vital functions going haywire.

Nurses and doctors rushed in, she was given an injection, and then suddenly nothing mattered and the world was wonderful. She felt she was floating above herself, like an out of body experience. But although she felt calmer, something still nagged at the back of her head – and it wasn't just the dull headache. She brought her hand up, felt the dressings, and then remembered. She'd been in the flat of the woman called Lotti when she must have been attacked from behind, just like their victim in Gorbitz. Through the fuzz of whatever sedative the medics had given her, she tried to get her thoughts in order, but couldn't.

The appearance of a familiar face – Tilsner – at her bedside was a relief.

'How are you feeling?' he asked. 'Someone had a right go at you.'

She struggled to get the words out. 'I've felt better.'

'Are you well enough to tell me what happened?'

Müller tried to sit up further in bed, then felt a thudding pain in the back of her skull and relaxed back into her previous position. 'There's not a lot to say. I found her flat in Sonnenstein.'

'I know. That's where I found you.'

'You came after me?' For some reason, the thought made Müller feel warm inside.

'Only because I knew it wasn't like you not to check in with me as to how I was getting on with the missing persons files. And the answer is, not very well. But I can't believe you just collapsed and hit your head.'

Müller started panicking again. 'My Makarov?'

Tilsner patted her arm. 'It's OK. Relax. I've got it. Whoever clobbered you didn't care about your gun. Now, are you well enough to tell me what happened?'

Müller tried to relax into her bed pillows. 'I went into the apartment. There was someone there – rifling through her desk drawers. But there must have been two of them and I didn't realise. The second one must have been keeping guard.'

'Descriptions?' asked Tilsner, taking out his notebook.

Müller shook her head, then regretted it, as pain pulsed through her body once more. 'I didn't see them clearly – even the one in front of me.'

'Male, female?'

'Male – medium build, dark clothing, dark hair – I think. His back was towards me, and when he turned he shone his torch into my eyes. I didn't see his face. Sorry. I'm worse than Petra Abt.'

Tilsner attempted a weak smile, but she could tell he was probably thinking the same thing. 'It can't be helped,' he said. 'The good news is, the doctors here think there's no lasting damage. But you were out cold for about four hours.'

'What time is it?'

Tilsner glanced down at his watch. His expensive, western watch. 'It's just coming up to one in the morning. I'd better be off now – someone will have to hold the fort in the morning, and you're in no shape to. But you've obviously got a nice thick skull – it's saved you.'

Müller attempted a weak smile, but just creasing her face was painful. 'Did you manage to find anything in the apartment – had they left anything to find?'

'Plenty, yes. I've bagged it all up but won't start sifting through it till tomorrow, and I've left Jonas there doing forensic work. He might be able to lift some prints. Were they wearing gloves?'

Müller defied the pain to furrow her brow, in a bid to remember. To recall something, anything. But she couldn't. 'Sorry, Werner, I just didn't see.'

15

When the morning doctor's round came, Müller was told they wanted to keep her in for another twenty-four hours for checks. Instead, she asked for the strongest painkillers possible and discharged herself. Then she wrapped herself up warmly in her still-bloodied police overcoat and took the short tram ride back to Dresden's police headquarters.

Tilsner's look when he saw her was more one of anger than surprise.

'I thought they wanted to keep you in longer for observation?'

'They did. But I feel fine,' she lied, trying to ignore the headache that still pounded despite the drugs to alleviate it. 'I discharged myself. How's everything going? Did Jonas manage to turn up anything?'

'He's got a match to some prints.'

'Really? Whose?'

Tilsner pulled her aside so they were out of earshot of any other officers, then whispered in her ear. 'You're not going to like it. Bahlow's.'

'The major from the *MfS*?'

'The very same. He's got a police record from way back, when he was a teenager.'

'Have we pulled him in yet?'

Tilsner snorted in disgust. 'What do you think? Half of the Stasi's agents probably have criminal records. A housebreaker would have exactly the sort of expertise they need.'

'So what do you suggest we do about it?'

'Nothing. It's useful knowledge to have, but that's about it. You didn't get a positive ID on him, did you? I doubt he's involved in whacking you over the head, either. If they wanted you off the case, they'd just insist on it with *Oberst* Reiniger back in Berlin, or with the *Kriminalpolizei* bosses here in Dresden. I'll have a quiet word with him and try to find out what's going on. In the meantime, I've uncovered something more interesting.'

'What?'

'We think we may be looking for a foreigner, don't we?'

'*If* what Petra Abt says she heard amounts to a row of beans – and if she was correct.'

Tilsner pointed to one of the plastic evidence bags on his desk. 'Letters to and from England. Dating back to the 1930s. It seems as though she was pen pals, perhaps more, with an English boy she met when he came over here on holiday. Although not all the letters were sent – some just seem to serve as a sort of diary. And the ones from England stopped when the war began. There was no direct mail between Germany and Britain during the war, although people sometimes got round it by using intermediaries in places like Switzerland. And it seems they rekindled the friendship more recently.'

'Do we have a name?'

Tilsner nodded. 'A certain Dr Arnold Southwick. Lived in Hull, wherever that is. Sounds like it got a pounding in the war, like Dresden. Anyway, I did some checking to see if the border guards had any records of an Arnold Southwick. They did. He arrived at Berlin Schönefeld last autumn to take up a visiting university research post.'

'In Dresden?'

'Exactly, at the University of Technology.' Tilsner started to get up and put on his jacket. 'I'm just about to go and pay his department a visit. Do you feel up to coming with me?'

Müller and Tilsner found themselves being ushered into one of the older buildings at the university, and then a wood-panelled room which looked as though it served as some sort of canteen or refectory where they were asked to wait for Arnold Southwick's boss, Professor Odenwald.

After ten minutes or so, a dishevelled, grey-haired bearded man arrived, slightly out of breath.

'Apologies. I've just come from a lecture I was giving. I gather you're from the police, asking after Arnold Southwick.'

Müller nodded, and introduced herself and Tilsner. They both showed the man their *Kriminalpolizei* IDs. Concentrating on this new lead seemed to have taken her mind off her headache. Either that or the strong painkillers had finally kicked in.

'*Kriminalpolizei?* Nothing's happened to him, has it?'

'We don't know at this stage,' said Müller. 'We're just making routine inquiries, and we believe Dr Southwick may be able to help us.'

'You're a bit late, I'm afraid,' said Professor Odenwald. 'Dr Southwick's research had come to a . . . a slightly premature end, shall we say. He's gone back to Britain.'

'When was this?' asked Müller.

'Earlier this month. Or was it late last month? Sorry, my memory's not what it was.'

'We'll need the exact date,' said Müller. 'Please check it and phone into the People's Police offices with it later. So what happened?'

'I can't go into any details, I'm afraid. Although the research was under the auspices of the Department of History, it also had government involvement, and was classified.'

'Classified?' queried Tilsner.

'As in secret.'

'Can you at least tell us the area of research?' asked Müller.

'The history of the Second World War.'

'That's a rather wide subject,' said Tilsner. 'We're going to need more than that.'

'I appreciate that. But I'm under oath not to break the secrecy around the project. There are government ministries involved, you see.'

'Ministries?' prompted Müller.

'Well, one ministry in particular. I can give you a contact there, if that's of any use. They have an office here in Dresden.

Here – he left me his card, if you need to copy down the details.'
He offered the business card to Müller.

She took it, then almost dropped it in disgust. Once again, she, Tilsner and Schmidt were being given the runaround.

The name on the card: *Major* Rüdiger Bahlow. Ministry for State Security.

When they got back to the incident room after the fruitless visit to the university, Bahlow was waiting for them, leaning back in Müller's chair, twiddling his thumbs. Müller almost expected him to stay there and let her stand, but clearly the man had some manners.

'Sorry, Comrade Müller. I was just resting my legs while waiting for you.' He noticed the dressing on the back of Müller's head, and seemed genuinely concerned. 'I hope you're all right. If this isn't a convenient moment, I can come back later.'

Müller drew in a long breath, then exhaled. 'No. We wanted to talk to you as well. And this is as good a time as any. The reason I've got a dressing on my head is that someone decided to whack me on the skull yesterday evening, a bit like our Concrete Man. Do you know where that happened?'

'No,' replied Bahlow, looking puzzled. 'Should I?'

'Perhaps,' said Tilsner. 'It was in an apartment where we found *your* fingerprints.'

'I hope you're not suggesting I had anything to do with Comrade Müller's injuries.'

'We're not suggesting that, no,' said Müller. 'I don't think even your lot would be clumsy enough to launch an unprovoked attack on a *Kriminalpolizei* officer. Nevertheless, your fingerprints were found in several places in an apartment we think may be linked to our inquiries.'

Bahlow shrugged, looking unconcerned. 'Would you care to enlighten me *where* exactly?'

'In Sonnenstein, on the edge of Pirna,' said Tilsner. 'At the apartment of a citizen named Lotti Rolf.'

Müller watched Bahlow's face. Trying to detect if there was any sign of alarm – that the man may have been involved in the raid on Rolf's apartment, and somehow made a mistake, forgetting to cover his hands with gloves, or taking them off at some point. But there wasn't a flicker in the eyes or facial expression.

'That's easy to explain,' said the Stasi officer. 'There's no reason why I have to tell you this, and it must remain absolutely confidential. She's an unofficial informer for the Ministry for State Security.' Then he looked hard at Müller. 'Ask your deputy if you're uncertain what one of those is, or what their function is.' He allowed himself a small smirk. 'I'm her handler – we sometimes meet at her apartment for briefings. It's as simple as that. So if she's featuring in your investigation, and you need to interview her, make sure you ask my department first. Is that clear?'

Müller gave the man as hard a stare back as he'd given her. 'We take our orders from Keibelstraße – from the People's Police. Not from you.'

Bahlow slapped his thighs, and then stood up straight from the radiator he'd been leaning against. 'Comrade Müller, you and *Oberleutnant* Tilsner here have a track record of *not* following orders. One day it may be your downfall. Perhaps you might like to ponder *why* you've been assigned to a difficult case such as this one. Maybe someone in Berlin is just waiting for you to fail.'

A silence descended on the room. What Bahlow said was meant to serve as a warning. The problem was, Müller was perfectly aware of the dangers they faced – she didn't need them spelt out by a Stasi man, whether he outranked her or not.

When it looked as though Bahlow was about to take his leave, Tilsner intervened. 'What about Dr Arnold Southwick?'

This time, Müller did detect a flicker on Bahlow's face. The question had ruffled him.

'What about him?'

'Is he our Concrete Man?'

Bahlow's brow creased in puzzlement. 'How should I know? The victim hasn't been identified yet.'

'Why was Southwick in Dresden?' asked Müller.

'He was a research fellow at the university – Dresden University of Technology.'

'Funded by whom? Invited by whom? Researching what?' Müller wasn't sure what she was hoping Bahlow would reveal – if anything.

'Such a lot of questions, Comrade *Hauptmann*. I'm afraid Arnold Southwick's research was confidential and I'm not at liberty to tell you any more about it. However, what I can tell you is that Normannenstraße are sending a senior officer here to liaise with me over our interest in the case. Once he arrives, I'll see if he's prepared to meet you, and I will put those questions to him for you in advance, to see if he can find you the answers. Does that seem fair?'

Bahlow hitched up his trousers, smiled at them both, and then left the room without waiting for a reply.

16

ARNIE

Pearson Park, Hull
Night of 7–8 May 1941

We'd had hours and hours of air raid warnings the previous
night, running to the shelter in the garden. Nothing happened.
We just had a terrible night's sleep – not least because Fred's hit
the terrible twos, so he's always trying to escape. Mother's angry
too. She said we should have evacuated to Walkington, where
we have family friends – Uncle Mick and Auntie Pam – or even
gone to Nana's or the great aunts' in Brid.

I suppose it was because of all the 'crying wolf' the previous
night that, if the sirens sound tonight, Mother has persuaded
Father we shouldn't go to the shelter. Instead, we'll all settle
down to sleep under the dining table and kitchen table that
Father and I manoeuvre into position in the back room.

The first siren sounds just after midnight, and it's only about
five minutes after that that we hear the ack-ack guns start up, so
we know this time it's for real. Then the whoosh and boom of

the bombs rattling the windows, getting closer and closer. The thunderous noise never seems to end, shaking the foundations of the house, and even round the edges of the blackout curtains we can see the glow in the sky.

At one stage, Father risks looking out. The room is suddenly flooded with orange – as though the sky is on fire.

'Jesus!' is all my dad says. 'Perhaps we should go to the shelter.'

'It's too dangerous to go out now, Arthur,' hisses my mother. 'Now close that and get back under here.'

Fred is screaming now, with my mum trying to shush him. My father puts his arm round me, pulling me close, and then is soon snoring despite all the noise. To start with, I just can't get to sleep, then eventually I drift off too.

The terror we felt when we heard the 'up-down' wail of the air-raid siren is in total contrast to the joy now when the sirens sound the all-clear – a low whine rising to a constant higher whine – almost like the howl of a wolf (well, how I imagine a wolf would sound – I've never actually heard one in real life).

Father's snoring away and misses it, and Fred's sound asleep too, but Mother can sense I'm awake.

'Try to get some sleep now, Arnold,' she whispers, so as not to wake the other two. But the adrenaline is still rushing round my body, and I wonder if my friends from school are all right, or if any of their houses have been hit. As Father did before, I get up and sneak a look behind the blackout curtains. The sky is overcast, so I know the orange light isn't the dawn. It's coming from the city centre – and it's obviously still ablaze. Although the all-clear has sounded, I hear other sirens – no doubt fire engines, ambulances and police. It must have been the biggest night of bombing yet. It seemed to go on for ever.

Then a noise that is out of place – or should be out of place by now. The drone of aircraft engines.

I just have time to dive back under the heavy oak dining table before there's a gigantic roar like a tornado, a deafening explosion, and the sound of glass shattering.

The next thing I know I'm pinned down by something heavy on my legs.

The orange glow from outside the house is inside now.

Bits of dust and debris are falling on my face like raindrops and I'm looking up at the sky.

Then screaming. Mother, Father, both yelling in pain. But nothing from Fred.

I see him, still held in my mother's arms, peacefully asleep I think.

I try to get to my feet but I can't.

Then my mother is wailing. 'Arthur, Arthur!' she's screaming. 'He's not breathing. He's not breathing.'

17

Dresden
February 1982

Tilsner's search of Lotti's apartment, after Müller had been taken to hospital by the ambulance, had yielded some other useful information – even though the raiders had got there before them. The principal thing they could work with was an address for Lotti's parents, if they were still alive. At one stage before the war, they had run the Pension Schönblick in Bad Schandau. Perhaps Lotti was lying low there given all that seemed to be going on in Dresden. Certainly, she hadn't returned to the apartment in Sonnenstein – Tilsner had made sure a uniformed People's Police officer would be stationed outside twenty-four hours a day with instructions to detain her if she turned up.

As soon as they exited the People's Police HQ and made their way to the Wartburg, Müller's internal antennae started twitching. She glanced round. No one there. Perhaps she was being paranoid.

But as they began driving through Dresden's still partially snow-covered streets, Tilsner indicated her fears were not ill-founded.

She saw him glance in the wing mirror, then the rear-view mirror.

'Company?' she asked.

He nodded. 'Do you want me to try to lose them?'

'No,' she decided. 'We're not even sure who they are. Is it Bahlow's lot? Or someone else? Maybe we ought to encourage them and then face them off. Do you think Bahlow was lying when he insisted he had nothing to do with me being hit over the head at Lotti's apartment?'

'Actually, I got the impression it was a surprise. I don't fully understand what the Stasi's motives are – but they want us on this case, they want us investigating, otherwise it would have been easy enough for them to take it over completely. Perhaps they're just using us. Perhaps they want to flush someone out – and we're the way of doing that.'

They wound their way by road along a similar route that Müller had travelled the previous day by train. As she watched the Dresden suburbs pass by, she found her head beginning to throb again. She opened the pack of painkillers the hospital had given her and popped another two into her mouth.

'You can't just treat those things like sweets, you know,' warned Tilsner.

Müller laughed. 'Don't worry, Vati. I'll be a sensible girl.'

'That'll make a change.'

Pension Schönblick had certainly seen better days. It appeared to Müller as though it was still in private hands: there was no mention of it being a Free German Trade Union holiday home. But as a result, the paint on the window shutters, frames and doors was faded and peeling, and the snow hadn't been properly cleared or swept from the entrance pathway.

Tilsner rapped hard on the door, as though to prove his manliness. At first there was no reply. Then Müller spotted a bell at the side and rang it. Still they waited with no response.

Then a flick back of one of the curtains in a first-floor window. Müller held up her ID. 'People's Police. Open up please,' she shouted.

Still they had to wait, until – eventually – they heard the lock on the front door being turned, then the door slowly opened. An elderly woman, hair covered by a dirty-looking flowered headscarf, began to mumble through a gummy mouth.

'I can't understand what you're saying,' shouted Tilsner, again brandishing his ID. 'We're the police. *Kriminalpolizei.* We need to talk to you.'

The woman gave a small nod, opened the door further, and ushered them inside.

'What can I do for you?' she asked in a quivering, nervous voice.

'We're looking for Lotti Rolf,' said Müller.

'Why? She's not in any trouble is she?'

'We hope not,' said Tilsner. 'But we need to talk to her. Is she here?'

'No,' said the woman, giving a good impression of looking perplexed. 'She doesn't live with us anymore. She lives in Pirna. Do you want her address?'

Tilsner had moved past the woman, intent on searching the bed and breakfast hotel, warrant or not.

Müller kept her talking while her deputy went about his business. 'That won't be necessary, Frau . . .?'

'Rolf. Elfriede Rolf.'

'We already know Lotti's address in Sonnenstein. She doesn't seem to be there at the moment.'

'Oh,' said the woman. But the look on her face was not one of surprise. Müller got the feeling that the mother knew more about what was going on with her daughter than she was prepared to admit.

'So you don't know where she is?'

The woman shook her head, but was looking at the floor, as though she couldn't bear to meet Müller's eyes. 'Would it be easier if we sat down while I ask you my questions, Frau Rolf?'

'Of course, of course. How silly of me. Please come through to the sitting room. There are no guests here at the moment. I've stopped opening in the winter, ever since I lost Waldemar.'

'Waldemar?'

'My husband – Lotti's father. He passed away some five years back. God rest his soul.'

The two women settled themselves in slightly threadbare armchairs at ninety degrees to each other. Frau Rolf perched on the edge of hers, hands clasped together as though to stop them shaking. The woman was a bag of nerves. The question was, why? Perhaps it was simply an unannounced visit from the police that had rattled her.

'So do you have *any* idea where Lotti could be?'

'Well . . . she'd started seeing that Englishman – the one at the university.'

'Dr Southwick?'

'That's the one. They were pen pals since the 1930s. Lotti was besotted with him as a girl – his family stayed here just before the war broke out. This was a much more popular area for tourists then. We were doing well as a hotel in those days.' The woman looked wistful for a moment, then covered her mouth with her hand, as though realising what she'd just implied. 'Of course I'm not saying it was better under Hitler. I hope you don't think that's what I meant.'

'I'm not here to judge, Frau Rolf.' She could hear Tilsner banging about on the floor above – and wondered if he'd found anything.

The woman was clearly thinking the same thing. 'He won't make a mess, will he? It's difficult to keep it all ship-shape on my own.'

'*Oberleutnant* Tilsner always does things in a very professional manner, Frau Rolf,' replied Müller. She wished what she claimed always held true. 'So other than trying Dr Southwick's digs in Dresden –' Müller didn't mention that the man was either dead, having been buried in concrete, or that he'd returned to the UK – 'have you any suggestions where Lotti could be? Do you or her own or rent any other property?'

The woman creased her already leathered, wizened brow. 'No . . . well other than the annexe, but that's not been used for years. It's hardly habitable.'

'The annexe?'

'It's a little cottage – well, not much more than a wooden hut, really – in the Kirnitzsch valley. Near the waterfall.'

'And how do we get there?'

'Oh, it's easy enough. There's a tram.' The woman had suddenly brightened up, as though she was in her element, pointing out Bad Schandau's attractions to a visitor – something she'd obviously done for most of her life. She moved swiftly over to the window and pulled back the net curtain, beckoning Müller to look.

'See there, on the other side of the Kurpark. That's the tram terminus – just take it all the way to the waterfall stop, and the cottage is the first you see on the path to the waterfall. Or you can drive if you've got a car. It's no more than eight kilometres or so. There's a pension next to it, but like us it will be closed in the winter.' She turned back to Müller. 'I'll go and get you the cottage key. But as I say, we haven't used it in years. It was Waldemar's project really. No one's been up there since he died as far as I know, and in his last couple of years he wasn't really in a fit state to look after it. So it's had seven years of neglect. I dread to think what sort of a state it'll be in.'

As she shuffled through to a back room to collect the key, Tilsner finally returned.

'Anything useful?' asked Müller.

Tilsner wrinkled his nose, as though he'd been assailed by a bad smell, and shook his head. 'There's no sign that I can see that she's been here recently. Only one bed looks like it's been slept in. The others are all neatly made. To be honest, the whole place has an unloved, un-lived-in air to it. Any joy in questioning the old woman?'

'Only that there's some sort of annexe or weekend cabin nearby. We can either drive or get the tourist tram. It's probably worth checking out.'

Although the tram looked tempting to Müller, they weren't on some tourist jolly, so they decided to drive. In any case, the tram departed just before they did, so that for a few metres they were level with it – and it was travelling at a speed befitting something which obviously dated back to the early part of the century, if not earlier. The carriages were empty, save for one man in a dark anorak whose hood covered most of his face.

The road wound through the narrow Kirnitzsch valley, with snow-laden trees on each side. Although the road itself was snow-covered, Tilsner seemed unconcerned.

He saw Müller frowning as she surveyed the route ahead. 'Don't worry. We've got snow tyres on. It'll be fine. I wonder if our friend behind has.'

Müller looked in the wing mirror, but it was adjusted for Tilsner's vision so she couldn't see their pursuers. She quickly swivelled her head, and saw a Lada with a driver and passenger on their tail. 'Is it the same ones following us as before?'

'Hard to tell. They didn't get as close as this before. A dark Lada – so probably, but then there are plenty of dark Ladas around. They're certainly not subtle. They want us to know they're there.'

Once they reached the tourist tram's valley terminus, they parked the car. Müller again glanced back along the road. The

Lada had pulled into a lay-by some two hundred metres or so behind them – its occupants showing no inclination to follow them on foot.

'They're just on a watching brief, I expect,' said Tilsner.

Müller took in their surroundings. The tram terminus platform was covered in snow, with only a few footprints stamped out on its white blanket. Clearly in winter – or at least in this weather – Kirnitzschtal wasn't a huge draw. As Lotti's mother had predicted, the inn opposite was closed and looked half-abandoned.

They tried to get their bearings from the old woman's descriptions, looking for the signs for the waterfall. Just a few metres along the track, before the falls themselves, there was what looked like the 'cottage' – though to Müller's eyes, to call it that rather overstated things. The single-storey building looked more like a run-down weekend allotment shed.

Tilsner rapped hard on the door. No response. He made to give it a kick before Müller held up the key admonishingly. She leant on the door as she made to unlock it, but before she had inserted the key, the door swung open freely.

'Frau Rolf!' shouted Tilsner as they stepped inside. 'Are you in? It's the police. The *K*.'

There was silence, save for the dripping of a tap in the kitchenette.

Müller scanned the work surfaces. There was a half-drunk mug of coffee on the draining board. She clasped her hands around it.

Still warm.

Someone had been here – perhaps within the last fifteen minutes. She handed it to Tilsner.

'So – if it's Lotti, where's she gone?' he asked.

Müller didn't answer, but instead opened the cottage's back door. Footprints in the snow – and they looked fresh.

She followed the tracks, conscious that Tilsner was close behind her, but not stopping to wait for him. The prints formed part of a narrow path through snow-covered ferns into a wooded area behind the waterfall. Müller couldn't see it, but could hear the roar of water and knew it was nearby. It might have been cold enough to snow, but the temperatures hadn't become low enough to actually freeze streams or rivers.

As they entered the wood, Müller realised the snow cover under the tree canopy was much thinner. Not only that, but the path – and the prints – had disappeared.

She frowned and stopped, then turned back to her deputy.

'It's not clear which way now,' she said.

Tilsner peered at the ground, trying to see what had happened. It was as though the footprints had evaporated into thin air.

Müller looked back down the hillside, beyond the little shack-like cottage, to the inn and the tram stop. The tram – after no doubt stopping at most of the stops en route – had only now caught up with them and reached its terminus. Two figures emerged. One from the driver's cab – the other from the rear of the two passenger cars. It was the same hooded figure they'd seen when they'd set off, but Müller still couldn't get a good look at the man's face. She saw, however, that he was following the exact same route they had, to the Rolf's rather grandly titled cottage 'annexe'.

She pulled Tilsner back into the cover of the trees. As she did so, two more figures emerged – from the Lada parked further along the road. Perhaps the men she'd assumed were Stasi agents hadn't been following Müller and her deputy after all. Perhaps they were more concerned with this new arrival. What everyone appeared to have an interest in was the whereabouts of Lotti Rolf. But she, along with the footprints – hers or not – had simply disappeared.

'Who's who, do you think?' whispered Tilsner, perhaps conscious that in a quiet valley like this one, echoes of their voices could travel far if they weren't careful.

'I don't know,' said Müller. 'But I get the impression they're not working together.'

Suddenly, from above them, Müller heard a crack of wood and a muffled cry that almost sounded like a baby.

'There's someone further up,' hissed Tilsner.

Müller felt her heartbeat pounding in her ears. *Had they finally found Lotti? And if so, was she the answer to this strange case?* The three men below them clearly hadn't heard anything awry – Tram Man had now almost reached the cottage, while the two from the Lada were hanging back, as though unsure whether or not to confront him.

Tilsner began to climb towards the source of the noise, with Müller following.

Then more rustling, another cry, and in her peripheral vision Müller saw something running off through the undergrowth. But it didn't look human.

'False alarm,' said Tilsner. 'Foxes getting into a fight.'

Müller sighed. 'But they didn't make those footprints leading from the cottage.'

'No. But the prints have disappeared. I don't think we're going to have any more luck up here. We'd be better off getting back to that cottage and catching our mysterious Tram Man red-handed, and seeing what he has to say for himself.'

They both knew they hadn't locked the back door to the cottage behind them. What Müller feared was that the visitor to the Rolf's annexe might also decide to use the rear exit – and catch them by surprise. But by the time they reached the door, there was no sign of him. There were – however – banging noises coming from inside, consistent with someone opening and shutting drawers and cupboards, looking for something.

Tilsner got his Makarov from his shoulder holster with his right hand and gingerly pushed the door open with his left, then switched to pushing it with his foot as he released the gun's safety catch. Müller did the same with her pistol, looking over his shoulder.

If he had been in the kitchen area, the man had now moved.

They heard noises from the mezzanine level.

Tilsner beckoned Müller with the Makarov.

As slowly as possible, to try to avoid making the boards creak, they climbed the stairs. They could see the man now, crouched down, his back to them, rifling through a chest of drawers.

Looking for something – apparently not, as Tilsner and Müller were, trying to track down Lotti herself.

Tilsner crept up behind the man, then suddenly grabbed him round the throat with his forearm.

Müller could tell he was beginning to squeeze – the man was fighting for breath, but Tilsner seemed possessed and didn't appear to want to stop.

18

ARNIE

Pearson Park, Hull
February 1942

'Surely you can look a bit smarter than that, Arnold?' My mother flusters over me, trying to straighten my tie, then when she's satisfied with that, she starts attempting to run a comb through my hair.

I wrench her off and shrug free. 'Leave me alone.'

My father lowers his newspaper and glowers at me over the top of his half-eye reading glasses. 'Don't raise your voice to your mother, boy.' He lifts his arm threateningly, the palm of his hand outstretched. 'Otherwise you'll get a taste of this. You're not too old.'

I let out a long sigh. It was bad enough having to write essays about the bombing at school. Describing the night when the whole sky glowed orange, and then the roof fell in, and my baby brother – seemingly untouched – stopped breathing. Some of my friends seemed to revel in reliving it all. I hated it.

But now a 'Man from the Ministry', as Father describes him, is coming round to interview us. Raking it all over again. Mother has been a bag of nerves ever since the night Fred was killed. Any little noise seems to spook her. Even the sound of a car or lorry driving past can be enough to set her off. I can see her face go white, her hands start to tremble, as though the German bombers are back to attack us again. But there have been far fewer attacks since that terrible night. Hull's still a complete mess, of course. The city centre's in ruins. But for the moment, the Nazis seem to be leaving us alone. The news from the rest of the war is a bit better too, with the Soviets putting up some fierce resistance. Perhaps the tide is turning and Lotti's beloved 'Führer' will finally be defeated. What would become of Lotti then? Is she even still alive? No letters get through to me anymore. Perhaps she's forgotten me.

I pull the net curtains aside and watch him come up the front garden path. He looks like one of those City gents you see in the newsreels and films, walking over the Thames bridges, brolly swinging, suitcase in hand, hat perched firmly on head. I'd rather just go upstairs to my room and hide, but then I really would get a belting from Father.

Father answers the door, puffing himself up, full of self-importance, the way he does when he answers the telephone in his posh voice, hiding all trace of a Hull or East Yorkshire accent, with its vowels lapsing into semi-coherent mumbles. As the man apologises for being late, my father says: 'Oh no, don't worry,' mouthing the 'o's in posh-speak, rather than the '*Err nerr, dern't wurry*' he'd usually use.

They set the man up at a table in the sitting room. He says he wants to interview us one by one. Mum looks absolutely terrified, so Father offers to go first. Mum ushers me into the kitchen with her, and then starts to prepare teas for everyone – using the best china, of course – and even, with shaking hands, opens the cake tin with the jam tarts in – somewhere I'm never allowed to venture without permission. 'We don't have enough on rations for you to be snacking all the time, Arnold,' Father will usually warn.

After she's taken a tray of tea and tarts through to the sitting room, Mum comes back and pours me one, and then let's me have the pick of the remaining tarts. She knows I like the lemon curd ones the best. It's proper lemon curd – although made with lemon juice, rather than real lemons – made by Nana, using up what little butter ration she gets. The pastry melts in my mouth, and I savour the tang and sharpness of the lemon, rolling it round and round on my tongue, feeling my salivary glands pumping out manically, as though they're fire hoses trained on one of the German bombers' fires.

When it's my turn, I brace myself mentally. I don't want to show any weakness in front of this grey man, who the government has sent to delve into all our sadness and grief.

Mother has set up the folding, green-baize-covered card table for him. Even that makes my eyes prickle. It was Nana's table, and she always said it would be mine. Now the fond memories of gambling games like Newmarket will be forever sullied. We only ever played for farthings – but Nana soon taught me it doesn't take too many wins of piles of farthings to turn them into sixpences, shillings and even – one time when all the luck was going my way – half a crown.

The man is going through his notes, wearing a pair of half-eye reading glasses like my father. The resemblance ends there, however. Father is thickset, muscly, and can whip a belt on my arse so that it hurts something chronic. This man doesn't look like he could hurt a fly. He's younger than I realised – his balding black hair, glued in strands to his head with some horrible oil, together with his glasses and sober expression, had made him seem older. I wonder if I'll have to do that one day. Get sent round by the government to dig into people's misery. I bloody well hope not.

Eventually he looks up and tries to smile at me. I don't smile back. As far as I'm concerned, he's the enemy.

'Now then Arnold, your mother says the war has had a bad effect on your nerves and schoolwork. Is that correct?'

'I suppose. But no different to anyone else.'

'But your house was badly hit in the last year's bombing, I believe?'

'You know it was.'

'I'm not here to judge you or criticise you, Arnold. I just want to explore your feelings about the war, and particularly the bombing of Hull, in your own words.'

'It's awful, isn't it? Those Nazis are barbarians.'

'And you've lost a family member?'

I can feel the tears starting already. 'I don't want to talk about that.'

'I can understand that, Arnold. But by talking about it, you will be helping the war effort. Everyone has to do their bit. As Mr Churchill has said, this is a war of unknown warriors. He didn't just mean soldiers by that. He meant every one of us – even those, like yourself, who are too young to actually fight.'

I glower at him then. What does he know – sitting in his pinstripe suit, with his fountain pen and inkwell? Why isn't he fighting like others of his age? Why isn't *he* doing his bit?

But he's like a dog picking at its own scabs, again and again and again.

'Was the loss of Fred particularly hard?'

I start curling my fingers into fists under the table. I want to give him a bloody good punch. How dare he ask such stupid questions?

'It wasn't just hard, it was awful,' I snap. Tears wet my cheeks, but I don't care. 'He was my baby brother. I looked after him. Protected him. Only I didn't do a very good job, did I? And it was all my fault.'

The man looks surprised at that, and stops taking notes. 'Why do you say that, Arnold?'

'I opened the blackout curtains to see the sky burning. The German bomber probably saw the light.'

The man gets out a handkerchief from his pocket and offers it to me. I take it and dab at my eyes and face. Then, from his other pocket, he gets out a packet of sherbet lemons and a paper serviette, puts three of the sweets on the tissue, and slides it across the table to me.

'Those might help,' he says in a friendly whisper. I don't want to take the sweets. It seems like a betrayal. But being presented with sherbet lemons in the middle of a world war is a bit like a man dying of thirst reaching an oasis in the desert. Grudgingly, I allow myself to think that he has a job to do, like anyone. 'Please look at me Arnold, and believe me when I tell you this. War is a terrible thing – but absolutely none of this, and certainly not what happened to your brother, is any of your fault. All right?' He lifts my chin up gently so that I have to look him in the eyes.

'All right,' I say, trying to choke back the tears.

'After what happened, did it change your attitude to the war, and to the Germans?'

'Not really,' I mumble. 'I've always hated the Germans.'

'But your mother said you had a German pen pal.' He peers through his glasses at his notes again, leafing back a couple of pages. 'Lotti. Did you feel differently about Lotti?'

'What's she got to do with anything?'

'In her letters, did she talk about her views on the Nazi leadership?'

I shrug. *What does that matter now? All this is irrelevant. My baby brother is dead and the bloody Germans killed him.* 'A bit.'

'What sort of things did she say . . . about Hitler, for example?'

The questions are so stupid I decide I want to shock him. 'She seemed to think the sun shone out of his bum, but I don't see what that's got to do with anything.'

My coarse language leaves him unruffled. 'So, going back to my earlier question, given the way she revered Hitler, did it make you feel different about her after the terrible bombing Hull suffered, particularly as you lost your baby brother?'

The question's too complicated. I find myself losing it – rage and despair whirling round my head. I jump up and try to grab at him.

'Leave her out of it, you bastard,' I shout, trying to pummel his face. In the commotion, his glasses fall off. 'They killed my brother, the Nazi fuckers. You've no idea what that means. You've no idea what it's like.' Tears are streaming down my face as if trying to douse the fire of my rage. He's not shouting for help, just holding my arms quite gently, trying to stop me striking and clawing at him.

Then my father bursts in, belt in hand.

'Arnold! Come here this instant.'

I try to cower behind the man.

'It's all right, Mr Southwick. It's not Arnold's fault. He's just a little—'

'Don't tell me how to look after my own son,' spits Father, and drags me from the room. I know what's coming next and I piss myself in fear.

19

When Tilsner had finally released the man sufficiently to allow him to speak, Müller realised they might have been presumptive in attacking him.

'Who the hell are you?' the man demanded after he'd caught his breath.

Müller produced her *Kripo* ID. '*Hauptmann* Karin Müller. And this is my deputy, *Oberleutnant* Werner Tilsner. Would you mind identifying yourself to *us*, Comrade? And can you explain why you are rooting around in a property which (a) doesn't belong to you and which (b) is the focus of a murder inquiry?'

The man held their gaze, then produced ID of his own. The shield, rifle and East German flag on the logo already told Müller what she needed to know. He was a Ministry for State Security agent.

'I'm *Hauptmann* Gustav Weiß,' the man said, stretching his neck from side to side and gingerly stroking it, as though to check that Tilsner hadn't done any permanent damage. 'And I will be reporting this.'

'Feel free,' said Tilsner. 'This is our case. Your lot just have a watching brief. Go and ask Bahlow in Dresden if you don't believe me. So why don't you just get out of here, now, before I actually squeeze your windpipe properly?'

The man started to move off, taking a folder with him.

'What's that you've got?' asked Müller.

'It's none of your business,' replied Weiß. Tilsner snatched the folder from his hands and began leafing through it.

'Oi,' shouted the man. 'That is Ministry for State Security property.'

'What is it, Werner?' asked Müller.

'More letters between Lotti and Arnold Southwick. Letters that are evidence in our murder inquiry.'

The man made a grab to try to snatch the folder back in turn, but Tilsner was too quick for him. With one hand, he shoved the man away by pushing into his face, with the other, he shielded the folder behind his body.

'As I said,' reiterated Tilsner. 'This is evidence for our murder inquiry. If you want copies, you'll have to talk to Bahlow.'

The man stared them both down for a moment, then turned on his heels. Müller followed him to the door, then watched him make his way back to the tram stop. To the side, leaning nonchalantly against a fence while enjoying a quiet smoke, were the two from the Lada. The two that Müller had assumed were also Stasi agents. Now, they were lazily watching Weiß but making no attempt to rendezvous with him. So if Weiß really was the Stasi agent, who the hell were the others?

Once they were back in Dresden, Müller's first move was to seek an urgent appointment for her and Tilsner with Bahlow at Bautzner Straße, the Stasi regional headquarters on the opposite – northern – bank of the Elbe, in Dresden Neustadt. Claiming she had important new evidence, she managed to secure a meeting within the hour.

The Stasi's administrative offices here were much like many others in the Republic. A fairly featureless, grey concrete affair, prettied up with screen walls of decorative concrete blocks. Müller had a fairly good idea what it would look like round the back of the building, however. Probably a mirror image of the Stasi prison in Bautzen itself – the town some sixty kilometres to the east which lent the street they were now on its name – complete with walls, barbed wire, and an internal brightly lit garage where new inmates would be processed.

Müller and Tilsner were led down a couple of corridors and then up a staircase before finally being shown into Bahlow's office.

As soon as they were through the door, Müller's heart sank.

If she and Tilsner knew what they were dealing with in Bahlow, the man sitting in front of them – with his slightly unfashionable sandy shoulder-length hair – was altogether harder to read. He was the man who Bahlow could easily have modelled himself on – Müller's old sometime nemesis, sometime collaborator, Klaus Jäger. Now reduced in rank to the level at which Müller had first encountered him: an *Oberstleutnant*, or lieutenant colonel.

As Müller and Tilsner entered, both Stasi men got to their feet and smiled. They could almost be an idealised Republic father and son, standing as they were under a portrait of Erich Honecker, and with a bust of that other communist stalwart Felix Dzerzhinsky on Bahlow's desk. Iron Felix was the former head of the Soviet secret service, the Cheka, on which the Stasi modelled itself.

'Karin, Werner,' said Jäger, extending his hand across the desk above the miniature white head of Dzerzhinsky. 'Good to see you again.' Müller took his hand and shook it, but she didn't echo his greeting of pleasure, and she wasn't very sure it was sincere in any case. Instead, she stuck to formalities.

'Comrade *Oberstleutnant*. What are you doing in these parts?'

'Ah. I thought your bosses at Dresden People's Police headquarters would have told you. I've been asked to take an overview of the case you and *Major* Bahlow here are working on. But I promise I won't be interfering.' Jäger said this last sentence with a thin grin plastered to his face. Both he and Müller knew it wasn't true.

'Now,' said Bahlow, 'what was it you wanted to see us about? I believe you have some new evidence?'

Müller tried not to look shamefaced. In fact, they had very little evidence at all. But they did have some new information.

'Not evidence, as such. More of a question, actually.'

'All right,' said Bahlow, pleasantly. 'Go on.'

'What was one of your men doing at the Rolfs' bed and breakfast annexe near Bad Schandau a few hours ago?'

Bahlow looked genuinely puzzled. 'I'm not aware of that. Did you get a name?'

'*Hauptmann* Gustav Weiß.'

Bahlow's frown deepened. 'The name doesn't ring a bell. Are you sure it was the Dresden department he worked for? Which section? Was that his real name or code name? Presumably his real name if he used his title.'

Now it was Müller's turn to frown. 'I'm sorry, I didn't get any of that.'

'No matter. Why don't you two sit with Klaus over there on the armchairs? I'll order us up some coffee, and make a few calls to try to find out what this Weiß bloke was up to, and who he works for.'

By the time the coffee arrived, Bahlow had got his answer.

'This is a little puzzling. I went up the chain as far as Normannenstraße. There are no agents of that name anywhere in the organisation.'

Jäger cleared his throat. 'In any case, to me that sounds more like a Swiss-German or Austrian name.' He turned to Müller. 'Are you sure you got it right, Karin?'

'Of course. He showed me his Ministry for State Security ID.'

Jäger shrugged. 'No doubt we'll get to the bottom of it eventually. Now I'm glad you two have come in for this meeting, because we *do* actually have some new evidence on our side.' He handed each of the detectives a sheet. On it was a list of printed numbers – one to thirty-two – each with a handwritten code alongside. The code letters corresponded to a printed key, while the numbers obviously referred to a diagram in the top left corner of the sheet. Müller had seen this sort of thing plenty of times before – as, no doubt, had Tilsner.

'As you can see,' continued Jäger, 'it's a set of dental records.' Then he lent back in the armchair, and folded his arms across his stomach. 'A perfect match for our Concrete Man.'

'Southwick, presumably?' said Tilsner.

Jäger shook his head. 'No. Someone entirely different. A middle-aged man – yes – but he lives ... well, lived ... in Gorbitz. There is no connection to this Southwick, or indeed this Lotti Rolf who everyone seems obsessed with.'

Müller took a long gulp of coffee to try to compose her thoughts. She was immediately suspicious. Jäger suddenly appears on the scene – and as if by magic he instantly removes one of the stumbling blocks to progressing the inquiry: the identity of the victim. 'How did you come by these records and the victim's identity?'

This time Bahlow answered. 'One of his neighbours reported him missing. Perhaps they'd seen all the police activity and put two and two together.'

Müller heard Tilsner sigh. He sounded as dubious as she was. 'So does this mean you're taking over the case?' he asked.

Bahlow shook his head. 'No. Nothing for us here, really. Here's the man's name and address.' He handed a typewritten note to Müller. 'I'm sure you two are perfectly capable of wrapping up the formalities. But I suspect there wasn't any foul play, or if there was, it was some sort of drunken fight.'

'Why do you say that?' asked Müller.

'He was probably the best customer of Zum grüner Heinrich. Their takings will be down.'

'What is Zum grüner Heinrich?' asked Müller.

'It's the new pub they've built in Gorbitz – in the Platz der Bauarbeiter. Near where the tramline will run and one of the new stations will be, once that's all sorted. It's just behind Leutewitzer Ring, where the man lived, and near where the body was found.'

It was all far too easy for Müller's liking. The whole thing stank of a Stasi stitch-up. But without proof, they would simply have to go along with it. She looked at the name and address on the sheet. Bodo Achterberg, aged fifty-eight, a refuse collector. Address: Hetzdorfer Straße 11, Gorbitz.

She eyeballed Bahlow. 'Have you questioned the neighbours who reported him missing yet?'

'No,' replied Bahlow. 'We didn't want to tread on your toes.' Müller turned to Tilsner and saw him rolling his eyes.

The two detectives began to get to their feet. As they did, one of the new pieces of technology in Bahlow's office beeped into life and started printing something out. He got up and tore off the sheet. 'Aha! That's interesting. Normannenstraße are specu- lating where our friend Gustav got his name from, assuming – as they suspect – that he's an imposter.' He handed the sheet to Müller. It was a fax – containing a representation of a painting of the Alps. 'Gustav Weiß was a Swiss painter – I suspect that may be where the name has been borrowed from.'

Müller handed the picture back. She couldn't help feeling she and Tilsner were simply pawns in a game – a game that was being controlled by the Stasi. 'So why was he at Lotti Rolf's?' she asked.

Now it was Jäger's turn to intervene, as he rose to see them out. 'We've no idea, Karin. Perhaps he was simply a burglar and that's his modus operandi – posing as a Stasi officer. Very few people would be prepared to challenge that.' As he guided the two detectives to the door, he took Müller to one side. 'There's something else I wanted to talk to you about, Karin. But perhaps we should go for a drink one evening.'

Going for a drink with Jäger was about the last thing she wanted to do. Better to let him say what he wanted here and have done with it. 'What is it now?' she asked.

'Nothing to be concerned about.' He lowered his voice, speaking softly into her ear. 'It's just we have a mutual interest in the Rosa-Luxemburg-Sportschule in Oberhof.'

'Oh yes.' The thought of the children immediately made her feel guilty. She would have to make time to visit her mother – and Johannes and Jannika – at the weekend.

'Yes. I don't think I've told you yet. My son was selected to go there last autumn. He's very good with a rifle – all those hunting trips with his father. And he's not a bad cross-country skier either – so they think they may be able to make something of him as a biathlete. And I gather your twins go there too now?'

It was never a surprise to Müller what Jäger or other members of the Ministry for State Security knew about her home life. After all, Emil – the twins' father and her ex-partner – had been a Stasi agent. That's why he'd become involved with her – because the Ministry wanted him to. Nevertheless, the mention of her children made her wary. 'Yes,' she finally replied. 'But they're probably in different parts of the school, I would think. I doubt they'll see much of each other.'

'Of course, you're right. But if you like, I could ask Jens to keep an eye out for them.'

Müller wasn't sure she wanted the son of a Stasi man *keeping an eye out* for any members of her family – particularly the children she'd fought so long to have. But perhaps it was an innocent enough offer. Certainly, there was no point in getting Jäger's back up unnecessarily.

'Thank you. That's very kind, Klaus.'

20

Hetzdorfer Straße 11 was part of one of the new blocks that had been completed within the last year in Gorbitz – just round the corner from the block where they'd found the witness to the fight, Petra Abt. So new, the supposedly 'green' areas between the blocks were still mounds of earth and rubble covered with patchy snow – rather than the lawned play areas they were shown as on the architects' plans.

Müller and Tilsner had brought Schmidt with them this time, hauling him off other work the Dresden *Kriminalpolizei* had tasked him with.

'It seems as though the inquiry is now going in a completely different direction, Comrade *Hauptmann*,' he said. 'May I ask, what has prompted this change of course?'

As Tilsner manoeuvred the Wartburg into a parking space in front of the block, Müller handed Schmidt the copy of Bodo Achterberg's dental records. 'The Ministry for State Security have conveniently unearthed these, Jonas. An exact match for the dental records of our victim.'

'Conveniently?' queried Schmidt.

'Perhaps that's unfair,' said Müller, climbing out of the car. 'But *Oberstleutnant* Jäger has arrived to take charge of the

Ministry for State Security side of our inquiry – and almost immediately, these dental records appear.'

Schmidt held the piece of paper up to the light. 'They seem to be genuine, although it's only a copy so it's difficult to tell.'

Müller turned and held her forensic officer's gaze. 'While Tilsner and I doorstep his neighbours, could you perhaps stay in the car and – from these records – draw up your best guess of what his teeth actually looked like? You know, if he smiled, and someone was looking him straight on. Any missing teeth, any visible fillings, any visible problems.'

'Of course, Comrade *Hauptmann*. With pleasure. Just a diagram – or does it need to be lifelike?'

'As lifelike as possible. From a quick glance at these, would you say he had good teeth?'

'I'd say reasonable for his age. The gold replacement tooth is a sign that – at some stage – he's spent some money on his dentistry, and from what I can see, there would be no obvious signs of teeth missing – that sort of thing. Plenty of people of his age would have at least one false tooth. Other than the gold one, there's no sign of that.'

'That's useful to know,' said Müller. Through the windscreen, she could see Tilsner stamping his feet in front of the car, showing signs of impatience. 'Anyway, if you can do your best with an artist's impression. We'll be back soon.' She tossed him the ignition keys. 'If it gets too cold, start the engine.'

Everyone seemed to know Bodo Achterberg – or at least know who he was. It became clear to Müller he was considered a bit of a local 'character' – principally because of his ability to sink prodigious quantities of alcohol. On its own, that wasn't that unusual in the Republic. But Achterberg had a reputation for turning violent when too drunk.

'He was a sad case, to be honest,' said one woman who lived on the same floor in the same block. 'There have been times my husband's found him when he was too sloshed to even manage to get the key in his own front door. At times like that, he'd always bang on about some "lost love" of his. I can't imagine that was recently. But maybe when he was younger he wasn't such a mess.'

'And you say he regularly got into fights?' asked Müller.

'That's what my husband reckons. And it looked like that from the state of his face, to be honest. Broken nose, plenty of scars.'

'What about his teeth?'

'His teeth? I can't say I ever got close enough to see – he certainly had terrible bad breath, I can vouch for that. But if you want to know any more, you'd be better off at Zum grüner Heinrich. That's where you'll find all his drinking buddies.'

Müller returned to the Wartburg to catch up with Schmidt, and retrieve his now-completed dental sketch.

She wasn't sure what the 'Green Henry' in the name of the pub referred to. From her police college days, she had a vague memory of a police truck for transporting prisoners that had the nickname – but if so, it seemed odd to then bestow the name on a bar-restaurant.

Like everything else in Gorbitz, Zum grüner Heinrich was brand new – a shining example of the Republic's efforts to improve the lot of its citizens. But to Müller, its square lines and modernist architecture gave it a slightly soulless feel.

One of the first things they discovered – thanks to the restaurant's manager as she showed them round – was the foundation stone plaque, on the side of the building, for the whole Gorbitz development, unveiled just the previous year.

The manager also showed them a mural linked to the origin of the restaurant's name. It was nothing to do with historic horse-drawn police vans – the mural showed a scene from the novel *Der grüne Heinrich* by the Swiss author, Gottfried Keller. The woman was about to outline the novel's plot when Müller felt she had to intervene.

'We're not here for a tour of your establishment, citizen. We're simply seeking information about one of your regular customers, Bodo Achterberg.'

'Of course,' said the woman, nervously pulling at the sleeves of her overalls. 'You did say as much. Sorry, we're just very proud of the new restaurant and it's not often we get a visit from the police. I think the best place to start is the skittle alley in the basement – Bodo spent most of his spare time there.'

From what they'd heard of the man so far, and his prodigious drinking habit, Müller couldn't imagine him having a steady enough hand for skittles, but she and Tilsner dutifully followed the woman down the concrete steps to the basement.

Even now – in the middle of the day – virtually every skittle lane was busy, but most of the customers were clearly pensioners.

The manageress approached one man, and brought him over to speak to the two detectives.

The man introduced himself as Albert Planck and claimed to have known Bodo well.

'Bodo was a wreck I'm afraid, but he still didn't deserve what happened to him.'

'And what,' asked Tilsner, acidly, 'have you heard happened to him?'

'Well . . .' The man hesitated, as though he knew he was repeating rumours. 'You know . . . buried in concrete and all that. Can't have been pleasant.'

'There's been no confirmation of Herr Achterberg's fate, dead or otherwise,' said Müller. 'So please don't go repeating tittle-tattle.'

'Sorry,' said the man. 'It's just, as you can imagine, it's all anyone's talking about round here.' A loud cheer rang out, followed by sustained applause. 'Someone must have scored a ringer. Let's move over there by the bar. It'll be quieter.'

Once they were seated on a circular red leatherette bench seat around a beige melamine table, Müller started to question him in more detail about Bodo.

'You say he was a "wreck". What do you mean by that?'

'Well, he'd never got over the loss of the big love of his life. Got ditched at the altar by all accounts. His wife-to-be went off with his best friend. Mind you, I never knew him then, and it must have been forty or so years ago – during the war I think – but that was what set him on such a self-destructive path.'

Tilsner leant forward. 'How did that manifest itself?' he asked.

'Drinking himself silly. Virtually every night. I don't know where he got the money from, to be honest. He must have had some stashed away. But if all this hadn't happened, I doubt he'd have lasted long anyway.'

'Why do you say that?' asked Müller.

'He didn't look well, he was always getting into fights because of the drink, and eventually I'm sure his liver would have given up, wouldn't it?'

'We're not doctors,' said Tilsner. 'We're police officers. But you'd be surprised how long some of these alkies can keep it up for.'

Müller tried to focus the questioning on what they really needed to know. 'So, on his face, were there visible signs of these fights and his alcoholism?'

'Oh yes. Come over here, I'll show you.'

Planck led them over to a side table filled with various trophies, above which were several official skittle team photos from down the years, together with some unofficial celebration snaps.

'Although Gorbitz – as in the new-build part of Gorbitz – has been here for less than a year, the Gorbitz skittle club's been going for decades.' He waved his arm over all the trophies. 'As you can see, we've had our fair share of success.' Then he pointed to one of the unofficial celebration photos. The team holding aloft the latest trophy they'd won. 'There's Bodo,' he said, pointing at a man in the back of the photo. 'He wasn't part of the team, of course, just the celebrations. But does that answer your question as to whether his drinking had affected his physical appearance?'

Müller could tell it had. It was a colour photograph – and the red, bulbous nose, the blood shot eyes, and the broken veins on the skin of his face were evidence enough. But that wasn't what really interested Müller. She was looking at the man's manic laugh, mouth open wide, terrible stained teeth on display. On display at least where he actually *had* any teeth to show off.

Because what was glaringly obvious was this set of teeth in no way matched the drawing Schmidt had produced based on Jäger's dental records for Achterberg.

Two of the upper incisors were completely missing.

Jäger's supposed copper-bottomed identification of Concrete Man was nothing more than a fabrication.

Whoever he was, he certainly wasn't Bodo Achterberg.

21

Dresden
15 June 1944

Dear Arnold,

I still think of you a lot even though you are never writing me. Perhaps you are writing but your letters are not delivered. I do not know. I wonder if this letter will ever reach you.

We get news of the war in the newspapers and the newsreels. We just saw one in the cinema in the centre of Dresden. Did I tell you I had moved to Dresden to be with my grandparents? My father has had to join the army and our little hotel in Bad Schandau has been commandeered for the war effort, so Mutti and I moved in with Oma and Opa (that is the German for Granny and Grandad – you see I am teaching you German too!). Many people think it is not as safe in the cities, but I'm sure Dresden will be safe. Even your Mr Churchill would not dare to bomb a city with so many architectural treasures. They call the city the Florence of the Elbe, and I can understand why. It really is beautiful.

So I suppose you have newsreels too. I do not know why your troops tried to invade us – it looked like you were badly defeated on the newsreel we watched ('Die Deutsche Wochenschau' – all that means in English is 'The German Newsreel'). We are much stronger. We saw how your landing craft were sunk, and your glider crews captured. Even though you are the enemy, I don't wish you ill, Arnold, but I hope your country will make peace with Germany and see Hitler for the great leader he really is.

Perhaps this botched invasion attempt will make your leaders finally see sense and then we will have peace and we will be able to visit each other again.

I still think of you a lot. You are much more interesting than all the German boys.

I hope you still think of me as your girlfriend, even though we cannot be together at the moment.

With much love and kisses.

Your Lotti XXX

22

Dresden
February 1982

Rather than immediately return to the city centre and confront Jäger, Müller decided they needed to have a debrief and try to pull all the strands of the investigation together. The best place to do that – where they could be sure of some privacy and where, hopefully, there were no recording devices listening in – was in the Wartburg.

'We've been lied to again and again,' said Müller. 'So let's try to work out what we actually know and what is – or may be – simply disinformation.'

'OK,' said Tilsner. 'All we know is that a middle-aged man has been killed – and we haven't yet identified him. Because it certainly wasn't that Bodo Achterberg character. Of that, we are now certain.'

Müller turned to Schmidt, who was sitting in the rear of the car, leafing through the pages of various files, as though he might find the answer in them. 'What's your feeling, Jonas, about those bus and train tickets – the only link to Lotti Rolf?'

Schmidt shrugged. 'I think you know as well as I do, Comrade *Hauptmann*, that it's a very tenuous link. It's so odd that the purse still had money in it. Perhaps she wasn't even the woman in the argument Frau Abt witnessed.'

'*Says* she witnessed,' interjected Tilsner. 'However, I do think there's something in the Lotti trail – even if it's some sort of strange set up by the Stasi. Let's face it, Karin. You were attacked in her apartment by assailants unknown – although Jonas has lifted Bahlow's fingerprints from the flat. Bahlow himself, though, seemed unperturbed by that and had a perfectly logical explanation – if we buy it.'

Müller gave a long sigh. 'The trouble is, we don't know what's true, and what isn't. Although we do know others had an interest in Lotti's whereabouts, because of our encounter with the fake Stasi agent at the cottage in Kirnitzschtal.'

The three of them sat in silence for a few moments.

'So if we're *not* barking up the wrong tree with Lotti,' continued Müller, 'we still need to find her. And perhaps when and if we do, we don't take her in for questioning straight away but just watch her for a period, to see if she leads us anywhere interesting. And then, of course, there's Arnold Southwick. Surely we should be able to establish if the body's his or not?'

Tilsner lit a cigarette, provoking both Müller and Schmidt to wave the smoke back towards him. 'To do that,' he said, after taking a long draw of nicotine-infused fumes, 'we might need the co-operation of the British police. That won't be easy.'

'Could you chase that up please, Werner?' asked Müller. 'And see if you can get hold of *his* dental records – if we can't establish that he's still alive.'

'I'll try. But it's easier said than done. Especially as the Stasi have now come up with their own alternative narrative that doesn't seem to involve either Southwick *or* Rolf. They won't give up on that easily. Perhaps the direct approach is best. How are your relations with Jäger these days?'

Müller laughed. 'Virtually non-existent. We've had no contact for ages until now.'

'But he's always held a torch for you,' insisted Tilsner.

Müller found herself reddening under Tilsner's gaze. 'I don't know how you work that one out. Most of the time he causes me nothing but problems. What are you suggesting, anyway?'

'Well, you have that knowledge of what he got up to in the war . . .'

'What you *both* got up to in the war.'

'Be that as it may, I don't have as much to lose as he does. You've already threatened to expose him in the western press once.'

Müller narrowed her eyes at her deputy. She didn't really want to discuss all that in front of Schmidt. 'So what are you saying?'

'Confront Jäger face to face. Call his bluff on this Bodo Achterberg – perhaps use what you know about Jäger's activities in the war to try to find out what's really going on. Otherwise we're going to be dancing like puppets on strings for the rest of this investigation.'

The trouble is, thought Müller, *we're always dancing like puppets on strings.*

She just wasn't sure if, this time, Jäger was really the puppet master – or if it was someone higher up the chain. If Jäger himself was having to dance to someone else's tune, and was as frustrated as they were, then it might offer them the glimmer of an opening.

As Tilsner was driving along Leningrader Straße on the way back to the People's Police HQ, a call came through on the radio.

'*There's a fatality at the TV tower. The colonel has asked that your team attend on behalf of the K, please, Comrade Müller.*'

'This is *Hauptmann* Müller here. Message received. We're on our way.' She didn't want to admit that neither she nor Tilsner knew the way to the TV tower, even though it could be seen looming over the city from plenty of vantage points. Western TV might be difficult or impossible to receive in Dresden's valley environment, but the Republic had made sure its own signal would come through strong and clear – positioning the tower on a plateau high above the Elbe.

'Jonas?' asked Tilsner. 'Are you going to provide directions?'

'Of course, Comrade *Oberleutnant*. You can stay on this road, cross the Elbe, and then head along Bautzner Straße as though you were going to Stasi headquarters. After a few kilometres we need to bear right, but I'll let you know when we get to the turning.'

Once they'd taken the right-hand fork, Müller realised they were entering a more exclusive part of Dresden – one that didn't look to have been as badly damaged by the bombing.

'Some very nice houses here,' said Tilsner, as though he was echoing her thoughts. 'Probably where the local party bigwigs live.'

'This is Loschwitz,' said Schmidt. 'And historically it *has* been more exclusive.' He pointed to the left. 'Up the hillside there, behind Loschwitz, is the Weißer Hirsch. That is indeed where bigwigs used to live – Nazi bigwigs, before and during the war. It was virtually undamaged during the bombings in 1945 – so most of the city's important Nazis escaped. One of the ironies of war, I suppose.'

Müller turned in her seat. 'How do you know all this, Jonas? Do you spend all your time studying history books?'

'Not *all* my time, Comrade *Hauptmann*. But when we're on assignment like now, away from the Hauptstadt and our families, it keeps me out of trouble.'

'Ha!' guffawed Tilsner, slapping the steering wheel. 'I shouldn't think you've ever been in any proper trouble in your life, Jonas. It's just not your style.'

They drove on through Loschwitz, following the line of the Elbe, with Schmidt pointing out the sights, such as the historic cliff monorail, the Schwebebahn. Müller made a mental note that if she brought the children to Dresden one weekend to see where she worked, she would have to take them up it. Schmidt insisted the view over Dresden from the top was unparalleled – with the exception of their final destination, the TV tower, and its own observation platform and restaurant.

The final few hundred metres to the TV tower itself saw them winding up the Wachwitzer Bergstraße until finally they reached the top and the grey concrete TV tower – a miniature version of the Hauptstadt's iconic landmark – came into view. The flashing blue lights of police cars and ambulances told them where the incident had occurred – directly at the bottom of the TV tower itself.

Once they'd parked the car and made their way past the onlookers and gawpers and through the police tape, Müller was surprised to see *Hauptmann* Magnus Schriver again overseeing proceedings.

'Do they give you all the sudden deaths?' asked Tilsner.

Schriver rolled his eyes. 'It certainly appears so at the moment. You lot too, it seems.'

'So what does it look like?' asked Müller.

Schriver beckoned them over to a tent – which presumably had been erected to keep the body out of sight from those gathered the other side of the police line. 'It's not pretty – so I hope you've got a strong stomach.' At the entrance to the tent, the three Berlin officers were urged to put on protective shoe coverings and gloves. 'There's a lot of mess around, if you know what I mean,' said Schriver.

When they got inside the tent, Müller had to shield her eyes from the flashes of the police photographer's camera. She was glad she had, and only gradually widened her fingers to allow sight of the body itself. While largely intact, the victim looked to have landed head first – his skull had shattered like a coconut.

'He really wanted to kill himself,' said Schriver. 'At least, that's what the pathologist says. Jumped from the restaurant. Normally, there'd be signs of trying to right the body – even in a two-hundred-and-fifty-metre fall. But he seems to have been determined to make sure his skull smashed into the concrete first.'

The result was clear to see – and Müller found herself having to swallow back bile. Grey matter – presumably his brain turned to jelly – was splattered together with blood over an area of about three metres diameter. Pretty much the whole internal part of the police tent. His legs and arms were still identifiable as such, but broken at unnatural angles.

'Do we know anything about him?' asked Tilsner, as Schmidt busied himself doubling up on the police photographer's work with his own camera.

'Yes. He was carrying ID. His name is Heinz Schenk. It appears he was a school director.'

Tilsner snorted. 'That figures. Trying to keep schoolkids on the straight and narrow is a thankless task. I know from my own.'

Müller frowned. 'Hardly enough to make you suicidal. How did he get out of the restaurant window? Aren't they locked to guard against that sort of thing?'

'He didn't, and they are,' replied Schriver. 'It looks like he had it planned. They clean the windows once a week, and he obviously watched the window cleaners climb out of the service door. They're supposed to lock the door after themselves while they're on the outside, but you know how it is, they get lazy and don't bother.'

'But no one actually saw him jump?' asked Müller.

'No,' admitted Schriver.

'Was he from round these parts?' asked Tilsner.

'We're checking on that. It looks like he might have had relatives around here and may have been brought up in Dresden. But he wasn't working around here. He was in Bezirk Suhl – Thuringia.'

'Where exactly?' asked Müller, beginning to feel a sense of unease.

Using his gloved hands, Schriver handed over a plastic evidence bag containing the man's identity card.

As she read his details, Müller immediately realised why she felt so apprehensive. She'd seen the man before, met him briefly, although now he was entirely unrecognisable. But the ID card spelled it out clearly. He had – indeed – been a school director. Not just any school, however. One of the elite ones in the Republic.

The Kinder and Jugendsportschule Rosa-Luxemburg.

In Müller's home town of Oberhof. The St Moritz of East Germany, so beloved of Erich Honecker's predecessor, Walter Ulbricht.

Where Jannika and Johannes were now amongst the youngest pupils.

23

LOTTI

Dresden
Night of 13–14 February 1945

We were just getting back from the Fasching parade – well, the slimmed-down, wartime version of a Fasching parade – when the air raid sirens started. I used to love the parades as a child, and I still feel like a big kid even though Mutti keeps on telling me I'm nearly a woman. Of course, there have been plenty of false alarms before, and even a few small raids on the railway yards. When they've happened, I've wondered if Arnold – who must be eighteen now – is up there, flying a British plane somewhere. Or perhaps he's with the infantry, maybe a dashing captain.

So I'm still wearing my witch's mask as we break into a half-hearted run, heading for our apartment block's cellar, me having to hold the mask to my face with one hand to stop it falling off. Mutti's laughing at how stupid I look. Earlier in the evening, I saw a boy – well young man, really – eyeing me up and down. That's the best thing about me; my figure. He sauntered over to chat to the 'witch', looking very dashing in his Hitler Youth uniform. I think he was a year or so younger than me, but definitely flirting. Then he dared me to lift up my mask so he could see my face. I shouldn't have done it really – I should have kept some mystery back. Always leave them wanting more. But he'd piqued my curiosity, so I obliged. I could immediately see the coldness and disinterest cloud his face as I gave in and showed him what he wanted. It's not that I'm ugly, I know. Just a Plain Jane. Soon he was moving on. Perhaps that's why I still hold a torch for Arnold, even though I know it's stupid, and still write him letters that I never send. Because I remember his look of wonder when I kissed him on the platform of the *Personenaufzug*, the way he was excited but scared when I tried to get him to make love to me in Kirnitzschtal, near the waterfall, and the little wooden cottage my parents wanted to buy as an overspill for the hotel. My imaginary love affair.

I'm thinking all this as we're running and laughing. It's been a perfect spring day – even though it's only the middle of February. But the laughter dies in our throats when we hear the sounds of the aircraft engines. Of course, it's an almost daily sound – enemy sorties. But this time they seem closer, louder than before.

We pile into the apartment block's basement – Mutti, me, Oma and Opa. It's somewhere that always fills me with terror – there's no electric light. Some families are already there with candles. Children are screaming and being shouted at to shut up by the parents, or just being held and rocked and comforted. There are probably around twenty of us down there, including a mother and her baby. The woman's perhaps only a couple of years older than I am, and – in the flickering candlelight – I see the fear in her eyes.

It's not a proper air raid shelter, but then no one ever expected Dresden – with all its architecture, all its jewels and riches, all its culture – to actually be attacked. In one corner there's a bathtub half-filled with water, and buckets of sand. Rudimentary, home-made attempts to get prepared.

One of the older men gets up and opens the basement door to look outside. He comes back, his voice quivering in terror, to say he's seen 'Christmas Trees'. I don't understand at first – then Mutti explains. They're the magnesium flares dropped by the vanguard of a bomber force to light up a target. I can imagine the scene, and it fills with me with horror – the whole city must be lit up as though there are tens of thousands of flood-lights trained on it.

Mutti tries to reassure me. She says it's probably only a reconnaissance mission – that they're just taking photographs of the city. I don't believe her.

Then the explosions start.

First, it's a series of whistling sounds, then the booms.

Mutti urges us to lie on the floor, me underneath her, to try to protect me. She tries to get Opa to lie on top of Oma but they're not interested. Perhaps they're too old to do that. There are explosions followed by explosions. The whole ground shaking, the whole building shaking above us. At some point the candle on the table must be blown over, because we're suddenly plunged into darkness, and that just makes things even more terrifying.

It feels like someone is hitting the back of my neck as each bomb drops, and the air pressure in the cellar changes.

It seems to go on for ever – bomb after bomb, explosion after explosion.

Eventually, the bombs stop falling, and the drone of the aircraft engines fades away.

There is stunned silence in the cellar. We gingerly get to our feet. All four of us seem to be none the worse for wear, but it is scorching hot and I'm struggling to breathe, as though all the air has been sucked from my body. The other three are panting and hyperventilating too and we realise we have to get out.

When we emerge from the basement, the scene is like nothing we'd ever imagined. Everywhere buildings are ablaze, and even above ground we're struggling for breath in the spark-filled air. Chunks of the burning buildings are falling down all around us. We turn back towards the cellar doors, but realise those are alight too. Oma moves as though to try to get into the apartment building itself, to try to rescue her things, but Opa and Mutti hold her back.

'Don't be stupid, Wilhelmine. You will get yourself killed. We need to get to the river.'

We try to advance a few metres, but the heat and burning debris beat us back.

We turn and see someone has kicked out the burning doors of our apartment block cellar.

Mutti drags me back there. 'We will be safer underground,' she shouts at Opa. But he doesn't seem to be listening. He in turn is dragging Oma in the opposite direction – towards the river, but also towards the worst of the flames.

That is the last I ever see of them.

I let Mutti take control.

Back in the cellar, we realise there are fewer people here now. It is still stifling, still difficult to breathe. Mutti takes my shawl, dunks it in the bathwater, and then wraps it round my face.

'You must protect your face, Lotti. Whatever happens, you must protect your face.'

24

Dresden
February 1982

As Müller perused the apparent suicide victim's ID card, she felt a tap on her shoulder. Turning, she was surprised to see Jäger standing there.

'Could I have a word, please, Karin?' His voice seemed totally shorn of menace, as though something had happened in the past three years to neuter him.

'Of course, Comrade *Oberstleutnant*.'

'In private.' He beckoned her out of the tent, and then wandered some fifty metres from the scene before stopping and lowering his voice.

'We have a joint interest in this particular death, Karin.'

'How so?' asked Müller.

'He was the director of the elite school which your twins and my son attend.'

'I know. It's unfortunate. But I'm not sure it has any relevance to our children. On a day-to-day basis, I doubt they would come into contact with him that much.'

Jäger nodded, thoughtfully. 'True. But I'm party to information that you may not have. On the face of it, it doesn't affect the
children – I agree. But if you knew what I know . . .'

'There's no point being all clandestine about it. If you have
some relevant information, you should tell me.'

Jäger paused, pursing his lips. 'I can't . . . directly. Let's just
say that in my line of work you come across information –
information that should not, in any circumstances, be shared
with the *Kriminalpolizei*. Some of it might just be harmless, or
harmful, tittle tattle. But some of the information that passes
through our hands can be very dangerous to the Republic.'

'You're not really making any sense.' She began to turn away.
'I'm not in the mood to be listening to riddles – especially from
you. Remember what I know about you.'

Jäger's face coloured a strange tinge of red, as though he
was about to burst a few blood vessels. 'I haven't forgotten,' he
said, slowly, holding on to Müller's arm. It was a light grip, but
Müller had no doubt it would become fierce if she moved away
any further. 'But believe me, we have a shared interest in this.
There are two things. One, this school director had certain links
with our Concrete Man.'

'Who you insist is Bodo Achterberg.'

Jäger nodded. 'The dental records leave no doubt.'

Müller wondered if this was the time to tell Jäger what they
knew – that those dental records had been faked. The trouble
was, Jäger almost certainly knew that – no doubt the Ministry
of State Security themselves had faked them. But why? The
only way she was going to find out was by continuing to play

along with the Stasi's game, whatever it was, and see how things panned out. So she simply nodded.

'And Achterberg and our latest victim had something in common.'

'What?'

'They both preferred the company of men.'

That didn't seem to tie in with what everyone else had said about Bodo Achterberg: that his alcoholism was linked to being jilted at the altar by the female love of his life. Müller couldn't help thinking this was another piece of disinformation. But she kept those thoughts to herself. 'And?' she asked.

'And therefore, it's perfectly legitimate for you to begin an inquiry into the death of Heinz Schenk, because of possible links to the death of Bodo Achterberg.' Müller had only just learned of the TV tower jumper's identity from his ID card. Why wasn't she surprised that Jäger knew it already? 'And in respect of any investigation into Schenk's life, you should speak to this woman.' He delved into his jacket pocket and produced a torn-off page from a pocket notebook.

Müller read the neat handwriting which she recognised as Jäger's own. *Frau Olga Voights, Room 1015, Kinder und Jugendsportschule Rosa-Luxemburg, Oberhof, Bezirk Suhl, DDR.* 'Is she a teacher there?'

'No. She's the head of the in-house cleaning and laundry service for the school.'

'And what will she be able to tell me?'

Jäger's face took on an even more serious look, if that were possible. 'You'll have to talk to her, I'm afraid. But believe me,

Karin, it will be worth it – for the sake of our children, and for the sake of this inquiry.'

Müller began to form another question, but Jäger had evidently finished, and turned on his heels, making his way back to his car, which Müller now realised was parked a few metres away. After a couple of paces, however, he turned back towards her.

'Oh, and please memorise that name and address, then destroy the piece of paper. I don't want anyone tracing it back to me.'

Müller gave a small nod. She wasn't sure why she was agreeing with him – she wasn't even sure she would do his bidding. On the other hand, it would be a chance to visit Oberhof on official business and get to spend time with her children at the same time. So while she never trusted any information Jäger gave her, perhaps this time it was worth taking him seriously.

The weather had become milder, so instead of facing snow on the drive west towards Thuringia, the Wartburg's wipers had to cope with driving rain. And they didn't cope terribly well.

'If I hear anyone else extolling the virtues of the Republic's cars, I'll be tempted to punch their lights out,' moaned Tilsner, leaning forward slightly, peering through the smeared glass. 'And I hope this isn't another one of those butcher's walks he's forever sending us on.'

Müller sighed. 'It probably is. But I got the feeling he might have been going slightly off script. Therefore, this time, perhaps there's more in it. Anyway, Schriver is perfectly capable of looking after the Dresden end of the TV tower suicide.'

'If that's what it was.'

'Indeed. You wouldn't have thought it would be easy to commit suicide at one of the city's most prestigious landmarks. That's another reason why it's worth following up Jäger's lead. In case this woman can tell us anything which might imply that Schenk was pushed, rather than jumped.'

They lapsed into silence. Müller couldn't help thinking that Tilsner might have better visibility if he slowed down, but he seemed to be doing his best impression of a Mercedes driver on a western autobahn, where speed limits were mostly non-existent. She wasn't entirely sure, as they rattled around in the Wartburg, that it was up to the job.

'What about this idea that he was linked to Achterberg via his sexuality?' Tilsner finally asked.

'I just don't see that. We didn't get a whisper of that when we were up at Gorbitz.'

'Maybe Achterberg kept very quiet about it. Most do.'

Müller shrugged. 'To be honest, from what we saw of him from those photos, I can't see anyone having taken a fancy to poor old Bodo – male or female.'

'True. But maybe he hasn't always looked like that. Perhaps it's something from his past. It could even be why his wife-to-be jilted him. Maybe the alcoholism was nothing really to do with losing her – but more that he couldn't face the reality of what he really was.'

'That's just idle speculation, Werner.'

'Idle speculation is all we have, Karin. So far, this case has just been one dead end after another.'

Müller wanted to ensure that Jannika and Johannes shouldn't see her until she could spend quality time with them – which she was determined would happen, whether it was against school regulations or not. So on their way into the school entrance, she pulled her coat lapels right up and her hat down over her ears and forehead, so that very little of her face was visible. Luckily, between the entrance and the director's office, they didn't encounter any children.

The deputy director was in charge, with Schenk having taken a couple of days leave. But news of his fate clearly hadn't reached his deputy. At first, she thought Müller was simply at the school in connection with her twins. When Müller revealed what had happened, the blood drained from the woman's face.

'But that doesn't make any sense. Are you sure it was suicide?'

'No,' said Müller. 'But it appears so. Had he been showing any signs of depression lately? Was he worried about anything?'

The woman frowned. 'Now you mention it, he had seemed a little distracted this past week or so. But he just wasn't the sort of man to do something like that.'

'How well did you know him?' asked Tilsner. 'Did he have a settled home life? A wife? Children?' Müller knew what her deputy was driving at, even though he didn't spell it out.

'He was divorced. No kids, no. He always said the children here were his progeny. He loved them – and loved to see them do well.'

'And this divorce?' continued Müller. 'Was that amicable? Any ongoing issues?'

'Well . . .' The woman hesitated. 'I mean, no divorce is ever entirely amicable, in my experience. But he never intimated there were continuing issues. From what he told me, he and his wife just grew apart. I think she felt he was too dedicated to his work, to be honest. That he didn't spend enough time with her.'

'And had he formed any new relationships since the divorce?' asked Tilsner. 'Any other women on the go?'

The woman paused to light a cigarette. Müller wasn't sure that was the correct image for the potential new leader of an elite winter sports school to project, and declined the offer of one herself. Tilsner, predictably, accepted. The woman lit her own with a match, then passed the lit cigarette across the table to Tilsner so that he could light his. Once they were both contentedly puffing away, polluting the room as far as Müller was concerned, the woman deigned to answer the question.

'I'm not aware of any.' The long pause. The fidgeting when she'd responded. Avoiding eye contact. As far as Müller was concerned, the woman was lying.

'What about men?' asked Tilsner. Müller found herself having to stifle a sigh. Subtlety was not her deputy's strong point.

The woman looked genuinely shocked, as though she'd never even considered the possibility. 'Of course not,' she said, with a note of disgust. 'How can you even suggest such a thing?'

Müller was inclined to believe her. The only evidence for the suggestion – and it wasn't even really evidence – were the claims of Jäger.

'We just need to explore all options,' said Müller. 'As part of that, we need free access to investigate any part of the school we wish to.'

'Well, I may need to refer upwards to the Education Ministry about that,' said the woman.

'You could,' said Tilsner. 'But then we could say you'd been obstructing our inquiries. Would you like to be arrested?'

'N-n-no,' stuttered the woman, looking round nervously, as though someone might be listening in. 'I mean, I'm sure you must do your jobs as you see fit.'

'Exactly,' said Müller. 'You're welcome to accompany us, but I'm sure you've better things to be getting on with. We won't get in anyone's way. We just want to talk to a few staff members to find out a little more about Herr Schenk.'

'I'm sure you won't hear a bad word said against him,' said the woman, nervously wringing her hands.

'I'm sure we won't,' agreed Müller. 'We just need to get to the bottom of what happened.' She started to get to her feet. 'Oh, one more thing while I remember. I've come all this way, so I want to take my children out for a meal in Oberhof this evening, and then have them stay with me at my mother's house. That won't be a problem, will it?'

The woman frowned. 'Well, normally of course it's against the rules. Pupils on weekly boarding arrangements such as Jannika and Johannes should really only leave the school at the weekend. Otherwise it disrupts their routine and that of other pupils.'

Tilsner leant forwards, blowing smoke in the woman's face. 'But then, you want to co-operate with the *Kriminalpolizei*, don't you? So that we say nice things about you in our report. So I'm sure you'll accede to Comrade Müller's polite request.' As he said this, Tilsner cracked his knuckles. The piece of theatre almost made Müller laugh out loud.

The woman sighed and gave a small nod.

'If you could deliver them back promptly in time for the start of classes tomorrow, please, Frau Müller, I'm sure I can overlook the rules this once.'

The deputy director didn't show any inclination to want to accompany them on their tour of the school, and Müller thought it would be better not to alert her to who they wanted to interview. So they didn't ask for directions to Olga Voights's office – Room 1015. Based on her knowledge of most buildings in the Republic, there would be plenty of signs showing which rooms were located where. If not, they could ask if they got lost by targeting a staff member who was less likely to become suspicious.

They followed the room signs down various corridors adorned with the sporting achievements of the pupils. Cups, shields, pennants – and ubiquitous photos of victorious children of all ages shaking hands with the great and the good. Erich Honecker, his wife Margot – now nicknamed the Purple Witch thanks to her strange-coloured hair rinse, but at one time, Müller had to admit, an attractive woman – and Honecker's predecessor, Walter Ulbricht. The former East German leader had been virtually airbrushed from history, despite doing so much to build up the reputation of Oberhof for elite winter sports. Müller tried to keep her collar up as they passed the classrooms and gyms, just in case Johannes or Jannika spotted her through any of the glazed doors.

Eventually they reached Room 1015, and Müller knocked on the closed door. No answer.

'What do we do now?' asked Tilsner.

Müller turned and furrowed her brow. Just then, another staff member passed and solved their conundrum.

'If you're looking for Frau Voights, you'd be best off trying the laundry,' he said.

'Which way?' asked Müller.

The man pointed to a sign on the wall. 'Just follow the notices. You're nearly there.'

In the humid, almost choking heat of the laundry, the two detectives were soon able to locate Frau Voights. When she realised who they were, the woman – in Müller's view – immediately became overly nervous, almost as though she wanted to run away.

She went into a side office, and then came out wearing a winter coat – which looked ridiculous given the heat of the room – and carrying a briefcase. Then she gestured with her eyes for Müller and Tilsner to follow her.

Müller thought she was taking them to another office. But they carried on walking, and were soon outside the building.

Still Frau Voights didn't stop. She walked at a furious pace on what looked like a cross-country ski track, straight into the forest. From the hubbub of the laundry room, they'd been catapulted into an eerie silence. The noise of the laundry machines, the noise of the pupils and teachers at the school, all replaced by a soundlessness – which the blanket of snow seemed to soften still further.

The woman turned off the track and walked for a few metres through the trees until they came to a clearing, which had a wooden table and benches – almost as though it was used by walkers as a picnic spot. It probably was. Voights cleared the snow off the table and one of the benches, and then invited Müller and Tilsner to sit down next to her.

'Sorry for all the secret squirrel stuff,' she said. 'But I didn't want to talk about any of this within earshot of anyone from the school. And to be honest, I hoped this day would never come.'

'Why's that?' asked Müller, noticing for the first time there were tears in Voights's eyes.

'Heinz asked me to look after some documents for him, in the laundry. He thought it was the safest place. Why would anyone look for anything like this in a laundry room?'

'And what documents are they?' asked Tilsner.

'These,' said the woman, pushing the briefcase along the table towards the two detectives. Then she seemed to have second thoughts, and pulled it back towards herself and clutched it to her chest. 'You're not from the Ministry of State Security, are you?'

'No,' said Müller. 'As we said a few moments ago, we're *Kriminalpolizei* detectives. We showed you our IDs.'

'Yes. But I think I'm still in a state of shock.'

'You heard what happened then?' asked Tilsner. 'To . . . Heinz?'

'Not exactly.' The woman stifled a sob, still clutching the briefcase tightly. 'But he rang me from a public call box last night. He sounded desperate. I knew he was going to do something. Or . . .' The woman let her unsaid thought hang in the crisp winter air of the forest.

'Or have something done to him?' ventured Müller.

The woman nodded, the tears starting to flow down her cheeks. 'Th-th-that's why you're here, isn't it?'

Müller laid her gloved hands over the woman's. 'I'm afraid so, Frau Voights. The body of . . .' The woman gasped and then started shaking uncontrollably. Müller gripped her hands more tightly, trying to calm her. 'The body of Heinz Schenk has been found. At the bottom of Dresden's TV tower.'

'Oh my God!' shrieked the woman.

'Shh,' soothed Müller. 'If you don't want to draw attention to this little meeting, you need to try to calm yourself, Olga.' Müller used the woman's first name to try to get through to her, even though she hadn't been invited to. It seemed to do some good. The woman tried to choke back her tears, and Müller could feel her physically bracing herself. 'Take some deep breaths,' said Müller. 'That will help.'

Voights proffered the briefcase once more, this time to Müller alone. 'Heinz said that if anything ever happened to him,

I had to pass this on to someone I trusted. Someone who would help the truth get out. And I needed to be sure that person didn't work for the Stasi. Can I trust you?'

'I hope so, Frau Voights. But before I take the briefcase, do you have any idea what the documents contain?'

The woman nodded, and lowered her voice still further. 'There's something strange going on here.'

'Where?' asked Müller, looking around her at the dense forest. Wondering if – despite everything – Voights might be nothing more than mentally deranged.

'Not here in the forest. At the school.'

Müller started to become alarmed. 'My twin children go to the school.'

'How old are they?' asked the woman, sounding concerned.

'Not even six years old yet,' replied Müller.

The woman appeared to sigh in relief. 'That's all right then. The really young ones aren't involved. You've no need to worry at the moment. But my advice would be once they reach puberty, their early teens, you need to get them away from here. Perhaps sooner.' Now it was the woman clasping Müller's hands rather than vice versa. 'Promise me you'll do that.'

Müller nodded, then started to open the briefcase. Voights slammed it shut again. 'Not here. It's not safe. Did you come from Dresden, where . . . Heinz . . . where Heinzi . . . died.'

Another nod from Müller.

'Take it back there, then. You'll need to get a scientist to go through it with you, anyway. Someone who understands chemistry, and biology, and can decipher coded information.

Otherwise it will just be sheets and sheets of meaningless data. But I need you both to promise me you will try to bring this out into the open, and put a stop to it.'

'Of course,' said Müller, giving the woman a hug. 'I promise I will.'

'And you,' said the woman, directing a fierce gaze towards Tilsner, who'd been unusually silent for the past few moments.

'Absolutely,' he said. 'I am *Hauptmann* Müller's deputy. Her word is our bond.'

In the end, taking the children to Rosamund's proved trouble free. And both Jannika and Johannes were thrilled to see her.

'Is he your new boyfriend, Mutti?' asked Jannika, staring hard at Tilsner.

'No, of course not. He's far too old for me.' Out of sight of the children, Tilsner gave her a nasty squeeze on the thigh.

Ouch, she mouthed at him, silently.

'Anyway,' she continued. 'You've met Werner before, when we lived in Berlin. We work together in the People's Police.'

'Is he your boss then?' asked Johannes.

Tilsner couldn't help guffawing at this. 'No, young man. She's *my* boss.'

'Women can't be bosses,' said Johannes.

'Yes they can!' shouted Jannika, punching her brother on the leg. He pinched her in return, provoking a yowl.

'Stop it you two, this instant,' said Müller. 'Otherwise I'll take you straight back to the school. And anyway, it's not that unusual to have women in charge these days. Once Jannika grows up, there'll be women bosses everywhere.' Then she added, *sotto voce*, for Tilsner's sole benefit: 'And the world will probably be a much better place as a result.'

Müller hadn't warned her adoptive mother about the visit, so Rosamund was all over the twins, offering them sweets, cakes and juice, even though they'd all be having supper within the hour.

It gave Müller and Tilsner the chance to look through the contents of Frau Voights's briefcase – or perhaps more accurately, Heinz Schenk's briefcase, as it had clearly been the director who'd collected all the information.

'She seemed very upset,' said Tilsner as they laid out all the sheets of photocopied paper on the kitchen table. 'More than many workers would be when their boss commits suicide.'

'I really don't think he was just her boss, do you?'

'Lovers?'

'Without a doubt. She was a broken woman. And she was taking a huge risk giving us these. What if we *were* secret Stasi agents . . .' Müller paused, smiling evilly at her deputy. 'Of course, in your case . . .'

'Give it a rest, Karin,' snapped Tilsner.

Müller laughed. 'Anyway, I've no doubt they were in a relationship. Which is why Jäger's claims about Schenk and Achterberg's sexuality seem so patently absurd.'

She shuffled the papers in front of them into something approximating date order, and then tried to make head or tail of them.

There were various initials – which could be acronyms for chemicals, or for pupils, or perhaps there was a mixture of both. And then various percentages and dates. But – as Frau Voights had predicted – to both Müller and Tilsner they were meaningless.

Müller had faith that Schmidt would be able to make more sense of them once they were back in Dresden.

What she did know, without doubt given the way the woman had been acting, was there was something sinister in these pages. Voights had assured her that her own children were too young to be at risk – Müller wasn't so sure.

She knew she would be spending a sleepless night worrying whether to take Jannika and Johannes – who both sounded so happy playing with their grandmother – back to the school at all.

25

LOTTI

Dresden
Night of 13–14 February 1945

For the second raid, there is no warning – yet the roar of aircraft engines is even louder than before. Then the boom, boom of explosions begins and even the cellar is rocked on its foundations. First the ceiling starts collapsing, with brick and plaster dust everywhere so that we're choking from the cloud of particles in the hot, airless cellar. Scores and scores of people who'd been above ground – perhaps trying to save their possessions from the inferno raging at street level – now crowd into our makeshift shelter.

Mutti is worrying that if we continue to lie down, we'll get crushed. 'We have to get up now, Lotti. There are too many people in here.' As she says the words, she's gasping, struggling to breathe. 'K-k-keep the shawl over your face. We need to dampen it with the bathwater again.'

But we can't get through the crush to the bath. Within just a minute or so, a flood of humanity has now gathered here, shoulder to shoulder, so we can barely move. In the first raid, the booms of the explosions and the pressure rush after each had felt like slaps on the back of my neck. Now it's like each one is crushing my lungs, and I'm fighting for breath. With each explosion, the foundations of the building shake so much it feels they will give way. The candles are blown out again so we are plunged into darkness, save for the orange glow from the cracks in the heavy cellar door. We don't have to ask what that glow is – we know it's the glorious city of Dresden burning to the ground.

As the blackness envelopes us, and the explosions seem not to end, people start screaming, thrashing about in the crush, not caring if they hurt their neighbour, desperately trying to secure some extra space so they can expand their lungs and try to gasp in more of the stifling air.

Then a cry goes up from near the doors. 'The ground floor of the block is on fire.' Instead of cramming together underground to escape the fire and explosions above, now there is a crush to try to get out before we too are consumed by the flames. There is no chivalry here. No ladies first. It is each man, woman, and child for themselves.

We finally make our way back to ground level but there is no real respite. The explosions have faded away along with the drone of the aircraft engines. But out here – if anything – everything is worse. Some people – confronted by the wall of flames – try to turn back, to re-enter the cellar.

I shout at them. 'You will die down there. At least up here we have a chance.'

Mutti pulls me away. It is no use reasoning with them. We have our own battle to fight – the battle to survive.

The bombers may have gone, but there is a new terror. Scorching hot currents of air, fanned by the flames, almost sucking us bodily through the streets. An artificial, superheated wind roaring in our ears.

'The river,' shouts Mutti, dragging me with her. 'We must get to the river.'

Turning into one street, towards Neumarkt and the Frauenkirche, we're confronted by a family running the opposite way – towards us. 'You can't go up there,' they shout. 'The flames are too bad.'

We turn down a side street. Above us, it's like there's an orange light in every window, but it's the flames. These are solid, stone houses, I think. Why are they burning so fiercely?

I'm holding the shawl over my mouth and nose, as some protection from the flame-filled, oxygen-depleted atmosphere.

Suddenly, a flaming window frame crashes down from above. I try to get out of the way but it catches me a glancing blow on the shoulder.

Then I realise my shawl is on fire. Mutti looks at me in horror, then she's ripping off her own coat, throwing it over me, trying to smother the flames. I feel terrible pain and heat on the left side of my face. Then Mutti is holding me, consoling me, but telling me we must get to the water.

As well as the pain from my face, my lungs are heaving as I struggle to breathe. My legs feel like they are too weak to carry me. But Mutti drags me onwards, past older people who have given up, who are just sitting in the middle of the street, arms outstretched, wailing at the angry gods in the sky, wondering what they have done to deserve this. Through all the pain, through all the desperation, for some reason I think of Arnold, and getting him to perform the 'Sieg Heil' for Frau Holzmann just so we could get that free ride up the *Personenaufzug* in Bad Schandau. When everything seemed lovely and innocent. Is that when it all turned evil and bad?

Then my mind turns back to our real purpose – to fight our way through to the terraces and water meadows of the Elbe. Yet this strange city of fire, this hell on earth, is unrecognisable and we aren't sure where we are going.

We turn down one street – I don't know which one because by now I've lost my bearings – but we're beaten back by the roaring, superheated wind and flames, as burning debris is sent flying through the air.

Mutti dives down another couple of small streets, dragging me with her, as though she *does* know where she is. I keep the remains of my shawl pressed to the burnt side of my face, despite the pain, trying to protect it from the flames.

Then at last, like a godsend, the first drafts of fresh, cooler air, and I know we must have nearly reached the river. There are more people here now, all going the same way, all hoping the great river that flows through our city – through Meissen, Torgau and Magdeburg before finally reaching the North Sea near Hamburg – will be their salvation.

It is wonderful to finally reach it and breathe the glorious, refreshing river air.

But no sooner are we there than Mutti seems to attack me.

Dunking the bad side of my face in the water, again and again. And I realise, through my foggy thoughts, she isn't attacking me at all.

She's trying to clean my face.

Trying to save it.

These are her desperate attempts to wash the disfigurement away and give her daughter a future that will not always be defined by her monstrous looks.

26

Dresden
February 1982

Despite her misgivings, Müller realised she had no real option but to return the children to the school. Her only other choice would have been to plead with Rosamund to look after them temporarily until regular school places could be found. But given her adoptive mother's obvious closeness to the ski trainer, Wolfgang Mayer, Müller wasn't prepared to discuss the matter with her in detail. In any case, until Schmidt or another scientist examined the documents handed over by Frau Voights, all she had to go on were the woman's warnings – and even she had insisted Jannika and Johannes were too young to be under threat, whatever or whoever that threat was from.

Back in Dresden, she sought out her forensic scientist. Schmidt seemed genuinely pleased to be able to work on something for her again, rather than being at the beck and call of the uniform People's Police team.

'It may take me a day or so to work everything out properly, Comrade *Hauptmann*,' he said as he took an initial look over the documents. 'It looks as though some sort of code has been used – it's not just chemical symbols, although I suspect the percentages *do* relate to chemicals in some way. Do *you* have any more information?'

'Not really, Jonas, no. From what I can gather the numbers and percentages refer to something being administered to some of the children at an elite sports school—'

'The one your children attend, in Oberhof?'

'Yes, Jonas. But that's not why I'm asking you to do this. It's not some sort of personal favour. This is connected to the apparent suicide at the TV tower.'

Schmidt nodded, and in doing so his thick-lensed spectacles slipped down his nose, making him look like a mad professor. 'Well, as I say, I'm sure I will get to the bottom of it, Comrade *Hauptmann*. I'll give you a ring as soon as I've cracked it.'

Returning to her office, Müller was surprised to see a note on her desk from her Stasi opposite number, Bahlow.

> As soon as you're back, please give me a ring at Bautzner Straße. Better still, if you've time, please pop by. I've an update on Lotti Rolf's whereabouts.

Müller turned the note over in her hand. She had no reason to trust Bahlow. On the other hand, he did seem – marginally – to be better than many other Stasi officers she'd encountered in her career. Jäger included.

Just the thought of the Stasi *Oberstleutnant* seemed to be enough to make him appear – he walked into the office as though he were the genie, and Bahlow's letter was somehow Aladdin's lamp. She hastily pocketed the note.

'Ah Karin,' he said. 'I hoped I might catch you. Any progress in Oberhof?'

Müller tried to keep her face as deadpan as possible. 'We're pursuing a number of lines of inquiries, Comrade *Oberstleutnant*.'

Jäger sidled up to her, lightly grabbed her arm, then brought his mouth close to her ear. 'What did Voights give you?'

Müller was determined not to be ordered about or bullied by him. If he wanted her to do his dirty work, then she would do it on her own terms – and only if she felt it could benefit herself, or the inquiry. The fact that he'd given her the tip-off about contacting Voights didn't mean he had the right to information in return. She wrestled her arm from his grip, and moved a pace away.

Then she held his eyes. 'As I said, we're pursuing a number of lines of inquiry.' She gave him a sarcastic smile. 'Was there anything else I can help you with?'

Jäger turned on his heels and stormed off, slamming her office door behind himself.

Müller decided to visit Bahlow in person, taking Tilsner with her. Instead of summoning them to his office, he came out to meet them in Bautzner Straße itself, away from the actual Stasi building, and then took Müller to one side – as though he didn't fully trust her deputy.

'OK,' he said, lowering his voice, 'this is strictly off the record and you didn't get the information from me, understood?'

Müller gave a small nod.

'By giving you this information, I'm going against what some in there want.' He flicked his eyes back towards the Stasi HQ. 'But I have my own reasons for trying to help you.'

'Just get to the point, please,' insisted Müller.

'We've managed to locate Lotti.'

'In Pirna, Bad Schandau, or Dresden?'

'The latter.'

'Have you arrested her?'

'That's not in our interests. However, I can tell you where you can find her.' He produced a Dresden street atlas from his pocket – Müller recognised the green cover. She and Tilsner had exactly the same one in the Wartburg. He turned to the maps section at the rear, and plate thirty-one. 'Very occasionally, she stays at the Rolf's run-down cottage in Kirnitzschtal – you know that. You very nearly caught her there.'

So the warm coffee cup *had* been Lotti's, as Müller and Tilsner suspected. And the two men watching from a distance had obviously been Bahlow's men.

'But most of her activity is in the confines of the city. Here, on the eastern edges of Dresden, there are a couple of passenger ferries. The first connects the northern end of Niederpoyritz to an area of common land next to the Elbe, by Tolkewitz. The second is about a kilometre upstream, connecting the south-eastern part of Niederpoyritz with Laubegast. She's been spotted using both of those ferries. She's also been seen on the Standseilbahn about three kilometres to the north-west of the first ferry.'

'The Schwebebahn?' asked Müller.

'No – not the suspension railway. The cable railway. It starts at virtually the same point in Loschwitz, goes up a similar hill to the Weißer Hirsch, but it travels along the ground.'

'All right,' said Müller. 'But what I don't understand is why you're giving me this information.'

'She knows we're on to her. Each time we've spotted her, she's managed to lose our agents.'

'But surely you can't expect the *Kriminalpolizei* to do a better job of tailing someone than the Ministry for State Security's own agents?'

'There are complications,' said Bahlow.

'Like what?'

'Like the man posing as a Ministry agent at the Rolf's annexe in Kirnitzschtal. He *is* an agent, but he doesn't work for us.'

'You know who he is, then?'

Bahlow nodded. 'His name is Gordon Breitmann – at least, that's the name he uses some of the time.'

'Gordon doesn't sound like a very German name.'

'He's not German, although his family were originally of German extraction. He's British. MI6.'

Müller stared hard at Bahlow. What game was he trying to play – and trying to get Müller and Tilsner involved in? If what he said was true, then this ought to be the Stasi's area of operation, not that of the criminal police.

She gave a long sigh. 'I still don't understand why you're giving us this information, rather than acting on it yourself.'

'The involvement of the British makes for complications. Also . . .' The man paused, as though wondering whether he could take Müller into his confidence. He glanced across at Tilsner, who'd lit up a cigarette and was smoking it while leaning against the Wartburg, apparently paying them no attention. Bahlow evidently reached a decision. 'The thing is, I have a personal interest in this. I can't tell you what at the moment, but I will, when the time is right. I'm going out on a limb to help you here. For my own reasons.'

He looked back at the Stasi HQ, and as he did Müller could have sworn she saw a shiver of fear in his expression.

'I take it,' she said, 'those reasons might not square with your superiors' motives?'

Bahlow didn't answer her. But he looked at her hard and gave an almost imperceptible nod.

'All right,' said Müller. 'Let's say Tilsner and I do your dirty work for you. Where does that leave you and Jäger? Isn't he supposed to be taking an overview of this on behalf of Normannenstraße?'

'Jäger?' Bahlow looked as though the name left a nasty taste in his mouth. 'He's nothing to me.'

'But Jäger's theory is the suicide at the Dresden TV tower is somehow linked to our original murder in Gorbitz.'

Bahlow simply rolled his eyes. 'You have more experience of working with *Oberstleutnant* Jäger than I do, Comrade Müller. You will know better than I do whether you can always trust what he says. Ask yourself, does he have any personal motives for you investigating that? Perhaps that will give you your answer.' He turned to go.

'That's it, then, is it?' asked Müller. 'We're just expected to do your bidding and follow Lotti Rolf?'

'That's up to you, Comrade *Hauptmann*. But I think you know she must be at the heart of all this – otherwise why are we and the British so interested in her whereabouts and movements?'

Back in the Wartburg, Müller discussed with Tilsner a limited amount of what Bahlow had told her. She left out the parts about the British agent, Bahlow's own motives – not that she knew what they were, but just the fact that he seemed to be going slightly off piste – and his distrust or apparent dislike of Jäger.

'Do you think it's another set up by the Stasi?' asked Tilsner.

'Possibly,' admitted Müller. 'But Lotti's bus tickets – if they were planted – did at least help us advance the inquiry.'

Tilsner looked at her with a slight smirk. 'You're sure about that, are you?'

Müller gave an ironic laugh. 'On *this* case, I'm not sure about anything.'

Müller considered a radio call back to Schriver at the People's Police HQ to ask for reinforcements from uniform to help mount a surveillance operation of the three places Bahlow had highlighted: the hill tramway and the two passenger ferries. But then she decided the best approach was to keep the information in a close circle. So instead, she hauled Schmidt away from his code-cracking duties temporarily.

'*I think I've nearly solved it, Comrade* Hauptmann. *Another day or so and you will get your answer.*'

'I need you for something else, Jonas. Get a tram to Körnerplatz in Loschwitz. We'll meet you there.'

'*Of course, Comrade* Hauptmann. *I'll have to check which tram I need.*'

'Number four from Pirnaischer Platz just by the back of the People's Police HQ, Jonas. It goes straight there.'

They divided the three points between the three of them. Müller took the hill tramway, while Tilsner took the furthest ferry crossing and dropped Schmidt off at the nearer one on the way. They would keep in touch via their handheld radios, but just using a number for each site – Müller at one, Schmidt at two, Tilsner at three – and not discussing anything else about the operation over the open line. If any one of them saw Lotti, or anyone who could be her, they would simply state 'target sighted' and give their location number. That way, hopefully, others would not take too much of an interest.

Müller wasn't quite sure why she'd chosen the tramway – although Tilsner claimed it was because she wanted the luxury of a covered tram car for her surveillance activities, rather than a freezing cold river bank.

The tramway was the less interesting of the two historic hillside lifts at Loschwitz that connected the riverside settlement and its beautiful traditional architecture with the settlements on the northern terraces above the Elbe – in her case the Weißer Hirsch. The settlement where, as Schmidt had explained, leading Nazis escaped the firebombing of Dresden during the war. What was Lotti's connection with the area, if indeed she had one? Did bigwigs still live there, but from a different party and political persuasion – officials from the Republic's ruling SED party, rather than Hitler's National Socialist party?

There were only five other passengers getting the tramway – and Müller knew immediately none of them was Lotti, not even in disguise. Nevertheless, she continued with the trip, the Standseilbahn trundling at little more than walking pace up the hillside. At the top, she exited and looked around. There wasn't a lot to see other than the upper station and a few surrounding houses, save for an inn, the Luisenhof. She'd heard of this. It was reputed to be a Stasi meeting place. Perhaps that was why Lotti made this journey regularly? The restaurant also enjoyed a panoramic view of Dresden and the Elbe Valley below.

Müller was considering going for a coffee in the restaurant on the off chance that Lotti was meeting another 'handler', given that it seemed unlikely it would be Bahlow, when the call came through on the radio.

'*Target sighted location two*,' barked Schmidt, for once limiting his verbiage to the precise alert the three of them had agreed on.

The chase, such as it was, was on.

27

Schmidt had – as agreed – stayed at the observation point on the northern bank of the Elbe, rather than follow the woman he'd identified as Lotti over on the ferry to the southern side.

Müller chewed over the wisdom of that in her head as they waited for the ferry to come back with its return passengers.

'I saw her get off and head downstream, Comrade *Hauptmann*, along the river bank,' said Schmidt. 'She was carrying a shopping bag and also had a rucksack on her back.'

'What is there that way?' asked Tilsner.

'Nothing much,' said Müller. 'If she was heading back to civilisation then by going straight on or turning left she'd have ended up in Laubegast. The other way it's the water meadows – for about a kilometre or so. Then you reach a few apartment blocks, opposite the cemetery.'

'Cemetery?' echoed Tilsner. 'That might be somewhere of interest.'

'For what?' asked Müller.

'For hiding out.'

'But she doesn't seem to be *hiding out*, does she? She was in plain sight on the ferry.'

'Well, not quite,' said Schmidt. 'She seemed to have changed her appearance from the photographs you gave us to recognise her by. She's dyed her hair dark, and was wearing glasses.'

'So how did you recognise her? Are you even sure it was her?' asked Tilsner.

'The disfigurement to her face. She'd tried to disguise that too, with make-up. But I could tell it was the result of serious burns.'

'The question is,' said Müller, 'do we wait for the ferry to come back, or do we take the car round to the other side?'

'Might as well wait,' said Tilsner. 'It'll be quicker and we might be able to pick up some info from the staff. Look, here it comes now.'

The two members of staff operating the ferry seemed particularly unobservant. Either that, or they were in no mood to help the police. Whichever it was, they failed to even recognise or remember Lotti – despite the fact that, according to Bahlow, this was one of her regular routes.

'We just mind our own business,' said the older of the two. 'It's no concern of ours who goes where or when, as long as they've got a ticket.'

'This is a murder inquiry,' countered Müller.

'Well, I didn't think you were just off for a picnic, officer. Whether you're chasing murderers or fare dodgers, my answer's the same. I don't know who you're on about. And you're not the first to be asking, either.'

Müller's ears pricked up. 'I don't suppose you can tell me what the other person questioning you looked like?'

'Ah, well that's where you're in luck. If people actually talk to me, I always remember their faces.' It turned out that lack of observation skill certainly wasn't one of the boatman's faults, even if general disinterest was. He proceeded to give a perfect description of the man identifying himself as Stasi officer *Hauptmann* Gustav Weiß – the man who, if Bahlow was to be believed, was in fact a *British* agent.

'When was he here?' asked Müller.

The man held her gaze. 'Yesterday, officer. About this time yesterday.'

They followed the riverside path in a north-westerly direction. Thankfully, a renewed cold snap meant the ground was frozen under the covering of snow, otherwise Müller would have expected them to be sinking into mud. As it was, she could feel her feet turning numb as the cold penetrated.

The snow did have another advantage. If Lotti at some stage had turned off the path, into the surrounding snow-covered water meadow, then they might be able to pick up her footprints. Or at least, a set of footprints. They would have no way of telling if they belonged to the woman they were looking for.

After about 300 metres, after crossing a footbridge, the path split into two – with the main branch continuing to follow the river, and the other following the line of a drainage ditch

towards the nearest settlement, the Dresden district of Tolkewitz. Both paths were reasonably well-trodden – there was no
indication which way Lotti had gone.

'How are we going to split it?' asked Tilsner.

'If you take that path, Jonas and I will continue along the
river,' said Müller.

Tilsner nodded and turned off the main route.

Müller and Schmidt continued along the path, keeping their
eyes peeled for any footprints diverting either towards the river,
or further into the meadows. There were none, save for a couple
of tracks obviously made by animals. And no sign of anyone in
the flesh, either.

'What do we do, Comrade *Hauptmann*? We could perhaps
take a look in the cemetery?'

Müller shook her head. 'We seem to have lost her, Jonas,
unless she went the way Werner's gone. It might be worth getting sniffer dogs involved, but then it will become obvious to her
that something's wrong. I'll try to raise Werner on the radio.'

She began to try to contact Tilsner, asking to be patched
through via the People's Police HQ. But neither they, nor she,
were able to get a reply.

'He could easily be out of range, Comrade *Hauptmann*. The
handheld radios are by no means a perfect system . . . yet.'

Müller nodded. In any case, Tilsner was a big boy. He knew
how to look after himself. Or he ought to.

They retraced their steps to where the path had split in two.

Müller had half-expected to see her deputy waiting there for
them. But there was no sign of him, and no one walking back

towards the passenger ferry. No one visible, either, on the path towards Tolkewitz.

Schmidt was by now sounding out of breath, their walking amounting to more exercise in the space of less than an hour than he usually managed in a week. 'Do you want to stay here, Jonas, while I check that way?'

'No, no, Comrade *Hauptmann*. I wouldn't forgive myself if something happened to you – I'll come with you.'

'Nothing's going to happen, Jonas. Werner will no doubt have found a bar and will be taking a rest. But thank you, anyway.'

It was only about a hundred metres down that track before they saw two sets of footprints in the snow to the left, leading towards the drainage ditch. But still no sign of anyone in the flesh. Müller didn't want to shout out in case Tilsner had managed to locate Lotti and was perhaps observing her from a hideout – trying to find out what she was up to.

She soon realised that wasn't what was happening. As they approached the ditch, Müller saw a shape slumped in the snow, just beginning to stir.

'Werner! Are you OK?'

He was gingerly rubbing the back of his head.

'There are . . .' His words tailed off as he tried to stretch, and then grimaced from the pain. 'God. My head. There are too many people getting whacked over the head in this case for my liking. And I didn't really want to be one of them.'

Müller and Schmidt got each side of him, then carefully helped him to his feet.

He gently traced what was obviously an emerging bump on the rear of his skull.

'Who did it?' asked Müller.

'Annoyingly, I've no fucking idea. I'd just found Lotti, challenged her, and then . . . whack! Someone got me good and proper.'

Schmidt started holding his fingers up in front of Tilsner's face, asking him to count them.

'Go away, Jonas. Your breath stinks of sausage as usual.'

'Well, you certainly *sound* like your usual rude self, Comrade *Oberleutnant*.'

'I am. I'll recover. Both of you, come and look at this. This is what I saw first, and then discovered Lotti . . . and then saw stars.'

He led them a couple of metres along the drainage ditch to a concrete tunnel through which the waters of the ditch – if they weren't frozen solid – would normally flow. On the left-hand – nearest – side of the tunnel was a concrete platform, possibly there so workmen could enter easily to do any necessary repairs.

Tilsner crouched low. 'I don't want to bang my bloody head again.' He got out his pocket torch. A few metres into the tunnel someone had made a rough sleeping area. There was a sleeping bag, blankets, a cooking stove, even a plastic washing-up bowl with a few pots, pans and plates neatly stacked alongside. 'Quite the home from home,' said Tilsner. 'Though I can't say I'd fancy it in this weather.'

'So is this where Lotti's been hiding . . . was it her who attacked you when you discovered her lair?' asked Müller.

'No,' insisted Tilsner, almost shouting. 'Ouch! I can't really raise my voice until this headache clears. But I've already told you that. I was talking to Lotti when someone else hit me from behind.'

'Possibly the person who *is* living here?' asked Schmidt.

'Possibly,' said Tilsner. 'I didn't see him . . . or her.'

Müller wiped her hand across her face, trying to concentrate. 'The other possibility, of course, is that it's our undercover British agent. After all, the boatman saw him coming this way.'

'Possibly,' said Tilsner. 'We'd better seal it all off, then Jonas you need to photograph the scene and dust as much of it as possible for fingerprints.'

'Of course, Comrade *Oberleutnant*. I'll get onto that right away. Can I suggest Comrade Müller takes you to hospital for a check-up while I get to work? Concussion can be a nasty thing, even if you feel all right. And I can easily get the tram back to the city centre when I've finished up.'

'Jonas is right, Werner. Why don't we do that?'

'I'm fine,' growled Tilsner. 'Let's just try to work out where the fuckers have got to. I'd like to see both of them behind bars.'

28

Stasi HQ, Normannenstraße, East Berlin
August 1981

Oberst Rainer Specht had prepared his case meticulously, and now he was about to present it to his superiors in one of the meeting rooms in House One in Normannenstraße. Perhaps even Comrade Minister Mielke himself would be in attendance.

His plan, Specht felt, was brilliant in its simplicity. He'd heard about the academic from his old Ministry contact in Dresden, Rüdiger Bahlow. Of course, it had been Bahlow's idea, but there was no point giving the credit to a lower-ranked officer. Specht himself had shaped the plan, finessed it, and would now present it as his own. He would of course congratulate Bahlow himself personally when it succeeded, recommend him for a minor promotion for the part he had played, that sort of thing. But the real rewards, the possibility of higher office here – at Normannenstraße – would be reserved for Specht himself.

He straightened his olive-green tie in the mirror. It gave him satisfaction that he could see the Weißer See reflected behind him, which he and his wife Monika's detached house over-looked. Perhaps if he played his cards right their next move could be to the forest settlement, the Waldsiedlung, where all the bigwigs lived. Although maybe he was getting ahead of himself.

'You look very smart darling,' said his wife, brushing some fluff off his lapel with her hand. 'I'm sure the meeting will go well.'

'Of course it will, *Liebling*. We will have to go out and celebrate this evening. I'll book us a table. Where would you like to go?'

Monika held both his cheeks and kissed him lightly on the lips.

'Whoops!' she said, wiping away some red lipstick. 'Surprise me, Rainer.' She gently squeezed his crotch. 'If you know what I mean.'

'You've got a date, honeybee.' He picked up his briefcase, and felt a renewed spring in his step as he made his way to his car.

Nearly all of those at the meeting in the wood-panelled room were his superiors. Major generals, colonel generals and the like. Sadly, Mielke himself was otherwise engaged. But these were officers who had already had stellar careers in the Ministry for State Security. Yes, there were a few colonels like himself, but he was determined to outshine them.

It was *Generaloberst* Udo Fischer who spoke first. 'Comrade Specht, we've all read your briefing note with interest and in principle there is a willingness to support your plan. Perhaps you could outline it in a little more detail, with emphasis on how it's going to work in practice.'

The signs were positive, thought Specht. *How it's going to work in practice.* It sounded as though the meeting was merely a matter of rubber-stamping. That the decision to go ahead had already been made.

'Thank you, Comrade *Generaloberst*. As you'll have read in the briefing document, the plan revolves around the research of a British academic, who is a visiting fellow at Dresden University of Technology. Now this man—'

'Dr Arnold Southwick,' said Fischer.

'That's correct, Comrade *Generaloberst*. Dr Southwick. Now, he is an expert both in history and international law. He holds doctorates in each.'

'Not someone to be trifled with, then,' said Fischer.

'Indeed not. He is a very well respected academic. His current area of research is the Anglo-American terror bombing of Dresden in 1945. Now, while I'm sure we'll agree that anything which hastened the end of the fascists and Hitler was a good thing, the bombing of Dresden – largely orchestrated by the British – has always been highly controversial, not least because of the city's unique cultural heritage and architecture, jewels of German heritage if you like, but also because Dresden was not a particularly strategic military target. Added to that is the fact that it is well known that in the early part of 1945 the city was home to tens, perhaps hundreds of thousands of refugees, many of them sheltering in exactly the targets the British and Americans attacked.'

Specht looked around the room as he spoke. He could tell he had his audience eating out of the palm of his hand.

When he mentioned the secret documents that Southwick had acquired, via a whistleblower, there were even low whistles of appreciation.

As he drew his presentation to a close, and retook his seat, Specht felt his eyes prickle when the great and good of the Ministry of State Security broke out into spontaneous applause. It hadn't just gone as well as he'd hoped, it had gone a hundred times better.

Fischer held his hand up to stop the clapping. 'Well, you can see that we're all very appreciative of your efforts, Comrade *Oberst*. Do you think you will be able to bring this plan to a successful conclusion – to the conclusion you outline?'

'I'm sure of it, Comrade *Generaloberst*. This will prove to be not simply an extremely prestigious project for the Republic, one that will raise its profile in the international arena, but also one that is potentially very lucrative. And by that, I mean in terms of raising hard currency.'

'Bravo, Specht. Bravo!' said Fischer. 'Well I'm sure we'll all drink to that.'

Fischer summoned an underling to hand out schnapps. For Specht, the warmth of the alcohol as he downed the shot in one couldn't add to the warm glow he felt inside. Monika would be very proud of him. His luck would be in tonight.

29

ARNIE

Dresden
June 1981

One of Arnie's first moves on arrival in Dresden was to survey the city – to try to imagine what it had looked like on that night. Of course, he'd seen the photographs of the horrendous devastation afterwards, the way the city had been turned into a grotesque collection of empty burnt-out shells of buildings, standing forlornly amongst the rubble – much how Nagasaki and Hiroshima looked after the bomb was dropped on each.

He could have gone to the obvious place – the TV tower, with its observation platform and restaurant. But that hadn't been there in 1945. The place he chose instead *had* been – the viewing platform at the top of the ancient Schwebebahn.

He parked his hired Lada near the entrance in Loschwitz, and then made his way across to the grand entrance. The lower terminus building had the same feel as the spa in Scarborough – the grand nineteenth-century architecture beloved of the Victorians, or indeed the Germany of Kaiser

Wilhelm II. After purchasing his ticket – which seemed unfeasibly cheap – he got in the carriage and waited for it to take him up the hill. He got the impression that he was the only tourist – or at least, the only person taking the trip for the experience, rather than as part of daily life. His fellow passengers looked slightly dour and grey – but then that seemed true of the whole of East Germany. They might have the highest standard of living of the whole of the Soviet bloc, but greyness predominated. At least here in Dresden some of the historic treasures and their flamboyance, such as the Schwebebahn itself, had survived, although much had been preserved only as symbolic ruins.

Once the carriage reached the top station, he made his way up the rickety steps to the viewing platform. The East German authorities might have deliberately kept some of Dresden's treasures as ruins as a reminder of the 1945 attack, but they didn't seem very adept at the upkeep of other – undamaged – heirlooms of past regimes, such as this one.

But although the structure itself had obviously seen better days, nothing could undermine the heart-stopping nature of the view – especially on a day like today. The vista of the Elbe Valley – stretching far to the north-west one way, and the south-east the other – was surely unparalleled. He could even make out the Altstadt, and from the rump of the ruins of the Frauenkirche, the position of the historic Neumarkt.

This would be his home for the next – what? – year, at least. Until his research had been peer-reviewed and published in a respected journal. It would make waves, of course it would. It was a controversial thesis, especially from a British academic, even though he didn't want to prejudge its outcome. But the documents he'd been provided, the documents that proved that psychological studies – studies he himself had been a part of as a young boy – had been traduced and perverted by leaders with particular aims, they were the proof. Yes, he had a personal interest in all this. His city, like Dresden, had suffered horrifically. His brother, who'd never had the chance to flourish into adulthood, never even properly enjoyed a childhood, he had been a victim. He owed it to little Fred that the truth should come out. Fred's death could, he supposed, be seen as a sacrifice, although it was one none of his family had wanted to make. But for that sacrifice to be perverted in the way it had been? Well, that was beyond the pale. And this was the city that had suffered the horrific, almost unimaginably diabolic consequences. Consequences that to its citizens must have felt like hell on earth.

As his head lighthoused from side to side, he tried to imagine what this view must have been like on 13 February 1945. Would anyone have been up here watching? He doubted it – but the nearby villas, reputed to have been owned by leading Nazis, would have also had a perfect view. First, the Lancaster pathfinder planes, dropping their magnesium parachute flares to light up the target – nicknamed 'Christmas Trees' by the Germans. Then the Mosquito marker planes whose job was to drop specific target indicators, whose red glow would guide the bombers. Finally, the main group of Lancasters – more than

250 strong – with their deadly load of nearly a quarter of a million incendiary bombs, and 500 tons of high explosives.

And that was just the first raid.

The city – seen from here – would have become a giant, lethal fireworks display. An awful spectacle. But surely even here you wouldn't have seen the actual firestorm, the deadly superheated winds cutting through the streets, sucking the air from Dresdeners' lungs, killing them as they ran.

It would have been an indescribable sight. And yet, the British had suffered the same thing on a smaller scale at the hands of German bombers earlier in the war. His home city of Hull reputedly the most heavily bombed outside of London – yet rarely mentioned in the news for fear of giving the Nazis succour. Only ever described – anonymously – as a 'north-east coastal town'. Britain had suffered that, Arnold and his family had suffered that, Fred had been killed, the psychologists had come and studied the effects.

And yet still they launched the attack on Dresden, when the war was already all but won.

His next mission took him to another town by the banks of the Elbe – but one some forty or so kilometres to the south-east. The town of Bad Schandau.

In many ways, the town – or large village, he'd never been sure which it was – had changed little. It still had the same feeling of being crammed in – the precipitous valley between the Elbe itself and the sandstone plateau that rose on both banks to too narrow a space for a settlement.

Before making his way to Lotti's parents' bed and breakfast hotel, he drove a little further along the road towards Czecho-slovakia, just so that he could be reminded of the cliff lift. He recalled his parents saying it was nothing special – just like the cliff lifts in Scarborough. But to him it *was* special. Not least because it always reminded him of the Tin Man in *The Wizard of Oz* – the book version, of course; when they'd visited in 1938, at the height of Hitler's power, the film had not yet been released.

And there he was. The Tin Man. Arm outstretched to the left, as though helping to prop up the cliff itself.

What had ever possessed him to go along with Lotti and Frau Whatever-her-name-was and give a Hitler salute, together with the 'Sieg Heil' shout? Surely, he knew even as a twelve-year-old how wrong that was? But perhaps his memory was coloured by the war itself and later events. There had been plenty of British adults, even in the late 1930s, who had been ready and willing to kowtow to the Nazi leader.

He experienced a strange feeling when he parked in front of Pension Schönblick. Almost like an out of body experience – as though he was a ghost visiting his past, and that that past had lost some of its colour, its vibrance. It was similar to the way colour photos – especially instant ones like Polaroids – tended to fade, so that reds became muddy, yellows turned to greens, greens to browns and nothing was quite as you remembered it. And that you were almost apologising to yourself for coming back and spoiling the memory. Because Pension Schönblick had certainly faded in the intervening forty-four years, as had Bad Schandau itself. Some of the changes were, of course, welcome. No swastikas hanging from the windows for a start. But the little hotel looked like it needed more than just a lick of paint. The front door looked part rotten, as did many of the window frames and shutters. Arnie wasn't even sure it was open, even though they were approaching the peak summer season.

He rang on the bell, then stepped back, feeling as though he was about to invade his own past.

He wasn't sure who he was expecting to answer. Would Lotti even remember him? In any case, surely she would no longer live here – she would have made her way in the world, married, had children, fulfilled at least some of her hopes and dreams? As had he. Not the children. Barbara and he had been unable to conceive. They'd just accepted it as fate.

Once again, he rapped on the door, this time a little harder, then had to rub his knuckles to ease the pain away.

Finally, it was half opened. A hunched old woman looked up at him quizzically.

'Frau Rolf?' he asked.

'Yes,' she replied, suspiciously.

'You probably don't recognise me. My name's Arnold Southwick. I came here on holiday with my parents in the 1930s. I became a pen pal of—'

'Of Lotti's? Yes, of course. I remember.' She peered at him myopically through her spectacles. 'Well I don't really recognise you, to be honest,' she laughed. 'But I do remember your name, the fact that Lotti was fond of you. Would you like to come in?'

She fully opened the door, and ushered him inside. 'You don't have any luggage?' she asked, her voice tinged with disappointment.

'Ah sorry, no. I'm not here on holiday. I'm actually working at the university in Dresden temporarily. For a few months, possibly a year or so. I just thought I might pop in and say hello, for old time's sake. Does Lotti still live with you?'

'Oh no. She's been gone a long while. I don't think she had any interest in going into hotel work. She was never one to wait hand and foot on people.'

The woman showed him into the lounge and pointed to a chair. Everything looked horribly familiar – as though there had been no real investment in the hotel since the 1930s.

'If you're happy to let me have her address, it would be nice to look her up. Presumably she's married with children by now?'

As he said the words, Arnie saw the cloud of sadness pass across Frau Rolf's face. He remembered the old rule too late: assume nothing, otherwise you'll make an 'ass' out of 'u' and 'me'. He'd obviously put his foot in it.

'I don't think Lotti was ever the marrying type really,' said the woman, sadly. 'She's had boyfriends, of course – well, one or two – but no one she's ever really fallen for.' Then her face brightened. 'She was always very sweet on you, of course.'

'Ha!' laughed Arnie. 'I'm sure she wouldn't be now. Anyway, I've been happily married for more than thirty years. I was just interested in getting back in touch for old time's sake.'

Frau Rolf got up and began rummaging around in a writing desk, bringing out a pad and a ballpoint pen. 'I'll write you down her address. She's in Pirna – Sonnenstein, on the edge of Pirna, actually. It's a new-build development of very nice apartments. She was very lucky to get one as a single person.'

Sonnenstein. The name immediately made Arnie shiver, as it would any historian of the Second World War worth his salt. One of the main euthanasia centres – part of the *Aktion T4* programme.

The woman wrote down the address and then handed it to Arnie. 'Will you stay for a coffee at least?' she asked.

'Thank you,' he said. 'That would be lovely.' It wouldn't be, of course. Now he was here, he was eager to get away from the sense of decay and sadness that seemed to pervade the hotel. But for politeness's sake, he knew he would have to at least drink her coffee. He just hoped it was drinkable – East Germany's excuse for coffee, with its ersatz ingredients, often wasn't. 'Milk and one sugar, if that's OK.' The next half hour would probably be the equivalent of watching paint dry – but it was only half an hour lost from his life.

The housing estate at Sonnenstein looked exactly how Arnie had expected. Identical blocks of identical flats. Already in the UK, such developments were passé – although Arnie knew there were plenty of examples of similar, brutalist architecture in Britain too, including in his home city. The Orchard Park estate, with its twenty-plus storey high-rises, was considered one of the worst places to live in Hull – built in the 1960s as part of a slum clearance, offering post-war modernity, just as the East German flats offered private bathrooms, toilets and kitchens – things that were often lacking in the DDR's older apartment blocks.

Here – unlike in Orchard Park – everything looked well cared for. Arnie could see four high-rises, but counting upwards he could tell they weren't quite as high as the hated ones in Hull. The other big difference here would be the level of employment. Unemployment rates in the Hull estate stood at nearly 20 per cent. Here, everyone who wanted a job would have one. Either at the energy and gas turbine plant – housed in the very buildings where the Nazis had carried out their euthanasia programmes – or at the nearby Leupoldishain uranium mine. Given a choice, Arnie knew where he'd prefer to work, history notwithstanding.

He quickly located Lotti's block, the one with the pharmacist's at one corner on the ground floor, and then entered the building and climbed to the third floor in search of her apartment, number 315. Was it fair to simply turn up unannounced? Would she even welcome the visit? Perhaps the past was better left alone.

He remembered that quote from L. P. Hartley, the opening line of his novel, *The Go Between*. 'The past is a foreign country: they do things differently there.' OK, Hartley had 'borrowed' the line from a historian friend – but it still held true. Arnie stood outside the flat feeling as nervous as he had when Lotti had first taken him on that tour of Bad Schandau back in 1938.

Then he rang the bell.

He wasn't sure what he was expecting. He wasn't even sure he should be doing this. After all he was – supposedly – a happily married man. And forty-three years had passed since he'd last seen her.

A middle-aged woman answered the door. He immediately realised there was something wrong with the left-hand side of her face, dropped his gaze, then felt embarrassed for having done so. So he tried to focus on her eyes, even though he wasn't sure if she was blind in the left eye.

'Ah, hello. I was looking for Lotti Rolf.'

The woman gazed at him with a peculiar expression. 'You've found her.'

'Ah.' Arnie could feel himself reddening. He should have known. The person in front of him looked nothing like the girl he remembered. She was dowdy, downtrodden almost. But then they had both been twelve – or perhaps Lotti had been thirteen, he couldn't remember. Now, he was fifty-five, middle-aged, with most of his life behind him. She was the same. Of course she would look entirely different.

'I'm sorry, I didn't recognise you.'

A slightly sad look passed over her face, together with something else. Almost a flash of anger.

'Why would you, Arnold? It's been a long time.'

'Ah, you remember me then?'

She peered at him oddly. 'Not really. We were only children. But my mother phoned ahead to let me know you'd be coming. And although your German is very good, you still have a trace of an accent. An English accent. So yes, I knew it was you.'

They were standing there, on her doorstep, the door only half open. Arnie had expected her to invite him in. But that didn't seem to be happening.

'Do you have time for a coffee, or something?' he asked, hoping to embarrass her into letting him enter her apartment. But she still stood there with the door half open, almost as though she was on guard.

She looked at her watch, and then nodded. 'Give me ten minutes to get ready. I'll meet you at the HO Gaststätte Glück Auf – in the Straße der Jugend.' She gave a vague wave towards the way Arnie had just arrived from. 'You can't miss it.'

Then she closed the door.

30

Dresden
February 1982

When they were back at the People's Police HQ – Schmidt having bagged up what he could from the underground den, and taken fingerprints from likely objects that couldn't be moved – Müller called an informal meeting in her office.

'Let's go through what we've got to go on now,' she said.

'Not a lot,' grumbled Tilsner, who Schmidt had said was showing no signs of concussion. 'Considering how long we've been going round chasing our own tails.'

Müller ignored him. 'Jonas, I want you to go through everything we've recovered from the drain tunnel. Check for fingerprints, clothes fibres, footprints, anything like that . . . see if you can establish who was using the hideout. Or if not who, then how many people. Was it just Lotti's lair, or has she been helping someone hide away from the authorities?'

'It doesn't make much sense,' said Tilsner. 'Why would you build a hideout there, on the edge of Dresden, near the Elbe?

Wouldn't you choose somewhere more remote – Dresden Heide for instance?'

Again, Müller chose to ignore Tilsner. If he didn't have anything positive to contribute, then she wasn't going to listen to him. 'Have you found anything of interest from your initial sift-through, Jonas?'

'There was one thing, yes, Comrade *Hauptmann*,' said the forensic officer. 'An expired works pass for SDAG Wismut in Königstein. In Lotti Rolf's name.'

'She was a *uranium* miner?' asked Müller. That was hard to believe.

'Not a miner, no,' said Schmidt. 'Although there are a minority of female miners. No, she worked as part of the administration of the mine.'

'Worked or works?' asked Tilsner.

'I've no idea, Comrade *Oberleutnant*. All I can tell you is that she possessed an out-of-date pass.'

'When did it expire?' asked Müller.

Schmidt consulted his notes. 'December thirty-first last year – so only a couple of months ago.'

Müller got to her feet and retrieved her coat from the back of the office door. 'Werner, you come with me. Let's pay the mine a visit. At least it's something to be going on with. Jonas, you go through the rest of the stuff please and, as I say, try to find out exactly who was using the lair in the Elbe water meadows.'

The contrast between the two sets of hills was striking: the beauty of the Elbe Valley, and the historic town of Königstein itself, with its imposing castle named after the king of Bohemia; and the moonscape and slag heaps of SDAG Wismut. Müller wasn't entirely sure why the enterprise had that name. Perhaps it was one of the Republic's many euphemisms, a little like the Anti-Fascist Protection Rampart. Wismut – or bismuth – did sound somehow much less frightening than *uranium*, which was known to be used in the Soviet Union's nuclear weapons.

Immediately, Müller could tell that security was strict. As well as plenty of radiation warning signs, there were guard-houses, barbed wire fences, and a general air of menace. They didn't have any authorisations, and they hadn't warned anyone about their visit.

As the guard at the gatehouse examined their IDs, they real-ised that was going to prove problematic.

'You will have to turn round and park in the visitors' car park over there, Comrade *Hauptmann*,' said the guard. 'Then come back here and wait in the waiting room. I will see if anyone can come and see you.'

They were indeed forced to wait, Tilsner regularly checking his watch – his expensive *western* watch – and then making sorties to the desk to demand some action. The guards looked disinterested.

'We've let the directorate know that you are here,' said the head guard. 'If they are able to come and see you, they will. If you don't have time to wait, then I suggest you write a letter asking for a proper appointment.'

Tilsner sat back down in a huff. 'I'm not even sure he's German. He seemed to have an accent to me. Russian?'

Müller shrugged. 'It wouldn't surprise me. I think the uranium mines are jointly owned by the Russians, aren't they? The place is probably staffed by KGB agents, rather than the Stasi.'

Eventually, a pasty-faced balding besuited man made his way over to them.

Müller and Tilsner stood up to shake his hand.

'I'm Horst Frank, one of the deputy directors of the mine. Come this way, Comrade *Hauptmann*, Comrade *Oberleutnant*, please.' He led them into a side office, closed the door behind him, and invited them to sit in two chairs placed in front of a desk. He took the seat behind.

'This is most irregular, I'm afraid. Visitors strictly need to make a prior appointment.'

'We don't need to actually visit the mine,' explained Müller. 'We're simply seeking some information about one of your employees.'

'Or former employees,' added Tilsner.

'Well, which is it?' asked the man.

'Well the woman in question had a pass to work here which expired at the end of last year,' said Müller.

'Mmm. And?' said the man.

'We need to know if she still works here,' said Tilsner. 'Her name's Lotti Rolf.'

Müller detected a flicker of apprehension on Herr Frank's face.

'You know her?' she asked.

'Well . . . yes, but she didn't have a particularly important role here. She was in charge of timekeeping.'

'Was?' asked Tilsner.

'Yes. She left her position towards the end of last year.'

'Why?' asked Müller.

'Ah,' said Frank. 'I'm not sure if I'm permitted to tell you that.'

'This is a murder inquiry we're working on,' said Müller.

'Still. There are questions of national security with an enterprise like this, I'm sure you understand.'

'We're working with the authority of the Ministry for State Security,' insisted Tilsner. Müller had to resist raising a quizzical eyebrow. 'If you'd rather speak to them direct, person to person, to explain how you came to be obstructing a murder inquiry, I'm sure they'd be interested.'

The man sighed, and leant forward on his elbows. 'I'm not being deliberately obstructive, Comrade *Oberleutnant*. But there are procedures we must follow. Unless you have a signed authority from the Ministry for State Security, you will have to put all your questions in writing for consideration in due course.'

Müller fully expected Tilsner either to give up at this point, or lose his temper and start resorting to physical threats. Instead, her deputy reached into his coat pocket and brought out an envelope.

'Here's the authority,' he said, handing it over to Frank. As the man studied it, Tilsner winked at Müller. She frowned back. *I'll explain later*, he mouthed.

The man pushed his glasses up his nose and steepled his hands together. 'This seems to be in order. You obviously have friends in important places.'

'No,' said Müller. 'It's simply that this is an important murder inquiry.'

'Very well,' said Frank. 'What is it you need to know? And I hope it isn't Frau Rolf who's been murdered?'

'It isn't,' said Tilsner.

'Who then?' asked the man.

'Ah,' said Müller, turning the tables. 'Well that's something we're not permitted to discuss.' The fact they still didn't *know* the identity of the victim, despite already being a couple of days into the inquiry, wasn't something he needed to know either. 'What we want to know is *why* Lotti Rolf ceased to be employed here?'

'It was partly health reasons, partly disciplinary reasons.'

'You'll have to give us more than that,' said Tilsner.

The man sighed. 'She developed a serious health condition.'

'Surely that's not enough to sack someone?' queried Müller.

The man shuffled in his seat. 'No, it's not. Not normally. But then she started to make a song and dance about it.'

'In what way?' asked Tilsner.

'Writing petitions about the health conditions at the mine, that sort of thing. Making a nuisance of herself. Given you say you're working in conjunction with the Ministry for State Security, I'm surprised you don't know all about it already. They certainly do. If you need to ask them anything, try the regional headquarters in Dresden. Now who was it who was looking after it?' He pulled a pocket diary from his jacket and flicked through it. 'Ah yes, a *Major* Bahlow was the man in charge.'

Müller and Tilsner exchanged knowing looks. Bahlow seemed to have a piece of meat in every bowl of soup.

'So what was her health condition?' asked Müller.

'Lung cancer.'

'Aha,' said Tilsner. Almost as though to wind up Müller, at the mention of lung cancer he reached into his pocket and brought out his cigarettes, offering one to Frank, who took it. Tilsner made a play of offering one to Müller too and got a sarcastic smile and long sigh in return. Then he lit both his and Frank's with his lighter.

'But she was a smoker,' said Frank, 'so her claims were without foundation.'

'Her claims?' asked Müller.

'That she and several other employees had developed lung cancer and other diseases as a result of conditions at the mine. That was something we could not tolerate. After all, who is to say she didn't develop her cancer through her smoking?' With that, he blew a cloud of smoke towards Müller, much to her annoyance and Tilsner's evident amusement.

'And how serious was this cancer?' asked Tilsner, once he'd choked back his laugh.

'That I can't tell you. You'd have to ask her, or her doctors.' He sat there, with a smug grin on his face. Müller was determined to wipe it off.

'*Do* you have a problem with cancers or other diseases amongst the miners or ancillary workers?' she asked.

The grin stayed in place. 'SDAG Wismut Königstein has an excellent record and strives to make sure its working environment benefits all its workers and allows them to meet their targets in a healthy, comradely way. Does that answer your question?'

It didn't, and Frank knew full well it didn't. He'd simply quoted a nonsense platitude from the corporation handbook.

There was a moment's silence.

'Is that all, gentlemen? Apologies . . . *lady* and gentleman.'

Müller wanted to punch the man. She wasn't entirely sure Tilsner wouldn't actually raise his fists. But she wasn't done with him yet.

'We'll need to interview her closest work colleagues, please,' said Müller, eyeballing the man levelly. 'I'd like a list drawn up and for any of them who are on shift to be brought here immediately.'

'Well, I'm not sure that will be possible. We can't jeopardise our targets.'

Tilsner lifted the phone handset on the desk.

'What the blazes do you think you're doing?' asked Frank.

'Ringing *Major* Bahlow, of course.'

The man put his hand over Tilsner's and pressed the handset back on to the telephone. 'There's no need for that. I'll get your list typed up, and round up anyone who's on shift.'

Once Frank had left the room and was out of earshot, Müller turned to Tilsner.

'I think we need to have another meeting with our *Major* Bahlow to find out exactly what's going on.'

'I'm sure he knows,' said Tilsner. 'But I'm not sure he'll tell us.'

'Well I'm sick to the back teeth of being taken for a fool.'

'As detectives with the People's Police, it seems to be our lot in life, Karin. The Ministry for State Security will always have the upper hand.'

Müller knew what he said was true. She also – to some extent – understood the Stasi's function. The revolution *did* have to be defended. Counter-revolutionaries, fascists; yes, they all should be targeted. Arrested if necessary. But it seemed as though all Lotti Rolf had been trying to do was draw attention to possible health risks at an important industrial enterprise. To protect other citizens and workers in the Republic. To fire her for that, well, that sounded more like something that would happen in the BRD or the west in general, didn't it?

The procession of co-workers, small though it was, failed to turn anything up of value for the two detectives, until the last person to be interviewed. She was the only one who claimed to be a friend of Lotti's – the others all claimed she didn't mix with people from work. But Ursula Horn was a similar age to Lotti, and did the same job, although they usually were on opposite shifts. As a result, at work they were like ships that passed in the night. But Ursula lived in Bad Schandau and knew Lotti's family of old.

'We'd meet up when she was visiting her mother. Lotti didn't want to stay at the bed and breakfast all the time – she found she was being roped into chores. So we'd meet up for a coffee in the village, or sometimes hang out at the Rolf's cottage.'

'The annexe, in Kirnitzschtal?' asked Müller.

'Yes, that's the one. It's a bit run-down, I know. But nice and private. We could just get away from it all, and chat about whatever we wanted, without fear of being overheard, if you know what I mean?'

'No,' said Tilsner. 'What do you mean?'

'You know. People who might report you if you were saying something slightly off.'

'Like what?' asked Müller.

'Well, you know about Lotti and her health, I expect?'

Müller nodded.

'Well, she wanted to expose everything. I warned her against it. Told her she'd never win. But she was very angry about her lung cancer. The poor woman has been through a lot – she's had an unhappy life, really.'

'What makes you say that?' asked Müller.

'What happened in the war. Her face. You know about that, presumably?'

The two detectives nodded again.

'So I think she felt she'd been dealt two unfair hands. First, the burns from the terror bombing, then the cancer at the mine.'

'But you don't *know* it was connected with her work, do you?' said Tilsner.

The woman lowered her voice. 'No. Of course not. I'm not a medical expert. But you should see the number of people here who get ill, especially the miners themselves. It can't just be coincidence, can it? Anyway, Lotti was determined she wanted to do something about it. She started writing official petitions, that sort of thing. And even asked other people to sign them. I did, with one of them, and that got me into a whole heap of trouble, so I told her never again. But she was firing them off left right and centre, even to Honecker. Word obviously got back to the directorate of the mine, and soon after that, Lotti was "let go".'

Müller frowned. 'And have you seen her since then? Since she left the mine?'

'Oh yes,' said Ursula. 'But she'd become involved with some old boyfriend or something. Someone who was helping her with her campaign.'

Müller's ears pricked up. 'Do you have a name?'

Ursula frowned, and rubbed her brow with her hand. 'Oh, what was it. I can't remember. But I can tell you a bit about him.'

'Go on,' said Tilsner.

'Well, he wasn't from the Republic for a start. He was British. Worked at the university. Quite an important man, I think. Well, Lotti certainly thought so. Oh!' The woman's face suddenly brightened. 'I've remembered his name. Arnie! Arnie somebody. Now what was his surname?'

'Southwick,' said Müller. 'Arnie – or Arnold – Southwick.'

31

Bahlow agreed to meet but said it needed to be somewhere well away from Bautzner Straße – preferably somewhere where none of them would be recognised. Müller almost laughed out loud when he suggested the Pioneer Railway in Dresden's famous Großer Garten. It was the sort of venue Jäger would suggest – indeed she and Jäger had met on Halle-Neustadt's miniature railway. But that was in the summer. In winter, she doubted it would be running, and expressed that doubt to him.

'*No, it won't be. You're right, but in the middle of the park, just by the railway, there's the open-air theatre. That's as good a place as any. I'll see you there in . . . what, forty-five minutes, would that work?*'

Müller decided to meet him on her own. She still wasn't entirely sure how Tilsner had miraculously produced the Ministry of State Security authority which had bought them some measure of co-operation from the uranium mine management. If he and Bahlow were somehow working together on something, and keeping her out of the loop, then she wanted to tackle the Stasi major about it face to face.

She made sure she arrived at the rendezvous point early. That way, she could choose her seat and watch. To see if Bahlow really was alone. She still didn't understand his full motives. He'd failed to tell them about Lotti's apartment, even though he claimed to be her handler. He'd pointed them in the direction of the drainage ditch hideout – but if it was so easy to find, how had the Stasi failed to uncover it themselves? And if he really *was* Lotti's handler, how did he apparently *not* know her current location? Müller still couldn't help feeling that the Stasi major was playing games with her. But even if that were true, what was his motive? What did *he* want to achieve? What did the Ministry for State Security want to achieve – and did it amount to the same thing, or had Bahlow gone rogue?

Müller felt she had a panoramic view of the park, sitting in the centre of the small, open amphitheatre. So she almost jumped out of her skin when Bahlow sat down next to her – without her noticing his approach.

'Sorry, Comrade *Hauptmann*. I hope I didn't startle you?'

She narrowed her eyes at him, and he gave a conspiratorial smile. 'It's part of the training,' he laughed. 'I thought you'd be impressed.'

'Still playing games with me, then?'

'Why do you say that, Karin? Can I call you Karin?'

'Of course, *Rüdiger*. If I can call you that?'

'Just Rüdi is fine. So, you wanted to meet. And you don't want to play games.' He stretched his arms above his head, as though he'd been working at a typewriter and was finally deciding to take a break. 'All right, I'll lay my cards on the table. Some of them, anyway.' He said nothing for a moment, looking left and right, as though checking that they really were alone. Then he seemed to come to some sort of decision. 'Let's move down to the front. I don't like the look of that hedge behind us. Anyone could hide there.' The joking levity in his voice had disappeared – Müller realised he was deadly serious. Even more so, when, as they got to the front row, he insisted they sat next to each other, but facing in opposite directions.

'How good are your observational skills?' he asked.

'Pretty good, I'd say.'

'OK, well sitting like this may seem stupid, but it gives us both a one-hundred-and-eighty-degree view. If you see any-one, pinch me to get me to stop talking, and I'll do the same. Understood?'

'It sounds like some children's party game,' laughed Müller.

Her laughter died in her throat as Bahlow replied. 'I'm deadly serious, Karin. Lives could be at stake. And not just in connec-tion with the murder you're investigating. So, you wanted to ask me some questions? Fire away.'

'Where's Lotti Rolf?'

'That, I don't know. She seems to have gone to ground. I gather you got close to her at the water meadows, but she gave you the slip.'

Müller nodded. Then realised Bahlow wouldn't see a nod. 'Yes. But if you knew her movements, why couldn't you have posted agents at all those points and intercepted her?'

'Because . . . as you've probably gathered by now, in some respects I'm acting on my own.'

'Why? And in what way? And how do I know I can trust you?'

Bahlow sighed. 'I'll answer the last part first. You can't trust me. You can't trust anyone. Certainly not Jäger. And probably not Tilsner either, although I gather you two are as thick as thieves. Nevertheless, although you can't trust me, I do want to help you.'

'Why?'

'Because some things are taking place that I find beyond the pale, Karin.'

She laughed ironically. 'Forgive me if I find that hard to believe. I'm sure you don't get to the level of major in the Ministry for State Security without plenty of experience in the dark arts.'

'That's true. But we all have our lines in the sand. Mine have been crossed.'

'Is it something to do with the cancer cases at the uranium mine?'

'Ha!' laughed Bahlow. 'Lotti's pet cause? No, not that. What do people expect working in a mine extracting radioactive material? She might have a point, in fact I'm sure she does. But there is no evidence that the development of her cancer was a result of working there. It's not as though she was at the coal face, as it were, is it? Although she did come into contact with miners, their clothing et cetera. So I suppose it's possible. But if you smoke as many fags as she does, most doctors are only going to point to one thing as a cause of lung cancer. But no, it's not that.'

'So does it involve Lotti at all?'

'Tangentially, yes. But it's more to do with history.'

'History?'

'Recent history – well relatively recent. I'm not sure how old you are and whether it was actually in your lifetime.'

'Something that happened here, in Dresden?'

'Very much so. Perhaps the biggest thing that ever happened in Dresden.'

'The bombing?'

'Exactly.' There was a catch in his voice, as though he was choked with emotion. Müller couldn't see his face, and she realised there might be a reason for that – a reason other than ostensibly watching out for spies and eavesdroppers. He didn't *want* her to see his face. Didn't want her to see the hurt that she could hear in his speech. 'I'm an orphan, Karin. You won't need three guesses to find out why. Yes, I was raised by loving, adoptive parents, but it's not the same, is it? You of all people would know that.'

Where Stasi officers were concerned, one thing never surprised her. The fact that they always did their homework. That they always knew everything about her. Possibly more than she did herself.

'OK,' she said. 'I can understand some of that. The strength of those feelings. But I still don't understand their relevance.'

'Think back to the start of all this.'

'What, in Gorbitz?'

'Exactly. Our Concrete Man who no one has, apparently, identified yet. Apart from some bungled attempt by Jäger to convince you it was a local drunk who'd got into a fight. You think your job is to identify the victim, and find out who killed him. Well that's true, but only up to a point.'

'Up to what point?'

'Up to the point of finding out who killed him. I know who the victim was – well, I know approximately who the victim was, *what* he was, shall we say. But he will never be positively identified. Certain people have made—' Bahlow stopped talking all of a sudden and pinched her leg, then changed the subject completely. ' . . . Of course we should co-operate more, Comrade *Hauptmann*. The Ministry for State Security and the *Kriminalpolizei* of the People's Police are . . .' Müller realised he was talking gobbledegook deliberately. The process of giving her useful information had come to an end.

She turned and briefly saw, just outside the theatre, the little that was showing of the face of the figure who had made Bahlow change tack. The man's hat was drawn down over his forehead, and lapels pulled up against his ears.

She couldn't be 100 per cent certain, but in the brief instant she saw his eyes she could have sworn she was looking at another Stasi officer, or at least someone who had claimed to be a Stasi officer, back at the Rolfs' annexe.

The fake Stasi captain. *Hauptmann* Gustav Weiß. Or rather Gordon Breitmann of the Secret Intelligence Service.

32

LOTTI

I'm angry with myself, really. Why did I answer the door? I'd only just got off the phone to Mutti – we're very lucky that both of us have private phones, she because of the hotel, me because of my work at the uranium mine – and hadn't had a chance to do my make-up. I don't like to keep it on all the time. I need to if I don't want to frighten people (ha! – I quite *like* frightening people, serves them right for being so squeamish), but the trouble is it itches, and I don't think it's good for my skin – or what remains of it – on that part of my face. It's already so damaged. But I could have just not answered, that would have been the sensible thing to do. All right, I know I'm no oil painting (actually, I've never understood the attraction of lots of oil paintings of women, including the *Mona Lisa*, ugly cow-faced bitch), but at least with my make-up properly done I can make myself presentable. Well, I think so, at least. Others may not agree.

So, I did answer the door. And I confess I felt a little disappointed when Arnie clearly didn't recognise me. I know it's silly holding a torch for someone I met briefly when I was only thirteen years old, but if you'd had the life I've had, perhaps you'd understand. Not that he's got film-star looks – he hasn't. His wiry hair is a bit unkempt and balding, his stomach could be more toned, and he could – quite frankly – have brought a present. Some chocolates, flowers, a bottle of something. Are the English just naturally rude? Maybe they are. Although of course, as well as being English, he's from Yorkshire. In books I've read about Great Britain, Yorkshire people – as well as those from Scotland – have a reputation for being 'careful with money'. In other words, downright mean.

It all leaves me a little flustered. And because I didn't get any warning – well not unless you count the phone call from Mutti, and that came far too late – I haven't tidied the flat, and my trouble is I can't bear to throw things away. It's probably something to do with what happened in the war, in Dresden, how we lost literally everything. Now I'm a bit of a hoarder. So there are piles and piles of newspapers on each surface, and various other pieces of pretty worthless bric-a-brac that I can't bear to be rid of.

And then, of course, there's my cancer room. It's not a treatment room. It's just where I collect all my information. All the cases where miners, or workers at the mine like myself, have either developed cancer, or silicosis, or both. I've noted the details of each one down. One day, people will learn the truth,

I'm sure of it. Whether I'll still be alive to see that . . . well, some-how I doubt it.

I check myself in the mirror before I set off. It's probably been more than the ten minutes I said I'd take, but then he's the one who sought a reunion with me, not vice versa, so I can afford to make him wait a little. In any case, absence makes the heart grow fonder, so they say. I don't particularly love the reflection that looks back at me, but it's about the best I can do for a middle-aged woman with fourth-degree burn scars on one side of her face.

When I finally arrive, I see him waiting in the corner, nursing a beer a little dolefully. Some of my neighbours try to catch my eye, probably surprised to see me out – no doubt even more sur-prised about me meeting a man sitting on his own, at least one that doesn't look like a complete gargoyle. They'll be gossiping about it tomorrow in the Kaufhalle, no doubt.

Let them.

He stands up when he sees me, gives me a kiss on the good side of my face because that's the side I proffer to him, and pulls out a chair for me. Then he asks me what I'd like to drink. A *proper* gentleman, not like some of the oafs I've been on dates with down the years.

'That's kind of you. I'll have a small *Sekt* please, Arnold.'

He calls the waitress over and orders for me, and another beer for himself.

'It'll have to be my last one. I'm driving back to Dresden.'

Oh don't worry, I want to say. *You'd be very welcome to stay over.* But I don't because (a) I know he's married although his wife's not with him in Dresden for some reason (b) the flat's still a terrible mess and (c) it would be horribly forward and I couldn't bear him turning me down.

'It's so good to see you, Lotti, after so long. How old were we?'

'I was thirteen, you were twelve,' I laugh. 'I suppose you could say I was a cradle snatcher.'

'I suppose so, but we shouldn't really joke about such things.'

Oh god! I forgot. He's a terribly serious academic these days. I'd better try not to make any of my feeble jokes.

'You were quite an eager little puppy, as I remember.' He looks slightly disapproving again. 'All over me like a rash.'

He laughs nervously. Perhaps I've put my foot in it again.

'I kept writing to you, you know,' I say. 'Through the war. I sent a few letters, but when I didn't hear back, I still wrote them, but I just never sent them. I was worried about you. We never got much specific information about attacks on Hull, but it was a port on the North Sea. I expect it got hit badly, didn't it?'

He looks terribly sad for a moment. I see his Adam's apple going up and down quickly a few times, as though he's struggling to compose himself. 'It was bad, yes. Not as bad as Dresden, of course. I lost my baby brother.'

'Oh Arnold,' I say, reaching over and touching his hand. 'I am so sorry. I didn't mean to remind you of it.'

'It's OK. It's not something you ever forget. The thing was, he looked so perfect. So undamaged. Just like he was sleeping and never woke up, which I suppose he was, really. They say that can happen – the blast wave destroys the internal organs, but outside, the body looks undamaged. That's what made it so hard to believe. It devastated my parents, of course. They stuck together during the war – mainly for my sake I think, although there were terrible arguments. But they got divorced soon after, and I went to live with my mum. I never really got on with my dad, anyway.'

'I remember you saying that, back on that holiday. It was almost like you hated him.'

'I think part of me did. He was a very selfish man. Got quite rich in later life, but then remarried and basically got swindled by his second wife. But he seemed besotted with her, as though he didn't care. She bankrupted him in the end.'

'Her own husband?'

He nods. 'Well her or her family did. I didn't get a penny in the will. Anyway, what about you? Your mother says you spent the war in Dresden. That you were caught up in the firestorm. That must have been dreadful.'

Suddenly I have a horrible thought. He's a researcher, a historian. Did he only want to meet up again because Mother told him about the burns? Is that all he wants – to hear first-hand what it was like? I don't think I can bring myself to go over it all again. 'It was. Awful.' I point to the bad side of my face. 'As you can see, I still bear the scars.'

He nods again. It's one of those prompting nods, the ones television interviewers give to encourage their interviewees to keep talking. But I've given all I'm going to give him. I don't want to be one of his research cases. So we lapse into silence for a moment.

'What about work, Lotti?' he says. I'm not sure he's really interested. In fact, he's probably wondering why he bothered having this meeting. What did he expect to find? A buxom, sex-obsessed thirteen-year-old as I was back then, trapped in some sort of time warp?

'Oh gosh. My work is very boring. I'm not really supposed to talk about it.'

'Ah!' he says, knowingly, with a wink. 'That sort of work. Say no more. My lips are sealed.'

Again, silence is the order of the day. I can see he's feeling uncomfortable, and wondering what to say. Whether to try to cut everything short. That's what they often do, my dates. Once they realise I'm not going to be an easy fuck just because I'm a Plain Jane. And not just a Plain Jane – a Plain Jane with a facial deformity. *It's thanks to you fucking British that I look like this*, I want to say. But of course I don't. That would be rude. He's fiddling with the menu now, turning it over and over.

'What about something to eat? Are you hungry?'

I realise this is the tipping point. It could go one way or the other. I can back out now, bring it all to an end, we say our goodbyes, and wonder why we've bothered to spoil what was probably a special memory for us both from more than forty years ago. Or I can say yes.

'Yes,' I hear myself saying. 'That would be lovely. The *Eisbein* with *Sauerkraut* and *Erbsenbrei* is particularly good here.'

He looks at me like a little lost lamb. 'Sorry,' he says. 'My German's not bad, but you've lost me there.'

'Well you know what *Sauerkraut* is?'

'Of course.'

'So the dish is pork knuckle with *Sauerkraut* and mushy peas.'

'Mushy peas. Great. A Hull delicacy – usually served with greasy cod and chips, but pork knuckle and *Sauerkraut* sounds much more appetising. Shall we go for two of those?'

The food, and more drink, relaxes the atmosphere. I stop feeling bitter, and start to feel quite warm towards him. After all, he's probably lonely, a Brit in the very strange country that the Republic is. For him, this was just calling on an old friend. A chance to catch up and gossip. I chide myself for my mean thoughts that he just wanted to use me as a subject for his research. Nevertheless, as I relax I do find myself opening up about that night. I always tell myself I don't like talking about it, but actually whenever I do, I find it all quite cathartic. So I give it him all – lock, stock and barrel. He even asks if it's all right to take some notes, and I say sure, why not?

And then I tell him about my job.

Then I lower my voice and tell him about my cancer, and he's holding my hand in sympathy and it feels quite nice. I know he means nothing by it, but it brings a little tear to my good eye, and he wipes it away. I only ever cry out of one eye these days. It means I have to use fewer tissues when there's a soppy film on TV or at the cinema. Although I don't go to the cinema that often – you just feel such an outcast sitting on your own. It's like you're a leper.

So I'm starting to feel a bit maudlin again, but he cheers me up by insisting we share a *Schwedenbecher* – a Swedish ice-cream sundae – for dessert. To be honest, I could have probably managed a whole one myself, but the act of sharing it with a spoon each is quite intimate.

Before I know what's really happening, we're standing outside my front door again. I'm tempted to invite him in, despite the mess. To ask him to stay over to avoid the risk of getting caught drink driving, even though the Vopos are terribly lax about it. But before I can, he's trying to kiss me goodbye on the cheek, accompanied by a light hug. As he leans in though, I turn my head so the kiss ends up on my lips, and I pull him in for a proper hug.

He feels good.

Really good.

33

'Care to join me for a snifter, Robert?'

'Don't mind if I do, old man. What are we celebrating?'

'How about that great victory at Headingley. Stirring stuff, wasn't it? That Beefy chap – magnificent. Turned it around all on his own. Margaret is apparently a bit of a fan, and the feeling is mutual. Shouldn't be surprised if he's an MP one day. Mind you, he's perhaps a little uncouth for the Tory party. Not really one of us.'

'No, perhaps not, Gerald. Anyway. I'm sure you didn't ask me here to talk about cricket, fantastic result though it was.'

'No. Quite right. Shall we go into the study? There's a few briefing papers there I want you to take a look at.'

The younger man sat down where his superior indicated, in front of his desk.

'We've got a bit of potential trouble in your neck of the woods, Robert, and we need it closing down. One way or another. It's something that – if it got into the wrong hands – could cause a bit of a stink. Margaret is particularly worried.'

The younger man always found it slightly affected the way his superior referred to the Prime Minister as Margaret, as though she was a personal friend. They both knew she wasn't. Behind the faux concern she could turn on with the slightest excuse – and the softly, softly voice – was an utterly ruthless politician. Brilliant – in some people's eyes – but utterly ruthless. From a personal point of view, Robert couldn't stand her. But then – despite what people assumed – he wasn't really a Tory at all. His sympathies lay much further to the left. But in this day and age, it didn't do to make that too public, especially in the Circus.

'In the German sector?'

'Exactly. Particularly the red side of the divide.'

'I thought we were of the opinion that relations were thawing. The talks on medium-range missiles last year, Reagan lifting the grain embargo earlier this year. We almost seem to be heading into a period of détente.'

'Perhaps, perhaps. But this isn't really an East–West thing.'

'No?'

'No.' The older man spread out some documents on the desk. 'No, this is more a British–German thing, a historic thing really, something that should be left in the past. But unfortunately the East Germans are pushing their noses into things that don't really concern them, or shouldn't really concern them. So, as I say, we need it shutting down. It's your job to come up with a strategy for that. Do you think you can do that, old man?'

'Well, let's have a look at all this and see what we can do, shall we?'

'Aha. Not committing yourself there, then. Sensible chap. I doubt it's that complicated though. As you'll see, it concerns an academic being feted by the East Germans for some of his historic research.'

'That seems a little . . . esoteric, shall we say?'

'Well yes, and no. If it goes the way we expect it to go *without* any intervention, it could bring some pretty big names down. Alive and dead.'

'Dead? Surely we've not entered the realms of protecting the reputations of the dead?'

His superior took in a long breath, then opened a box of cigars and offered Robert one. He shook his head. Couldn't stand smoking the things, and couldn't stand other people smoking them either, but here he didn't have a choice. He would have to suffer the other man's foul-smelling smoke, like it or not.

There was a moment's silence, with only the steady tick-tock of the no doubt priceless mahogany inlay longcase clock breaking the quietude.

'That rather depends, old boy. On who the dead person is. In this case, he was a national hero, a Conservative Party hero, and Margaret is rather eager to make sure nothing is done to sully his reputation. For the national good. Even though he's long gone. The other person in question, well, he's alive, but to be honest we're not too bothered about it.

Not too much of a reputation to protect, if you know what I mean.'

Robert took a quick look at the documents. At first glance, there was nothing that looked insurmountable, but as always, it would come down to resources.

'How much help can I have on this?' he asked.

'Whatever it takes. Whatever it takes. Those were Margaret's words.'

Each time his superior said the name 'Margaret' it was like someone had scraped a piece of rough chalk down a blackboard. That horrible shiver of discomfort. It was known that Gerald was not long off retirement – perhaps he was angling not just for a knighthood, but something even more grand.

'And the object is what? Destruction of reputation of this academic?'

'Something like that. The East Germans themselves are rather good at that – perhaps we could employ some of their techniques.'

'What, gaslighting?'

'*Zersetsung* is their term for it, I'll think you'll find.'

As head of the German section, Robert was perfectly well aware what *Zersetsung* meant. He'd just deliberately chosen an Anglicism instead. He kept his counsel.

'But no,' continued Gerald. 'We need something rather more than that. A successful result for us would be that this never sees the light of day, not that it sees the light of day but is discredited, although the latter would be better than nothing. Anyway, can

I leave it with you? Will you get back to me by Monday with your proposals, there's a good chap.'

Although the last sentence had been phrased as though it was a question, Robert knew that it wasn't.

It was an order. Plain and simple.

34

Dresden
February 1982

After her meeting with Bahlow, Müller decided she'd had enough for one day. The case seemed to be constructed of lie upon lie upon lie. The truth? Well, from what Bahlow was saying – *if* he could be trusted – the truth was something they would never really uncover. It was as though the truth, solving the murder, was something that just didn't matter. And that left a nasty taste in Müller's mouth.

The flat she, Tilsner and Schmidt shared looked out onto the Neumarkt and what remained of the Frauenkirche. Before 1945, this would have been a sought-after address in Dresden, with either sky-high rents, or let out to tourists as a holiday flat. But being here wasn't some reward. It was just conveniently near the People's Police HQ, a walk of less than a hundred metres.

Tilsner had also arrived back, although Schmidt was nowhere to be seen.

As a result, when she looked in the fridge there was actually some food left.

'Do you want me to cook tonight?' asked Tilsner.

'Wonders never cease. It's not like you to offer.'

'Well, greedy guts isn't back yet, so I'll have less to make, and won't have to suffer him scoffing with his mouth open. Besides, you look utterly knackered, if you don't mind me saying. How was the meeting with Bahlow?'

'Less than satisfactory, as you can imagine.'

'Care to tell me more?'

'Not really.' She kicked her boots off and flopped down onto the sofa with her legs up.

'Are you making space for me?'

'I thought you were cooking.'

'I thought you might like to relax first.'

Müller gave a snort. 'No thank you, Werner. I've got a headache. And I'm utterly fed up with this case.'

'Suit yourself. Do you want a beer? Or something stronger?'

'No. But if you're making a coffee . . .'

'Whatever Madam requires . . .'

Once her coffee came, Müller relented and briefed Tilsner on what Bahlow had said, including the untimely arrival of the man she thought was the fake Stasi captain, Weiß.

'So Bahlow knows who Concrete Man is, but won't tell us?'

'And he implies it doesn't really matter, anyway, as we'll never manage to properly identify him.'

'Well that's just a heap of shit. The whole case is a heap of shit. My advice is this – you get on to *Oberst* Reiniger back in Berlin. He's always had a soft spot for you. Well, hard spot, probably.'

'Don't be disgusting.'

'You can't deny that he's sweet on you.'

'Not in that way. He treats me more like a naughty daughter.'

'Whatever floats your boat. Anyway, we'll agree that – until our little fall from grace on the frozen Ostsee – you had the ability to wrap him round your little finger. So now's the time to use your charm. We might still be in disgrace, but he won't like the fact that we're being played for fools by the Stasi. Get him to pull us off the case. Bring us back to Keibelstraße. I'd rather be pushing files, or pens, or even licking Reiniger's arse than spending any more time in this godforsaken shithole.'

Müller laughed. Tilsner had a way of bringing things down to their most basic level. 'I don't think that's any way to talk about the Florence of the Elbe, do you?'

'I don't give a flying fuck about the Florence of the Elbe, or the Florence of anywhere come to that. I just want to be off this case and back in Berlin where we belong.'

35

Müller had almost dozed off when the jangle of the phone jolted her awake. Tilsner was slumped in the armchair, still pretending to be asleep, so she answered it.

'*Zum grüner Heinrich. Thirty minutes time. Be there.*'

The caller immediately rang off, just as Müller was about to ask who it was.

She kicked Tilsner awake. 'Get up. We've got to go up to Gorbitz.'

'Who says?' he groaned, shielding his eyes from the main light Müller had switched on.

'Anonymous tip-off.'

'Oh, great. Another wild goose chase, then.' Despite his grumbling, he started getting into his boots. 'Did you recognise who it was?'

'The voice was muffled, as though the caller was holding a handkerchief or similar over the mouthpiece. But if I had to hazard a guess, I'd say Bahlow.'

'That's all we need. I'm dog tired. And not really in the mood to play the Stasi's games anymore.'

When they reached the Platz der Bauarbeiter and parked the car, they decided to wait outside Zum grüner Heinrich, rather than inside. That way, they could keep their anorak hoods tightly drawn, with less chance of being identified other than by the anonymous caller, who – having known the private number for their police apartment – would almost certainly recognise them. They'd both already taken the precaution of drawing their Makarovs from their holsters. Müller's hand gripped hers in her anorak pocket.

A bearded man in darkened glasses walked by – a ridiculous piece of apparel for a winter's night in February – but at first they deliberately paid him no heed. He drew close and hissed *Follow me, but stay back!* without actually turning his head or greeting them, and it was then they knew, from his tone of voice, that it was Bahlow.

In the half-light and shadows of street lamps and new and partially built apartment blocks, they followed Bahlow as he picked his away along wooden duckboards – the makeshift paths that had been threaded between the piles of building materials, muddy waste ground, and the new-builds themselves.

Müller led the way for her and Tilsner, making sure she stayed some twenty metres or so behind the Stasi officer. Both of them knew this might be another trap, or another piece of gaming. But each of Bahlow's tips – or deliberately planted pieces of evidence, if he was responsible for those too – had so far advanced the case. Müller had weighed it up in her head, as she was sure Tilsner had too. They had little to lose, and everything to gain.

Bahlow's weaving, seemingly tortuous route had taken them to a part of the residential area which – although newly built – almost appeared to have been abandoned, at least temporarily. The apartment blocks were just shells – no windows, no doors, no street lights. The concrete blocks rose like ghostly shapes in the gloom, the slightly lighter colour of the concrete fractionally picked out by the ambient light of the centre of Dresden, in the valley a few kilometres to the east. In the dim light, Müller could make out a street sign – Amelie-Dietrich-Platz – and a sign below explaining that the woman had been a nineteenth-century botanist and explorer.

Then – in one of the empty shells – a flickering light from one of the windowless openings on an upper floor. Bahlow had stopped and was pointing to it. Müller counted the floors as her head panned upwards – one, two, three . . . thirteen, fourteen, fifteen. Just one floor before the very top.

She turned back, intending to draw closer to Bahlow to ask him what this was all about.

But he'd disappeared into the night.

Slipped away behind the pipes, blocks and construction material, some of which were already weed-infested – as though the site hadn't been touched for weeks.

She looked back up to the fifteenth floor and the dim, flickering light. Then glanced at Tilsner, drew close, and cupped his ear.

'We're going to have to go up,' she whispered. 'He's clearly brought us here for a reason.'

She could sense Tilsner's reluctance. 'Yes, but what reason?' he hissed. 'Probably to do exactly the same to us as they did to the director of the sports school at the TV tower.'

Müller drew back from him, aghast. 'What makes you think *that* wasn't suicide? There was no indication of foul play.'

'Except for those documents the laundry woman gave us. Has Schmidt managed to decipher them yet?'

'He's been busy with other stuff. But I will chase him up about it.'

'*Scheisse!*' hissed Tilsner into her ear. He was suddenly pointing up towards the fifteenth floor. Her gaze swung upwards. *The light had gone out.* While they had been standing here discussing the merits of the case. But they'd kept their voices inaudible, surely? Perhaps whoever it was up there had been keeping a lookout.

They had the same thought at the same time. Müller saw Tilsner draw out his Makarov as she did hers. They slowly advanced into the shell of the building's lobby.

The lift shaft was simply that, an empty shaft with no mechanism whatsoever. They would be climbing up the stairs, which appeared to be complete. Why had this block been abandoned part-way through construction? It didn't make sense. Perhaps some vital parts were missing, or some structural defect had been discovered. Or – given the rumours about the Republic's dire need for hard currency – maybe the money was just running out.

They slowly climbed the stairs, taking extra care as they arrived at each new concrete floor that someone wasn't about to leap out and attack them.

They tried to keep noise to a minimum. But each false step they made sent clanging echoes through the empty building.

Müller accidentally kicked a metal bolt or screw off the stairs, into the adjoining lift shaft void. They stopped, stock still, as they heard it clatter to the floor far below, like a stone tossed down an empty well.

Finally, trying to control their panting breath, they reached the fifteenth floor.

Müller edged her head round the pillar of the lift shaft, which gave them some protection. She could sense Tilsner doing the same behind her. This storey was an almost complete void both ways, and to the right she immediately saw what had caused the flickering light.

An open fire on the floor, encased by a makeshift structure of grey concrete breeze blocks. It was now just glowing red rather than flickering with yellow flames, as it presumably had been earlier. A human shape covered in what looked like rags or sacks lay to one side of it, with another shrouded human crouched beside.

As quietly as possible, Müller and Tilsner advanced. The two figures didn't seem to have noticed them yet – either that, or they were beyond caring.

Müller could see, though, that there was no escape for their prey. The staircase she and Tilsner had just ascended was clearly the only way in or out.

'Freeze, *Kriminalpolizei*!' she suddenly shouted. 'Get up slowly, with your hands above your head. You're both under arrest.' There was no evidence of any serious crime, of course, but just sleeping or living rough in the Republic – and not contributing to the socialist workers' and peasants' state – was crime enough.

The hunched figure slowly rose to a standing position and raised his or her arms. Only when she spoke did Müller realise it was a female.

'He can't get up, he's too weak.'

'What are your names?' asked Tilsner.

'I'm . . . I'm . . .' The woman hesitated, as though wondering whether or not to construct a lie. Then any defiance, any hesitance seemed to disappear from her voice. 'I'm Lotti Rolf. This man is—'

'I'm . . . Arnold—'

'Shut up!' cried the woman.

'It's too late now, Lotti,' the prostrate man croaked. The woman sobbed. 'I'm Arnold Southwick. A research fellow—'

'It's all right,' said Müller. 'We know who you both are. We know what you do – or did.'

Tilsner moved next to Rolf, and handcuffed her arms in front of her. Müller knelt next to Southwick. 'Can you stand, or do you need help?'

The man shuffled himself into a sitting position, tried to get higher, then his legs gave way and he slumped back with a cry of pain. 'Help me with him,' she said to Tilsner. Her deputy moved over and roughly pulled the man to his feet. Once he was standing, Müller realised his leg was injured. It stank as though it had already turned septic, or – even worse – gangrenous.

As they tried to move him, both supporting a shoulder, Rolf saw her chance.

Müller watched almost in slow motion as the woman made a run for the stairwell. Tilsner loosened his hold on the man for a second, and raised his gun.

'Stop right there, Lotti! I won't hesitate to shoot.'

The woman stopped and turned round. 'Go on then,' she shouted. 'Open fire. I've a death sentence over my head anyway.' She started to turn back to the stairwell.

Tilsner slid the safety catch on the Makarov.

'Please, Lotti,' said Southwick, as loudly as his feeble voice would allow. 'I'm begging you, don't let them do this. Don't let it end like this.'

The woman stood stock still for a second, then slumped to the floor – like a marionette whose strings had suddenly been cut. As though she'd finally accepted everything was over.

36

LOTTI

Dresden
August 1981

I didn't think that kiss on the doorstep of my apartment would lead to anything, but it's important to let people know how you feel. At least I'd let Arnie know what I wanted. At the time, he pulled back, embarrassed. He's married, after all. He'd told me that, but I still felt this connection that I'd felt when we were teenagers – well, he wasn't quite a teenager then. Of course, I've never married because I've never found the right man. That's just the luck of the draw, isn't it? But I'd be horrified if any husband of mine started kissing an old girlfriend – what is it they say? *New flames burn brighter, but old flames burn longer.* That's it.

Anyway, for the first couple of months of his new posting, we've continued to meet for coffees about once a week. Well, we had a bit of a break from the coffee last month when the Elbe flooded. Apparently, Arnie said it was well over the Terrassenufer, right in front of the historic Brühl's Terrace, and up to the top of some of the bridges. So I decided then it was safer to stay in Pirna, even though Arnie was trying to get me to come and have a look.

But now he's invited me out for a meal again, at the Fresswürfel – the eating cube – in the centre. I try to doll myself up as nicely as possible. All right, I know it's a bit like old wine in a new bottle, but you've got to at least make the effort. My new haircut helps – permed but worn long, behind the ear on the good side of my face but flopping over the burnt side to hide it a bit. In the bathroom mirror, I tell myself I haven't scrubbed up too badly.

Oh clever him! It's a lovely warm summer's evening, and he's only managed to bag us one of the tables on the terrace overlooking the Zwinger itself. I wonder which waitress he bribed to arrange that. I hope it's not the pretty young thing coming towards us with the menu cards, smiling sweetly at him and getting a shy grin back. I almost want to kick him under the table.

But his attention is soon back on me once we've ordered our food and drink and are waiting for it to arrive.

'You're looking well, Lotti. If you hadn't told me, well, I wouldn't have known.'

We both know what he's referring to. Is it safe to talk about it here? Perhaps it's safer than at either of our flats. He's a foreigner, so he might be a target. I know at work I'm increasingly being seen as a troublemaker, so I might be too. But here, it just seems to be families or lovers meeting in a beautiful spot. Of course, we're not the former, or the latter . . . yet.

'I feel well. It's been lovely to meet up with an old friend.' He keeps on insisting we're just friends, so I humour him.

'Have you thought any more about what you're going to do about it?'

Last time we met, he was urging me to leave my job. That's all very well, but what would I do? Everyone knows that everyone has to work in the Republic. You can't just choose to be a layabout. 'I can't leave. I need to earn money.'

He looks at me earnestly through his spectacles, and lays his hand on mine. 'Not if it's making you ill, Lotti. It sounds like a very dangerous place.'

I look round nervously from side to side and frown at him. 'It's OK, I can write an *Eingabe*.'

'What's one of those when it's at home?'

'A citizen's petition. All you Westerners think we don't have any freedoms here, but we do. We can write *Eingaben* – petitions – to the government, and then the government responds.'

He looks at me, thoughtfully. 'That sounds like a good idea, then, Lotti. You have to do something. Perhaps I can help. Through my contacts at the university, I might be able to find other studies, other evidence. We need to get you out of there and we need to get you proper treatment.'

There's fire in his eyes. A burning desire to do something to help me. As he looks at me, I hope he's saying all this for the right reasons. That it's not just pity for an old friend.

Of course, we don't spend the whole evening talking about my work and problems. Arnie's also very excited about his own research. He says he's uncovered something 'mind-blowing' that might help people like me – people whose lives were ruined by the bombing in 1945.

That's the point when I kick him under the table. At first, he grimaces, moves as though to rub his leg. Then slowly it dawns on him. He shouldn't be talking about that here. We've been talking in English – though sometimes we switch between English and German, both of us at approximately the same level in each other's second language – but even so, I could detect a lowering of conversation round us when he began to talk about the 'terror bombing'. All right, most East Germans learn Russian as their main foreign language at school. But there's plenty like me who've tried to improve their English in their own time. I did it for my own reasons – the hope that one day I would see him again.

That stilts the conversation for a while, but as we down more glasses of *Sekt* we're soon gibbering away again, although we keep the talk on safer ground.

In the alcohol haze that accompanies the evening, I rather lose track of time. It means Arnie and I have to run to the Hauptbahnhof so that I can try and get the last train to Pirna. I know I'll look a sight – the sweat will play havoc with the make-up on the bad side of my face – but we've been having so much fun, I don't really care.

'Quickly, Lotti,' urges Arnie, after I drop some coins on the floor while scrabbling in my purse to find my ticket. 'You're going to miss it.'

We get to the platform just as the minute hand of the clock clicks to the departure time. Unfortunately, for once, the Republic's trains seem to be as prompt as they reputedly are in the west. We see my train pulling away.

'Oh God!' I cry. 'What am I going to do now?'

Arnie's head scans round. 'Where's the taxi rank? I don't mind paying for a taxi.'

'Ha! Finding a taxi in Dresden at any time is virtually impossible, but at this time of night . . .'

There's a moment's silence. I realise this is a critical point – but I have to let him suggest it, not me.

'Look, come to mine,' he says, finally. I can understand there's a bit of reluctance. But without his wife here with him, it must be difficult. 'I can sleep on the sofa – you can have the bedroom. And then you can get the early train to Königstein and work in the morning.'

I punch him lightly on the arm. 'Duh! It's Saturday tomorrow, and I'm not on shift, so I don't have to rush back. What about you? Will you be at the university tomorrow?'

There's a slightly frightened look in his eyes, as though I've trapped him. I suppose I have, in a way. But he's not to know I threw the coins on the floor deliberately, just to make sure I *couldn't* catch the train.

'No,' he says, finally. 'I haven't got any teaching to do, not yet anyway.'

'Great,' I say, linking arms, although he's slightly uncomfortable about it. 'I can treat you to breakfast, then.'

*

The apartment the university has provided is in one of the long blocks in Leningrader Straße. Much sought after because they're so near the centre, and it's only a few minutes' walk from the station. When we get there, I hope he's going to suggest coffee or a nightcap before we turn in, but instead he seems determined to go to bed – alone. I hide my disappointment, and when he tries to take the sofa, and begins tugging out some blankets and a pillow, I yank them off him.

'Don't be silly,' I say. 'It was my fault I missed the train. *I'm* going to take the sofa. You go to your own bed. It's kind enough of you to allow me to stay, you being a married man and all that.'

He's on the point of insisting, but I won't have any of it, and finally he gives up. He gives me a peck goodnight on the cheek. I try to turn my lips towards him like last time, but he's wised up to that trick now and moves away before I can.

'Good night, Lotti. I enjoyed tonight.'

'I did, too, Arnold. Good night.'

I try to get to sleep, but I keep on playing the evening over in my mind, wondering if I could have done anything different. The curtains are too thin, so the lights of the city below cast shadows on the walls. I get up and try to pull them together, but they've not been fixed to the curtain rod properly, so that just produces a gap at each end. Eventually I give up, and settle down on my back.

I try to concentrate on the lights playing on the ceiling from passing traffic, hoping my eyes might eventually tire of them and that I'll nod off that way. I try to imagine what the people driving those cars and lorries could be doing in the middle of the night. Shift workers, delivering food and newspapers, I suppose. But I'm still no nearer getting to sleep, and my mouth and throat feel dry and itchy. I can feel a coughing fit about to come on – so I get up to get myself a glass of water.

I've only just settled down again when I hear his door click open.

My shuffling around must have disturbed him.

'Everything OK, Lotti?' he whispers, as though not wanting to wake me if I'm really asleep.

I snort a bit, a kind of half snore, pretending I've been asleep. I don't want him to blame me for waking him, thanks to my night-time marauding.

'Sorry, did I wake you, Arnie? I sometimes have these bad dreams,' I lie. 'You know, from the night of the terror bombing.' I don't know why I say that – perhaps I'm just looking for his sympathy.

'Oh no,' he says, full of concern. 'I know what you mean. I still often dream of meeting Fred as a young man, believing in my head his death was all a mistake, and then I wake up. And realise he is really dead. It's a horrible feeling.'

Now I'm the one who feels bad. I draw back the blankets, showing him my half-naked body in flickering light from the street below. 'Do you want to come for a little cuddle?' I say.

'I'd better not, Lotti. Just as long as you're all right. I hope you get back to sleep OK. Good night.'

I let the covers fall back, feeling my face burn from the shame and rejection.

'Good night, Arnold,' I reply. Even I'm slightly shocked by the cold, slightly menacing tone of my voice.

I still struggle to get to sleep, although I've probably dozed a little. But from the sound of his snores through the closed door, I can hear that Arnie is well away.

I open his door as quietly as possible, trying to be light on my feet. Then I move across to the bed, trying not to disturb him, gently pull the duvet aside and climb in beside him. The rhythm of his snoring is disrupted for a few moments, and I hold my breath. But he doesn't wake. As he enters deep sleep again, and the rhythm settles, I curl up against him, feeling his warmth, imagining what it must be like to be loved. Normally I can't stand snoring, but his become more like regular snuffles. They soothe me, and I soon find myself drifting off.

Sometime in the night, he's turned against me. I can feel his hardness. I know it's just a Pavlovian, physical response, and that it means nothing. But I can't help myself getting excited. Then I hear him mumble his wife's name. I should be annoyed – I know I should be. But instead that excites me still further. I take a huge risk, and start to caress his penis, just very lightly rubbing the back of my hand under his glans. I feel him start to respond in his sleep. He seems to get even harder – impressive for his age. I duck my head under the covers, move the fly of his pyjamas aside, and – very softly – use my tongue instead of my hand, gliding it round. I feel him responding, and then take him fully into my mouth. Before he really realises what's happening, he's unloading in the back of my throat, while making anguished cries.

'Oh God, Oh God. No!' Then he's trying to throw me off. 'Lotti! What the hell are you doing?' He might be complaining now. But I know he wanted it. I know he needed it. And I know he wants and needs me – he's just given me the proof, and I swallow it down urgently.

37

Interrogation room, People's Police HQ, Dresden
February 1982

'How's Arnold?' asked Lotti.

'We're the ones asking the questions, Citizen Rolf,' replied Tilsner.

Müller sighed. Sometimes her deputy was aggressive and abrasive just for the sake of it, when a subtler approach might bear more fruit. 'He's getting treatment at the hospital as we speak,' said Müller. 'They'll do the best they can for him. But he may lose the leg. You realise you should have sought hospital treatment earlier?'

Lotti held her head in her hands. 'He wouldn't let me take him. He knew he'd be arrested, and that all he'd worked for would be lost.'

'Why would he have been arrested?' asked Tilsner.

Lotti stared at him as though he were mad. 'It's obvious, isn't it?'

'Why don't you tell us in your own words, Lotti?' said Müller, as gently as possible.

'Well, after what happened in Gorbitz.'

'You mean illegally squatting in the empty apartment block?' asked Tilsner.

Again, Lotti looked at Müller's deputy as though he'd lost his mind. 'No, of course not. Because of what happened earlier. The argument with one of your lot at the building site nearby.'

Things were starting to become clearer in Müller's head, but the elliptical way Lotti was giving her answers wasn't helping. 'The man who died? You're saying he was a People's Police officer?'

'People's Police. Ministry for State Security.' The woman shrugged. 'Same difference, isn't it?'

'Not necessarily,' said Müller. 'Anyway, in your own words, tell us what happened.'

If Lotti Rolf suspected the police knew less than she thought they knew, she didn't seem to be showing any inclination to withhold the facts. In fact, she seemed all too ready to tell Müller and Tilsner everything – which itself left a nagging doubt at the back of Müller's brain.

'This policeman, or Stasi officer, asked me to arrange a meeting for him with Arnie.'

'This was after Dr Southwick's research at the university was supposed to have come to an end?' asked Tilsner.

'Yes. Of course.'

'Why did they ask you to get involved?' prompted Müller.

'They must have known we were close. That I had some influence over Arnie. And also, that I knew where he was.'

'And where was he?' asked Tilsner.

'He was hiding out in another half-built building in Gorbitz. Near the one you found us in at Amelie-Dietrich-Platz.'

'Why the hell did you go back there again?' asked Tilsner. It was something Müller couldn't understand either, although it wasn't the most pressing question that needed to be asked.

'It was Arnie's idea. Something about hiding in plain sight. But we moved between there and the culvert in the water meadows every few days to try to keep safe.' She eyeballed Tilsner. 'You know. The one you found.' Then the woman gasped, and held her hand over her mouth. As though she'd said something she hadn't wanted to. Possibly because one of them had been responsible for assaulting Müller's deputy when he stumbled across their riverside lair.

'Tell us more about this meeting with the police or Stasi officer,' said Müller, trying to draw the interrogation back to the key part. 'What went wrong?'

'Arnold lost his temper. Said he'd been tricked. That his life's work had been ruined.'

'He lost his temper with this official?' asked Müller. Then she stared hard at the woman. 'Or with you for luring him to the meeting?' Müller remembered Petra Abt's testimony – the punky art student. She hadn't mentioned a second man being involved – the argument had been between a man and a woman – presumably Rolf and Southwick. She saw a look of guilt pass momentarily over Lotti's disfigured face.

'With the policeman, or whatever he was, of course,' said Lotti, a sneering note in her voice. 'The man made Arnold an offer – it really angered him.'

'What offer?' asked Tilsner.

'That he would make sure Arnold got safely back to Britain. And that he would ensure he got a comfortable and lucrative professorship at a university. I think he said a "red brick" university – I didn't really understand what that meant. But Arnold had to forget about all his research in Dresden. If he didn't, then his and his wife's life might be in danger.'

Müller heard Tilsner draw in a sharp breath beside her. But something in Lotti Rolf's statement didn't ring true.

'How would a People's Policeman, or indeed an agent from the Ministry for State Security, be able to come good on such an offer? Did you stop to wonder that, Lotti?'

The woman was sobbing softly now. 'There wasn't time to think about things like that. It all happened so quickly. Arnie flew into a rage. The man was trying to arrest him or something. Anyway, they got in a terrible fight. The man fell over and hit his head at one stage. But then he got up again. They were grappling on some duckboards where the new build was going on. Then the man slipped and we suddenly realised the concrete hadn't set yet. He was sinking down into it. Arnie grabbed his hand, tried to pull him out, but it was no good. I could tell the man couldn't breathe, that it was too late. I had to pull Arnie away in the end. He didn't want to leave him. None of this was his fault.'

'So you're saying it was all just a terrible accident?' asked Müller. There was still something about the woman's account she didn't fully believe. When Southwick himself had recovered enough to be questioned, they'd have to see if his account tallied with hers or not.

'Exactly. We weren't even sure who this man was. He was very aggressive. But Arnie didn't mean for him to fall into the concrete. We didn't even know the concrete wasn't set. We tried to save him. That was when Arnie injured his leg, on a rusty piece of concrete-reinforcing mesh.'

Müller looked hard at the woman. So much of the story didn't really square with what they already knew. The pathologist had insisted Concrete Man had suffered a blow to the back of the head that had been inflicted with a blunt weapon. He'd been adamant it *wasn't* the result of a fall. Now Lotti was trying to claim the exact opposite.

She looked across at Tilsner. He shrugged, but had a resigned expression. As though he didn't really believe the woman either, but might be prepared to swallow her story just to bring some closure to what had been a particularly frustrating case.

38

LOTTI

Dresden
October 1981

The car picks me up at the bus stop – a black Lada.

I suppose I have a good idea who they are, even as they bundle me in despite my protests. Thankfully, there's no one else waiting for the bus to see my shame.

They immediately pull a hood over my head, and tell me to lie down on the back seat, out of sight of other citizens. I try to ask them what's going on, what I've done wrong – but they tell me to be quiet. From the motion of the car, and the noise of other traffic, I can guess they're taking me from Pirna to Dresden itself. But they don't tell me that. They won't tell me anything – just order me to keep my mouth shut.

Eventually – after I suppose half an hour or so – there are a couple of sharp turns, I hear a metallic gate rolling open, and the car comes to a stop. I'm manhandled out of the car, but still can't see anything as they keep the hood in place. From the change in acoustics, the harsh echoes, I realise I've been taken inside. Then the hood's pulled off. Immediately, I have to shield my eyes from a harsh, penetrating light coming from very bright strip lights overhead. I'm in some sort of garage below a building.

Then I'm being taken down the corridors of what looks like a prison.

'Why are you taking me to jail?' I scream. 'I haven't done anything wrong.'

'This isn't a jail,' the guard who's holding me insists. 'We just want to ask you a few questions.'

We go down various corridors, stopping until the control lights change colour, up at least one flight of stairs. I'm beginning to lose my bearings in this prison that my guard insists isn't a prison.

Finally, we arrive at what appears to be our destination.

I'm bundled into the room and ordered to sit on a stool in the corner. It's as though I've been a naughty child at school. The guard stays with me for the time being. The paintwork in here is the same as the corridors outside – an unappetising mix of cream and olive green. There's no window as such – just patterned glass blocks, which allow in the natural light but mean you can't see any detail of the outside. So although I believe I'm in Dresden, I could be wrong.

The door opens, and two uniformed men enter the room. They sit down next to each other at the desk in the middle of the room, their faces stern. One of them – the one whose uniform looks somehow more important, even though I don't know

what rank is what – gives a head gesture to the guard, who with-
draws, closing the door behind him.

'Good morning Frau Rolf,' says this man in a serious tone,
opening a file which he's pulled from his briefcase. 'I'm *Oberst*
Rainer Specht and my Comrade here is *Major* Rüdiger Bahlow.
We want to see if we can help you.'

'Help me?' I cry. 'Your goons pulled me in off the street, put a
hood over my head, and brought me here against my will. How
is that helping me? And what the hell is this place?'

The other man speaks now, in a friendlier tone. 'Yes, we're
sorry this meeting had to be arranged in such an underhand
way. But we assure you, we do want to help you. As for where
we are, we're in Dresden, as you've probably guessed. This is
the regional headquarters of the Ministry for State Security in
Bautzner Straße.'

So, the Stasi, not the police. It confirms what I suspected.
'And exactly how are you, the Stasi, proposing to help me?' My
voice sounds strong, challenging, even though I'm sitting like
a little girl on this stupid, uncomfortable stool in the corner of
the room.

Serious one answers this time, turning his file and lifting it
slightly to show me something familiar. 'It's about your *Eingaben* here – your petitions about working conditions at SDAG
Wismut in Königstein. You make some pretty damning allegations, and of course we're concerned about your health.'

'Exactly,' says the friendlier, younger one. 'We want to make
sure you get the best medical treatment for your cancer. And

it sounds as though, for your own good, you should no longer work at the mine.'

The feeling of foreboding that's been increasing ever since I was pulled in off the street now becomes all-out panic. 'I never said I wanted to leave the job. I enjoy the job. I just want it to be made safer, that's all. For everyone, not just myself.'

The colonel nods. 'Of course. A very comradely sentiment. And we will look closely at your allegations about working conditions. But you have to understand the importance of SDAG Wismut's operations to both the Republic and our Soviet friends. Nothing can be allowed to get in the way of that.'

Aha! The usual story. I feel emboldened now. What do I have to lose? The cancer is almost certainly a death sentence anyway. 'So you don't really want to help me, you just want to shut me up and make sure I don't rock the boat. At the same time as taking away my job so I have no way of earning an income.'

The friendlier one – the major – sighs. 'Please don't prejudge us, Frau Rolf. We do want to help you, and can indeed help you. We want to be able to get you the best medical treatment, give you the best chance to survive. And although – yes – you will have to leave your existing employment, we can make sure you don't lose out financially. Nothing is off the table, and everything is possible – as long as you co-operate with us.'

'Co-operate?' Now I see their game. But if they want something from me, it will have to be worth my while.

'Yes,' says the colonel. He's not that old himself. A lot younger than I am. But, for his years – not a single grey hair on his head – he seems to have climbed the greasy pole remarkably rapidly. 'For a start, the petitions must stop. And we need your help in another matter, something where you can do great service for the Republic.'

Now I'm getting really suspicious. 'Oh yes?'

'Yes,' says the major. 'It concerns the English friend of yours.'

Immediately my defences go up. I'm not going to betray Arnie, if that's what they want. 'What about him?' I ask, warily.

Again, it's the slightly younger one, the major, who answers. If they're playing good cop, bad cop, he's certainly been given the 'good' role. 'His research is of great interest to the Republic. To be honest, it's important to the whole world. And we know it's very close to your heart.'

I know what he's driving at. For the first time, I feel terribly self-conscious about the bad side of my face. Their eyes seem to be trained on it, like hungry wolves eyeing their prey. I feel myself reddening, and try to rearrange my hair to hide the burn scars as much as possible. 'I don't really know that much about his work,' I lie. 'He never really talks about it.'

Now the colonel intervenes. 'Nevertheless, we know you are close to him. Very close.' He pulls something from his briefcase. Photographs. Strange shadowy photographs that almost look like negatives. I realise what they are – infra-red, low light images. Captured by some sort of bugging device inside Arnie's apartment on Leningrader Straße. Showing me – at least my back – hunched over his prone body. You don't see anything too revealing, but it's obvious what's going on. I feel the nausea rising in my throat, and start to get up from the stool.

'I'm not playing these sort of games with you.' I turn towards the door, to make my way out. I try to turn the handle. It's locked, of course.

'Please sit down again, Lotti,' says the major, using my given name for the first time. 'We don't want to have to use these photographs, and we don't intend to. They're not something we set out to catch you doing. Dr Southwick's flat was under surveillance as part of our normal operations, simply because he is a foreigner in an influential position.'

I slump back down onto the stool. I feel like bursting into tears but don't want to give them that satisfaction. The colonel lifts up the phone and summons someone. Then the guard is back with a colleague – wheeling in an armchair. They place it in front of the desk.

'Come and sit here, Lotti,' says the major. 'It'll be more comfortable.'

Like a robot, I get up and obey. Already I feel broken by their mind games.

'Now, as I say,' continues the major, still using his faux friendly voice, 'that photograph isn't going anywhere. In any case, you're a single woman. You've done nothing illegal here.'

'No, but he's not single,' I sob. 'He's married. I don't want to be the one accused of ruining his marriage.'

'He's a big boy, Lotti,' says the major. 'He can make his own decisions. If he did split up with his wife, that wouldn't be such a bad outcome for you, would it? He clearly has feelings for you.'

This time I don't answer. Why would I want to win him that way?

'Anyway,' continues the major, 'as we say, these photographs are going nowhere. And despite what you may think of us, we really do want to help – both you and Dr Southwick. That's why we have a proposition to put to you. Would you like to hear it?'

'Do I have a choice?'

The colonel sighed. 'We're trying to do this in a co-operative, comradely way, Frau Rolf. This *isn't* a prison as such, but it does have remand cells, and some inmates have found themselves incarcerated here for some length of time while their actions have been investigated. Now, your many petitions about SDAG Wismut could be interpreted as trying to foment insurrection against a vital state enterprise. I'm sure that wasn't your inten-tion.' The man wrings his powerful hands together. I imagine them round the neck of a chicken, or pheasant, squeezing out the last bit of life.

'No. Of course it wasn't.'

'So,' smiles the major, 'let's try to work co-operatively. We will make sure you get the best medical care possible for your condition. We will pay you an allowance while you are under treatment. In return, we are not asking for very much. We have some documents which will strengthen Dr Southwick's research. Give him the incontrovertible proof he needs that his thesis is correct. Clearly, if those documents came directly from us, he would be suspicious. We will construct a story about how they come to be in your possession. Or it may be simply that you introduce him to someone who has the documents in his or her possession. That's all we require from you. We and Dr Southwick want the same outcome – a positive outcome for his research is a positive outcome for the Republic, and a righting of some of the wrongs that happened on the thirteenth and fourteenth of February 1945.'

Put like that, what they're asking me to do doesn't seem so unreasonable. What happened that night – when I suffered the scars that will stay with me forever, physically *and* mentally – was something awful. Terrible. Whatever Hitler had done, whatever Germany as a nation had done, the German people, the people of Dresden, did not deserve that.

'What about those photographs?' I ask, glancing at the desk.

The colonel picks them up and theatrically tears them into little pieces. I'm not stupid. I know that means nothing and that the negatives will be stored in some safe somewhere. 'These will never be seen again,' he says. 'You have our word. In return, we need your word that you will not reveal to Dr Southwick that he was under surveillance.'

I give a small nod. 'What about . . .' I feel my voice breaking, even though I try to swallow back the emotion. 'What about my cancer? Will . . . will they be able to cure me?'

The colonel is stony-faced, but the major looks at me with what seems like genuine sadness. 'Cancer is a terrible thing, Lotti. We're not medical men, and we can't make hollow promises to you. All we can say is that we are being genuine when we pledge you will get the best possible treatment. The sort normally reserved for party bigwigs and VIPs.' I see the colonel shoot an angry glance towards his colleague, as though he might have overstepped the mark. 'It still might not save you, you know that. But it will give you the best possible chance.'

39

Schwebebahn viewing platform, Dresden
February 1982

When she'd contacted him, Bahlow had sounded distracted – frightened almost. She'd asked if they could meet, but he wouldn't give her an answer over the open line. The invitation to meet here – high above the city of Dresden, on the viewing platform of the historic Schwebebahn suspension railway – only came some thirty or so minutes later, in a sealed envelope brought to her office by a motorcycle courier.

'Things are becoming more complicated, Comrade *Hauptmann*,' he said, by way of introduction. 'I'm not sure it's a good idea for us to have further contact. In any case, you have your suspects under arrest now, I believe?'

The question was, of course, redundant. The Stasi would know about every move they'd made. It was Bahlow himself, after all, who'd led them to Rolf and Southwick's squat, in his ridiculous sunglasses disguise, even if he wasn't admitting it.

'We do have two people under arrest, although one of them is being treated in hospital. However, I'm not sure I buy their story – or at least, *her* story – which is why I wanted to talk to you.'

The Stasi officer grunted. He didn't turn to face her. Instead, he seemed to be intent on solemnly gazing at the Dresden cityscape below, bathed in the wan morning light.

Without eye contact, Müller focused on the back of Bahlow's head. 'Lotti Rolf claims that Concrete Man was – in all probability – a Stasi officer. She claims he died *accidentally* in a fight with Southwick . . .' Bahlow snorted in disbelief. Müller ignored him and continued. 'And that, contrary to what the pathologist says, he hit the back of his skull in a fall rather than being struck. And that both of them tried to save him from his concrete grave, without success.'

This time Bahlow gave a small laugh, and started shaking his head. He turned to hold Müller's gaze. 'She's a one, that Lotti Rolf. I'll give her that. A game girl. But a seasoned liar. Let me ask you something, Comrade *Hauptmann*; in all your dealings with pathologists in the Republic, have you ever known any of them to deliberately lie? Or – to put it another way – did Dr Giesler seem like the sort who would change his findings, no matter what pressure he was put under?'

'No,' admitted Müller.

'No, precisely. There is only one liar here, and that is Lotti Rolf. For my own part, I'll admit I haven't been open with you about everything, but for my own reasons I've tried to point you in the right direction. In fact, I've put my own job in jeopardy in doing precisely that.'

He turned back to look at the city far below. Its historic buildings – ruined, semi-ruined, or rebuilt – could be picked out one by one. In the centre, the festering sore left as a reminder: the blackened remains of the Frauenkirche. Müller wondered what was going through his mind – was he reimagining that awful night that had killed both his parents and left him an orphan? Were the bellows of his memory reigniting the flames of the firestorm in the scene before him?

'There are two people in all of this who want – who need – the truth to come out, warts and all. One is Dr Arnold Southwick. The other is myself, for personal reasons. But both of us need you to be a third, Comrade *Hauptmann*. We're relying on you to find and expose the truth.'

40

It was all very well for Bahlow to talk about 'the truth', but he worked for an organisation which Müller knew too well often engaged in concealing truth. Whether that was necessary for the security of the Republic was of course another matter. No doubt its agents – and even unofficial collaborators such as Tilsner – would argue that was exactly why they did what they did. Müller's own views down the years had become increasingly jaundiced.

Her musings were interrupted by a young uniformed female officer, carrying an envelope in her hand. She placed it on Müller's desk.

'Someone left this for you at the front desk, Comrade *Hauptmann*. They said it was urgent.'

'Thank you, Comrade,' replied Müller.

She tore the envelope open and began to read its contents. As she did, she was aware of Tilsner having got up from his own desk, and hovering over her shoulder.

'Anything interesting?' he asked.

She didn't answer immediately, and instead began to read, shielding the note from her deputy.

I have some information for you in connection with the death of the middle-aged male
in Gorbitz. I believe you are the investigating officer. You'll find me in Room 619
at the Hotel Lilienstein between 2-3 p.m.
Please come alone.

She glanced at her watch – 1.45 p.m. The Lilienstein was the first of three near identical Interhotels arranged in a row along Prager Straße – all named after topological features in nearby Saxon Switzerland, not far from Lotti's family home and former place of work. The Lilienstein and its neighbour, the Königstein, were reserved mainly for international guests and would there-fore be closely watched by the Stasi. The third and furthest hotel, the Bastei, was mainly used as a union holiday home for guests from within the Republic. She gathered her coat and started to get up.

'Are you going to tell me what's going on?' asked Tilsner.

Bahlow's monologue about 'the truth' had reminded her of her deputy's divided loyalties. So she probably would have gone on her own anyway, despite the risks. She got her Makarov from her locked desk drawer and slid it into her shoulder holster. 'I've got to meet someone at the Hotel Lilienstein.'

'Who?'

Müller wasn't going to admit she didn't even know the iden-tity of the person who'd summoned her. So she ignored the question. 'They want to meet one to one. If for any reason I'm not back within a couple of hours or so, perhaps you ought to send a search party. Room six-nineteen.' With that, she was gone, before Tilsner could insist on going with her.

For Müller, it was hardly worth getting a bus or tram. The hotel was little over a kilometre distant – a fifteen-minute walk. She knew she was almost there when she saw the infamous 'Tin Can': the Centrum department store which had earned its nickname thanks to its bizarre covering of metallic silver, shaped into honeycomb spikes. The Lilienstein was the next building on the right of the pedestrianised street – the city's prestigious shopping area.

She managed to avoid reception. Not having the name of her contact might have proved problematical. When she was challenged by the lift attendant – who for all she knew may have been a Stasi agent himself – her *Volkspolizei* ID seemed to suffice as a passport.

Walking along the sixth-floor corridor, searching out room 619, reminded her of her visit to see the French 'businessman' in a similar hotel in Magdeburg a few years earlier. This time was different – she was expected. She'd been lured here, even. She didn't need to play a role. Nevertheless, as she knocked on the door for room 619 she made sure she used her left hand – her right was gripping the handle of her Makarov.

She wasn't sure who she expected to open the door. At the back of her mind, she wondered if it might be the man who'd posed as *Hauptmann* Gustav Weiß. But the door was opened by a smartly dressed man in a dark business suit she'd never seen before.

The man's eyes were immediately drawn to Müller's right arm, still attached to the gun in her shoulder holster.

He laughed. 'It's all right, *Hauptmann* Müller. You won't be needing that. This is just a friendly chat. Won't you come in?' His German was precise. Grammatically correct. But almost too perfect – and there was the faintest hint of a foreign accent.

Müller still didn't release the gun, and swivelled her head left, right, and then behind her – trying to make sure there was no repeat of what had happened at Lotti Rolf's apartment in Sonnenstein.

The man gestured for her to sit on the sofa, while he turned the desk chair around to face her, then stretched out his hand.

'Sorry, I didn't properly introduce myself. My name is Brian Jones.' He drew his hand back when it became obvious Müller was in no mood to shake it. 'I'm an English business-man – computers and electronics mainly – regularly doing deals with the Republic. Particularly with your VEB Robotron.' Robotron was the Republic's biggest electronics manufacturer – as deeply embroiled in Dresden as the optical firm Carl Zeiss was in Jena. Müller hadn't had any dealings with any of the Robotron factories during her stint in Dresden – but she knew how important the organisation was to the city. 'Now I said I had some information for you. I'm afraid that was a bit of a white lie. Really, I just wanted a chat.'

'And why did you need to drag me all the way here for that, Mr Jones? Why not just call in at People's Police headquarters, as presumably you had to do to deliver your note?'

Jones dismissed the notion airily. 'Oh, that. No, that wasn't me. I got a motorbike courier to deliver that. It can go on expenses. Wonderful thing, expenses. Very elastic, as long as you don't stretch things too far.'

Müller sighed. 'Why am I here, Mr Jones?'

The man failed to answer for a moment, then moved to the minibar and opened it. 'Can I get you anything to drink. Beer? Wine? A soft drink?'

Müller rolled her eyes and shook her head.

The man selected a sparkling mineral water for himself, poured it into a glass, and then sat down again. 'I always hate these sorts of conversations – after all, we don't really know each other. Why should you listen to anything I have to say?'

Müller tapped her foot on the floor.

'The reason you should listen,' he continued, 'is that it might be in your interests to do so. You see, rather by accident you've stumbled on something that could be embarrassing both to foreign powers and to East Germany itself.'

Müller stared at him levelly. 'And why would you – a businessman specialising in computers and electronics – know anything about what my team has or hasn't "stumbled upon", as you put it? Why do you have any interest at all in my investigation?'

The man gave a weak smile. 'A fair question, of course. Let's just say I do some freelance work on the side. Freelance *government* work.'

'For the East German government?'

'No. For a foreign power. But our interests on this are aligned with East Germany.'

'If you're saying you're a spy, Mr Jones, then perhaps we ought to end this conversation now. I'm an officer with the Republic's People's Police. I don't want to be arrested for espionage. Neither do I want to get involved in international power games. I'm just a detective, investigating a murder, and that's what I'll continue to do.'

The man turned to his desk and pulled out a bulging brown envelope. He placed it on the low table in front of Müller.

She laughed and shook her head. Then ostentatiously looked at the centre light of the hotel room, then in each corner of the ceiling, so that 'Mr Jones' – if that was even his real name – knew exactly what she was doing.

'Don't worry, *Hauptmann* Müller. I'm fully aware that this conversation may be being monitored. Interhotels are notorious for it. It goes with the territory. As I say, I have nothing to hide. My employers' motives mirror those of your good Republic. The contents of that envelope are yours to keep. The case you are investigating is – for you – a no-win situation. My information is that is precisely *why* you were assigned to it in the first place. People here are fed up with you. They want you to fail. But it doesn't have to all end badly for you. The contents of that envelope will help you build a new career outside of the police – either within the Republic, if that's what you want. Or even outside it. Should that be your choice, my employers could help facilitate things.'

Müller snorted with derision. She pulled on her gloves and started to stand up. As she did, she leaned across the table, then curled her right index finger against her thumb and flicked the envelope back towards the man – a bit like she'd seen her son Johannes doing with his Tipp-Kick table football players. 'I'm not interested in bribes, Mr Jones. I'm not interested in threats. If I discover you have any link to the death in Gorbitz, then – mark my words – you will be arrested and will face the full might of the Republic's legal system. Please have no doubts about it.'

She strode towards the door.

As she did, the man tried one last tactic. 'By the way, how are your children *Hauptmann* Müller? Johannes and Jannika, isn't it? It can't be easy for you being separated from them while they're in that sports school in Oberhof.'

The words did make Müller halt, just before she opened the door to the corridor. But she still wasn't going to give in. 'If my children come to any harm, and I find out you have anything to do with it, then I won't be just arresting you, Mr Jones. I'll be making sure you never leave this country alive.'

41

Back at the People's Police headquarters, before she could even brief Tilsner on the strange Interhotel meeting, she found herself having to deal with a slightly breathless Jonas Schmidt.

'Ah, Comrade Müller. I'm glad I've found you. I've finally had a chance to study those files of encoded data in detail, and I think I've cracked the code and worked out what it all means.'

'Go on.'

Schmidt looked pointedly at Tilsner at the adjoining desk. 'I think it would be easier if you came down to the lab and we went through them there, Comrade *Hauptmann*. Some of the information is a little sensitive.'

Tilsner laughed. 'That's OK, both of you. Keep me out of the loop, why don't you? I'm obviously utterly untrustworthy. I might as well go out to the nearest bar and start cracking open the beers.'

'Don't be like that, Werner,' said Müller. 'I'm sure that's not what Jonas meant.' Despite what she said aloud, privately she knew it was *exactly* what her forensic scientist was implying. 'I'll fill you in on everything in a few minutes' time.'

As they descended to the forensic laboratory in the elevator, Müller could tell Schmidt still wasn't going to talk publicly about his findings until they were actually in the sanctuary of his work environment. But even there, the *Kriminaltechniker* was taking no chances. As he'd done on previous cases in Berlin, he ushered his commanding officer into the lab's dark room, switched on the eerie red safety light, and closed the door.

'Can't you just put the normal light on, Jonas?'

'The bulb's gone, I'm afraid, Comrade *Hauptmann*, and I haven't got round to fixing it yet. You should be able to see all you need with this.'

Müller sighed, and gave a small nod. 'Come on then. What have you found?'

'Well I've managed to decipher the documents. They're written in a form of what's known as a Caesar cipher – a very early version of coding.'

'What does that mean?' asked Müller.

'Well, for example, each letter might be transposed by three spaces in the alphabet. So the letter "a" becomes the letter "d", a "b" is an "e" and so on.'

Müller frowned. 'That doesn't sound as though it would be a terribly difficult code to crack. I might even manage it.'

'Precisely, Comrade *Hauptmann*. But it can be made almost indecipherable by using a Vigenère cipher.'

'What's that when it's at home?'

'It's just a way of – if you like – disrupting the Caesar cipher in a particular order, that can only be solved using a special alphabetical table – a *tabula recta*. The table shifts the alphabet along, and which position you use depends on a repeating keyword.'

Müller sighed. 'You've lost me, I'm afraid, Jonas. Do I really need to know all this detail of how the code was constructed and how you deciphered it?'

For a moment, under the strange red lighting, Schmidt looked slightly hurt. Then he shrugged. 'No, Comrade *Hauptmann*. You're quite correct. Perhaps I was showing off. You simply need to know what the documents say, and I'm afraid they make for pretty grim reading.'

'In what respect?'

'Widespread doping of children, presumably to increase their sporting prowess and performance. The documents – once I'd managed to crack the cipher – show the percentages of which drugs or hormonal supplements have been administered to which children. There's also a rather chilling appendix listing the noted side-effects. And we're not just talking about post-pubertal children. Some of the pupils here are aged under ten. None as young as your twins, but even so, if I was you, I would be taking steps to remove Johannes and Jannika as soon as possible, Comrade *Hauptmann*.'

Under the red control light of the dark room, Müller knew her facial colour wouldn't have changed obviously to Schmidt. Under normal lighting, he'd have seen her face had gone deathly pale. She'd expected something bad – but not this bad. 'You'd better fill me in on some of the details, then, please, Jonas.'

Schmidt started to reel off a list of chemicals, and percentages or dosages in milligrams. The names flew over Müller's head in a bit of a blur – all she could think about was Jannika and Johannes, and how she'd let them down by allowing them to go to the special boarding school in the first place. There was no question but that, at the first opportunity, she would be removing them. If it meant leaving her job, so be it. She had been on the point of quitting so many times. She tried to bring her focus back to what Schmidt was saying.

'By far the most prevalent drug seems to be Dehydrochloro-methyltestosterone, 4-chlor-1-dehydro-17α-methyl-testosterone, Comrade *Hauptmann*.'

'That just sounds like a lot of scientific gobbledegook, Jonas. What does it actually mean?'

'Its non-scientific name is Oral Turinabol – it's an andro-genic-anabolic steroid, made by VEB Jenapharm in Jena. It increases muscle strength, aggressiveness, that sort of thing.'

'So for male athletes?'

'From what I know of it, that's how it was first used. But these documents make it clear it's being administered to girls too. And as you can imagine, the side effects are pretty horrific.'

'Such as?'

'Hirsutism in girls, far beyond the hair growth that normally comes with female puberty. The thighs, for example, would become hirsute, as well as muscular. It can cause havoc with the reproductive system too – infertility is a real possibility. And then in boys, evidence of breast development and nip-ple enlargement. In the documents, there's also a secret report from a Stasi unofficial collaborator, which shows how pupils are threatened with expulsion from the school if they refuse to take what are euphemistically known as "vitamin pills". But Oral Turinabol is not the only drug used. There's mention of steroid substances with various numbers attached which correspond to slightly different chemical compositions: 646, 648, 482, 12 et cetera, et cetera . . . the list just goes on and on.'

Müller realised these documents, and their horrific contents, were highly dangerous to her and Schmidt – as well as to Frau Voights.

As for the school's director, who'd launched himself to his death from the top of Dresden's TV tower, here was more than sufficient motive. If – as the deputy director had claimed – her boss, Heinz Schenk, loved the children almost as though they were his own, finding out they were being treated as sporting guinea pigs, with horrific effects on their health, might have been the final straw. Either that, or he had been complicit in the doping, and couldn't live with his conscience. Or perhaps there was an even more sinister explanation. Perhaps Schenk had been trying to put a stop to it all, perhaps he'd been trying to expose it, so that his leap from the TV tower wasn't as accidental as it looked.

For Müller, it was more evidence that the Republic was rotten at its core. As well as rescuing her own children from the school as soon as was practical, she would have to inform Jäger. It was only fair. Jannika and Johannes might still be too young to be administered these so-called vitamin pills. Jäger's son Jens, however, was a teenager already – and therefore right in the firing line.

42

Although Tilsner had given the impression to Müller and Schmidt that he was annoyed at being kept out of the loop, in reality it gave him the space to do something he'd been wanting to do for some time. In fact, ever since it became obvious their current case was – at best – heading for a messy, compromised resolution controlled by the Stasi.

To some extent, it was unfinished business. What he'd almost achieved some three years ago on the frozen Ostsee. Guilt, and his loyalty to Karin, had thwarted him then. But since that time, he and an old friend from his childhood in Gardelegen had been preparing.

He wasn't going to use the phone lines at *Volkspolizei* HQ. Instead he got out the Dresden street atlas and looked for a public call box in a more obscure part of the city. He chose the area of Übigau – on the north bank of the Elbe – a quiet back-water known for little except its shipyards. Going out there wouldn't be a complete defence – the Stasi probably moni-tored most public call boxes – but it was still safer than having the conversation he wanted to have inside the People's Police building.

He checked the mirrors of the Wartburg as he drove through the city's backstreets, trying to go as circuitous a route as possible, all the time making sure he wasn't being followed. Once he reached the call box he'd chosen, on the corner of Sternstraße and Scharfenbergerstraße, he parked the car and approached it. Rather than one of the rounded modern designs, it was one of the older types: octagonal with a witch's hat roof.

Tilsner fed in his coins, then dialled the number.

After a few rings, the line was answered.

'Manfred?'

'*Werner. How are you doing?*'

'OK. But I'm keen to go sailing as soon as possible.' It was the agreed code. Manfred would know what he meant. Tilsner heard a sharp intake of breath on the other end of the line.

'*I'm not really ready to go sailing.*'

'Why?' asked Tilsner, alarmed. 'What's the problem?'

'*There's no real problem. But the sailing club is short of material to make the sails.*'

Tilsner thought for a moment. 'I might be able to help. Do you want me to buy some?'

'*If you want to go sailing soon, then yes, you'll need to. Very few stores have the necessary material, but there's one in Leipzig.*'

'Leipzig?' It was more than an hour away. Tilsner looked at his watch. Not impossible, the shops would still be open if he got a move on, and he was on the right side of Dresden centre to make a quick getaway, before any early evening traffic built up.

'*Well, just south of Leipzig, so perhaps a bit nearer for you. Markkleeberg to be precise.*'

'OK – tell me what you need.'

'*Have you got a pen and paper?*'

As Manfred listed the various pieces of material he needed, and the sizes, Tilsner started to worry whether he'd have enough cash to buy it all. Placing the handset back on the receiver, he pulled out his wallet and counted out the notes. There ought to be enough – just about.

He reached the store with about a quarter of an hour to spare before closing time.

The shop assistant initially queried how many square metres of material Tilsner was asking for. 'Are you sure that's right?' she asked. 'We don't normally get asked for such a large amount – not without advance notice.'

He could see her looking towards her manager. Tilsner didn't want someone else interfering – and possibly vetoing the sale.

'As I said, it's for our sailing club. Our *police* sailing club.' As he emphasised the word, he pulled out his *Kriminalpolizei* ID and raised his eyebrows. 'We're used to people co-operating with us.'

Mention of the police seemed to be enough of a catalyst to make up the woman's mind. She stopped trying to catch the manager's attention, and instead found the relevant roll of material and started measuring it off.

Once Tilsner had staggered back to the Wartburg with his prize, he was faced with another dilemma. How to get the material to Manfred. He looked at his watch. Karin and Schmidt had probably already finished their tête-à-tête. By rights he should be getting back to Dresden as soon as possible in case they now had anything worth following up. Diverting to meet up with Manfred – who lived at Bad Lobenstein, not far from the Republic's southern border with Bavaria in the BRD – would add at least two hours to his journey, even if he put his foot down. But Tilsner knew things were coming to a head – there might be no option but to start their 'sailing' adventure soon. Without the material, Manfred couldn't complete the job. He would have to drive there this evening, and just front up any consequences with Karin later.

Arriving at Manfred's small farm, Tilsner could tell he was anything but welcome. Manfred's wife Sissi wouldn't meet his gaze, and instead of the usual hug, there was just a curt hello, before she turned back to preparing the family's supper.

Manfred – too – seemed curiously unfriendly. He gestured with his eyes to Tilsner, indicating that they needed to talk in private.

He led Tilsner into the adjoining cattle barn. Tilsner had to hold his breath to stop himself retching from the stink of cow muck. Manfred sat on a straw bale and gestured to Tilsner to sit next to him.

'Don't mind Sissi,' he said by way of explanation. 'She and I have had a bit of a falling out over all this.'

Manfred was also finding it hard to meet his old friend's gaze.

'What's happened?' asked Tilsner. 'Is she getting cold feet?'

'I wouldn't put it exactly like that. We've had a thorough talk about it. Both of us feel it's not the right time for us.'

Tilsner felt his anger rising. 'What the fuck does that mean? I thought we had an agreement? And now I've splashed most of my spare cash on all this material. Why did you let me do that if you're backing out?'

'I'm not backing out. I'll still keep to our deal – I don't want to let you down. It was just a bit of a surprise when you said you were ready, and when I talked it through with Sissi she decided it was all too much of a risk.'

'So what are you saying?'

'I'm saying we're not coming. But I'll still help you. I'll still get everything ready. I'll still stick to my side of the bargain.'

Tilsner could hear the pent-up emotion in the man's voice. This was the death of a dream for his friend – something they had both secretly planned together, ever since Tilsner's aborted dash across the Ostsee ice some three years earlier. It wasn't really his style, but Tilsner put his arms round the other man, and gave him a gentle hug.

'Sorry, Werner.'

'No worries, friend. I understand. Looks like I'm driving on my own for this one – but if you're still prepared to get everything ready, I'll be eternally grateful.'

43

Back in the office, Tilsner's absence didn't initially strike Müller as being odd. In any case, her head was full of Schmidt's figures, chemical names, and dire warnings. She knew she had to get Jannika and Johannes out of the school as soon as possible – even if their age meant they weren't in imminent danger. But she also owed it to Jäger – and his son, Jens – to reveal the results of Schmidt's code-cracking to the Stasi colonel. And there was a murder case Müller and her team were on the point of solving – even if the conclusion was looking messier by the day. So it might take her a day or two to come up with a plan to safeguard the twins.

Tracking Jäger down at Bautzner Straße proved more difficult than she expected. His name clearly didn't carry the weight it once did – the man was a shadow of himself, and so was his reputation. Eventually, the telephonist found Jäger's extension, and patched Müller through to him.

Müller didn't want to give any details over the phone about what Schmidt had discovered. Instead she kept the conversation elliptical.

'I wondered if you were available for a quick chat, Klaus?' she asked. Just the use of his first name, rather than his title and honorific that she usually used, would alert the Stasi colonel that this was something out of the ordinary. But to spell it out further, she left no doubt what she wanted to talk about. 'It concerns the education of our children, and that talk you said you wanted which might be beneficial both to Jens, and to Johannes and Jannika.'

Müller could immediately hear the eagerness in his reply. *'Of course, Karin. Do you know the Bogenschütze statue, by the banks of the Elbe in Dresden Neustadt?'*

'The archer?'

'Exactly. Meet me there in thirty minutes' time.'

The statue was only fifteen minutes' walk away, across Dr-Rud-Friedrichs-Brücke, on the northern bank of the river. But by the time Müller reached the centre of the bridge, and the biting northerly wind started to penetrate her clothing, she wished she'd brought the Wartburg. Once she actually reached Jäger, who was standing in the shadow of the bronze archer, she felt thoroughly frozen.

'Whenever we have these meetings, Karin, you always look as though you need a more suitable winter coat. Still, at least you've got rid of that ridiculous red raincoat.'

Müller was too cold to take umbrage at the Stasi colonel's unnecessary comments about her wardrobe. 'I haven't really got time for verbal jousting, Comrade *Oberstleutnant*. But as you probably gathered from the phone call, I have some more information about those documents.'

Jäger nodded, while turning his head to scout round the park, checking for anyone taking too close an interest. 'Let's walk then,' he said, and set off in the direction of the rose garden.

The ambient light from the city cast their shapes into several shadows, so that at one stage Müller wondered if there really was just the two of them. Jäger had set off at a furious pace, and she struggled to keep up with him.

When he was satisfied they had sufficient privacy, he sat down on a park bench and indicated for Müller to join him.

'Is it as bad as I suspected?' he immediately asked her.

'Yes, Comrade *Oberstleutnant*. Perhaps worse. I don't know how much you knew before you asked me to talk to Frau Voights.'

'I had come across rumours, but my department of the Ministry is not involved in this. And my wife was pushing for Jens to go to the sports school – she said it was a fantastic opportunity. I was always more wary. When a small country like ours wins so many medals – and when some of its female athletes look so masculine – well, who wouldn't be suspicious?'

Müller patted her briefcase, which contained Schmidt's findings. 'The suspicions are correct. The dosages for the children were written in code, but Schmidt managed to crack it. They confirm exactly that – the administration of drugs that in effect change the childrens' gender, for both girls and boys.'

Jäger nodded grimly in the half-light. 'So it's as I suspected. But I needed the proof. I had heard on the grapevine that the director of the school was unhappy about the programme, and creating trouble. I just steered you in the right direction – because I knew of his close links, shall we say, with Frau Voights. If I'd have gone investigating myself, then my career – already in the doldrums, as you know – wouldn't have lasted much longer.'

Müller didn't entirely buy the sob story. When Jäger had been more of a power at the Ministry, he'd been ruthless – crushing those in his path. Getting Müller to do his dirty work for him wasn't a particularly noble act, even though – with the twins as pupils too – Müller had her own reasons to get to the truth. She reached into her briefcase and pulled out the couple of sheets she'd photocopied of the summary of Schmidt's findings.

'What will you do with this information?' she asked, as she handed the document over.

'I will try to expose it and put an end to it.'

'But won't that mean an end to both our careers?' Not that Müller was too concerned for her own part. This latest case, taken together with the ones in Rügen and Gardelegen three and four years ago, meant that she had already reached the end of her tether.

'I will try to keep your name out of it. But as you're aware, I don't have much of a career left. I'm not sure you do either. And then we clearly each need to get our children out of that environment as soon as possible. By whatever means necessary, Karin. By *whatever* means.'

44

Jäger waited till the next morning before trying to contact Normannenstraße to arrange an appointment to discuss Schmidt's findings about the sports school. When he finally got through on the phone, he found himself being given the run around. No one was prepared to talk to him, or make time for him, another sign of how far he had fallen. Eventually he was told to try to arrange a meeting with *Oberst* Rainer Specht.

'Well, can you put me through to Specht, then?'

'*I'm afraid we can't do that, Comrade* Oberstleutnant. Oberst *Specht has gone on a mission to Dresden. If you want to talk to him, you would have to contact the district MfS headquarters there, at Bautzner Straße.*'

Eventually, Jäger managed to arrange his meeting. But as soon as he entered the room – which looked more like one of the Ministry's interrogation suites – he had an inkling it wasn't going to proceed in the way he hoped.

'Ah, Klaus,' said Specht, showing him to a chair. 'I was meaning to catch up with you in any case to discuss how the Arnold Southwick case was progressing. I'm sorry I didn't give you advance warning I was coming down from Berlin.' The levity in Specht's tone sounded insincere to Jäger, and it probably was.

'Not to worry, Comrade *Oberst*. It was another matter that I wanted to talk to you about.'

'Oh yes? Fire away, then.'

'You know the suicide of the director of the sports school from Oberhof, Heinz Schenk?'

Specht appeared to turn his nose up, as though Jäger had just admitted to having dog shit on his shoes. 'I'm vaguely aware of it. I can't say it's any concern of ours – the man was obviously mentally disturbed. He probably shouldn't have been placed in charge of an elite sports school in the first place. Perhaps he just couldn't take the pressure.'

'There was more to it than that.'

'Pray enlighten me, then, Comrade *Oberstleutnant*.' Jäger could remember a time not so long ago when he talked in a similar dismissive manner to his subordinates. Now the tables had been turned on him.

'I believe Herr Schenk had uncovered something illegal that was happening at the school.'

'Illegal? Really? What are we talking about – paedophilia or something similar? Was the man involved in that? If so, how are you so intimately acquainted with it?' The fake smile on Specht's face did little to disguise the menace in his tone.

Jäger reached into his briefcase and extracted the document Müller had given him – the summary of *Kriminaltechniker* Schmidt's findings. 'Not that, no.' He passed the document across the desk. 'This paper outlines the findings of my investigation. In short, children at the school are being administered dangerous, body-altering substances. Already, there have been numerous accounts of serious side effects. In short, that girls are virtually being turned into boys and vice versa.'

Specht took the document and looked at it briefly.

'Your son goes to that school, doesn't he?'

'He does, Comrade *Oberst*. He's a promising biathlete.'

'So you have a personal interest in this?'

'Yes, but that's not the point.'

'What is the point then, *Oberstleutnant* Jäger? Is it that you carried out some sort of secret investigation without telling me, your superior, when you are supposed to be overseeing the Southwick case? Overseeing it so badly, by the way, that Berlin saw it necessary to send me here to clear up your mess.'

'That's a ridiculous accusation.'

Specht opened a desk drawer and retrieved something from it that Jäger couldn't quite see behind the clutter on the desk. 'I don't think it is, Jäger. You're treading on very thin ice. Now you come here questioning the techniques of our sports schools. Techniques, I'd remind you, that led to our small country rubbing the rest of the world's noses in it at the last Winter Olympics. We won more medals than any other country, Jäger. Think what that means. It's an incredible success, and our sports schools are without parallel. The fact that they sometimes administer a few vitamins to the athletes is neither here nor there.'

'They're not vitamins, they're dr—'

Specht held up his hand like a traffic policeman. 'Enough, Jäger. Which department do you think oversees this "vitamin" programme, and takes the credit for its success?'

Finally, Jäger realised his stupidity.

'Exactly, Jäger.' Specht rubbed the white bust of Dzerzhinsky on his desk, identical to that on Bahlow's, and countless others in Ministry offices around the country. 'Iron Felix would be proud of us. But not, I'm afraid, of you. I suggest you get back to what it is you're supposed to be doing, otherwise your time working for the Ministry might be shorter than even you envisaged. You're some way off retirement. If you lost your job now, what the hell do you think you would do?' Then he picked up the object he'd retrieved from the desk drawer, and Jäger finally realised what it was.

A cigarette lighter.

'I shall file the results of your investigation most carefully, Klaus, thank you so much. That will be all. See yourself out.'

As he got up to leave, realising any more discussion was futile, Jäger watched Specht set fire to a corner of Schmidt's document, and throw it in his waste paper bin. Once he was satisfied it had been destroyed, he doused the fire with a glass of water on his desk.

Jäger stood there, paralysed, watching.

Then he finally turned and left, realising bitterly that Specht's unique brand of 'filing' was a metaphor for what had happened to his own career.

45

ARNIE

People's Police HQ, Dresden
March 1982

At least my leg is hurting less, and the doctors reckon they've managed to save it, although they said it was touch and go at one point. By the time the police found us in the empty block in Gorbitz, I think I was already drifting in and out of consciousness so it was probably for the best that we were arrested. What is the penalty, though, for killing an East German officer, even though we're not sure whether he was Stasi or police? If they still use the death penalty, I guess it would be for something like that. Would I have more chance of receiving clemency as a foreigner? I'm not sure. In any case, I'm not going to rat on Lotti. I've let her down enough – although perhaps she was expecting too much.

If my German has been good enough to understand the guards correctly, I'm now in some sort of remand cell in the main People's Police building in Dresden – the one that overlooks the Neumarkt and looks a little like an Aztec temple with windows. It's given me ample opportunity to think about everything, and where it all went wrong.

I don't think I was set up from the start. That came later.

First there was the meeting with the whistle-blower in London, before I even got to Dresden. I still believe he was genuine – that the documents he handed over were genuine, or at least, copies of the real thing.

Seeing the documents felt like a punch in the guts. It was a betrayal, a perversion, of the sacrifice that had been Fred's death: my baby brother, with his whole life ahead of him – too young to have dreams, ambitions. So perfect and untouched in death that you couldn't believe he'd breathed his last breath. My parents certainly never did. And in my dreams, Fred often appears as an adult, and I'm full of joy about what a wonderful human being he's turned out to be. I'm overcome by love – and then I wake, in a sweat, my heart thumping, and the loss is as painful as ever.

We'd arranged to meet in the Lyceum Tavern – my contact was apparently coming in by train from the Guildford area. He insisted the pub was convenient – he could just walk across Waterloo Bridge to it – but still had plenty of hidden corners. I knew of it vaguely from interviews I'd done at the World Service in Bush House – killing time there either before or after.

He wouldn't give a name, or a telephone number, but insisted it would be 'worth my while'. He said the fact that I was from Hull, the fact that I'd survived the Hull Blitz, and my area of historical specialism – the bombing of Dresden – meant that

I was the ideal person to bring this all out into the open. Little did I know how difficult that would be.

I found him in a tucked-away corner of the pub. He was already waiting for me. He was a nervous looking chap – quite slight, white-haired, perhaps late sixties or early seventies – with those round wire NHS specs that people only wear when they can't afford anything else. His blazer was threadbare at the elbows too – which started alarm bells in my head. Perhaps that was what this was all about. Money. Or the lack of it, in his case. And the chance to earn some from me, in exchange for what he'd insisted in his letter was 'historical dynamite'.

But as he explained the background to how he came to have the documents, I realised I was doing him a disservice.

'It's something I've felt guilty about all my life,' he said, his voice barely above a whisper. It felt at the time almost like a piece of theatre – how could the events of nearly forty years ago still pose a threat now? But the man appeared genuinely frightened, and was determined our conversation shouldn't be overheard. 'Of course,' he continued, 'the Dresden bombing's been exploited at times for propaganda. You know, the Nazis adding a zero to the death toll, taking it into hundreds of thousands rather than tens, then people like David Irving regurgitating those figures. But it was still a terrible, awful thing. And I witnessed some of the thinking behind it, and it's always preyed on my mind.'

'Witnessed how?' I asked him.

'During the war, I worked for Frederick Lindemann.'

'Churchill's chief scientific adviser? Viscount Cherwell?'

'That's right. Not a particularly pleasant man. Brilliant, but arrogant – like a lot of top people in their field. Anyway, I was his secretary. Everything he was involved with passed my desk. Including the psychological study in Hull for which you were one of the subjects.'

I looked at him aghast. 'You know that I was involved?'

He nodded. 'I remembered your name.' Southwick's not that unusual a name in East Yorkshire, but perhaps for a mandarin from the Home Counties, it would have stood out. I felt myself start to shake then, the memories of Fred coming back, the memories of that meeting with the man from the Ministry in the front room, how I lost it with him, and then the belting from my father.

It's the opening he wants. The proof that he's not talking nonsense – how would anyone without an intimate knowledge of that psychological study of children in Hull, and the effects of the bombing on them, ever know that I was involved? It certainly wasn't something I'd ever advertised – it brought back too many painful memories. He began to pull various documents from his briefcase, and then leafed through them.

And there I was. In an appendix to the main study – reference to my fifteen-year-old self.

'You were one of the exceptions,' he said, pushing his glasses back up the bridge of his nose.

'What do you mean?' I took a couple of large gulps of my pint of bitter. I'd wanted a beer because I'd known parts of this might be personally painful. Lindemann's former secretary – he still didn't have a name because he evidently didn't want to give me one – had insisted he only wanted a mineral water.

'The Hull study was quite remarkable. The psychologist in charge of it concluded that the children and people of Hull were amazingly resilient. That despite it being the most heavily bombed city outside of London, even though at the time the rest of the country didn't realise—'

'A "north-east coastal town".'

'Exactly. Hull was almost never mentioned by name. But despite all the bombs, despite the loss of life, despite the massive number of homeless, there was no sign that the people of Hull would break. That's why you were noted as an exception.'

'The guy who interviewed me felt I *had* broken?'

'I'm not saying that, but he concluded your reaction wasn't typical and might have been due as much to an unhappy home life as to what had actually occurred as a result of the Hull Blitz.'

'So the study concluded that mass bombing *wouldn't* break a population's resolve? Interesting. I'd not heard of the results before.'

The man leafed through his documents. 'More than interesting. There were forty psychologists involved in the team, and as well as interviewing children like yourself – and getting them to write essays about their experiences – they also interviewed around seven hundred adults. So it was a very comprehensive study, and hard to argue against the results.'

'Yet Churchill still gave the go-ahead to Bomber Harris's campaign?' It seemed astonishing. 'Why?'

'The results were misrepresented – turned completely on their head, initially by Lindemann. I know because I was there. Instead of being used as a reason why carpet bombing was pointless because it wouldn't undermine the morale of a population, the data from Hull was perverted to show that if enough bombs were dropped – *ten times as many bombs* – the German people would crack.' He tapped his documents. 'And it's all clear in these documents. Minutes of meetings between Lindemann and the psychologists. Records of exchanges between Lindemann, Churchill and Harris. When you see all this, you'll see the bombing of Dresden in a new light.'

I nodded thoughtfully. The man was right – *if* the documents backed up what he was saying. I could see the man's hands shaking as he held the papers. Keeping all this bottled up for years – when it meant so much to him – had clearly had a profound effect.

'What I don't understand,' I said, 'is why you're giving me this information now. You're still taking a huge risk in breaking the Official Secrets Act. What's in it for you?'

'I don't want money, if that's what you're implying. I just want to right a terrible wrong. I've lived with the guilt of this for years. The bombing of Dresden wasn't just a mistake. It wasn't just a miscalculation.'

'So what was it?'

'A war crime. An horrific, predetermined war crime – and some of Britain's most revered and lionised wartime leaders were simply that: war criminals.'

46

That, of course, was why the East German authorities were so interested in my research. I wasn't naive. If they could cultivate an eminent British academic, whose research included secret papers that appeared to show Britain's wartime leaders had deliberately and illegally flouted the rules of war, just how valuable could that be? Not just as a propaganda tool, but also – potentially – as a way of receiving reparations, despite the fact that Nazi Germany had been the initial aggressor.

Where did it all go wrong? Why am I languishing here, in a People's Police holding cell? The answer to that is Lotti, or rather my mistake in reviving our friendship – and to me that's all it was and would ever be. How was I to know that the Stasi would manage to blackmail her into joining them, and that – bizarrely – they would use her to undermine my research, not strengthen it?

I hear the metallic clang of the cell's observation hatch being slammed open. A pair of eyes peers through at me, as if to check I haven't managed to discover some secret passage, and escaped, like in an Enid Blyton novel.

Then the sounds of the door being unlocked, and two men enter who I've never seen before.

'Please stand, Dr Southwick,' says the younger-looking man – speaking in English, but with a distinct German accent. I struggle to get to my feet, wincing from my bad leg. 'I am Colonel Rainer Specht of the Ministry for State Security. And this is Gordon Breitmann – here on behalf of . . . of the British government, shall we say.'

'A pleasure to finally meet you, Dr Southwick,' says Breitmann, who – despite his German-sounding surname – speaks in a clipped Home Counties accent. 'You've proved quite elusive these past few weeks – almost as though you didn't want us to find you.'

Specht goes back to the door and opens it again. Two uniformed guards enter. They immediately begin to search the cell – pulling up the straw mattress and patting underneath it. One of them pulls out an odd-shaped object, wrapped in some sacking material. He unwraps it, taking care that he uses the material to grip it, presumably so as not to transfer any of his fingerprints. My stomach flutters – it's a gun. *How the fuck did that get there?* Then I remember my first chance of a shower in the communal block after weeks in hiding, how I was so grateful for what I saw as a small act of kindness. It obviously wasn't. It was simply the opportunity to plant the gun in my cell.

The guard hands it to the Stasi colonel.

'What were you planning to do with this, Dr Southwick?' he asks. 'Aren't you in enough trouble already?'

'I-I-I've never seen that before.' Immediately I realise that – although I'm innocent – I *sound* guilty and terrified.

Specht gestures with his eyes to the guards, indicating they should leave. Then he pulls over the cell's stool – the only place to sit, other than the bed – and pushes me down onto it.

'You're in a spot of bother, I'm afraid, old chap,' says Breitmann, towering over me. 'We can only help you so far.'

'Who's we?'

'I suppose you could say the Foreign Office, after a fashion. The point is, you've angered the British government by contravening the Official Secrets Act in propagating classified documents, and handing them to a foreign power.'

'I did no such thing,' I splutter.

'Well, actually, you did. You made them available to the East German authorities via your research thesis, for which you were paid, I believe.'

'Paid?'

'You received a salary from Dresden University of Technology,' continues Breitmann. 'That salary was in turn paid for by the Ministry for State Security.'

I can't help the gasp that comes out of my mouth. 'Well, I never for a minute suspected that.'

The younger, German man, intervenes. 'Your signature is on the agreement.' He pulls a document from his briefcase and hands it to me. 'Are you saying that's not your signature.'

It clearly *is* my signature. If it's a forgery, even I couldn't detect it. 'But I never signed anything with the Ministry for State Security.'

'Unfortunately,' says Breitmann, 'it's here in black and white.'

I don't want to play their game, but this all must be leading somewhere. I sigh. 'What exactly is it you want?'

'Where is your final research document?' asks Breitmann. 'The rewritten one. The one you changed after the first draft was rejected for containing fake sources.'

'I don't know what you're talking about.'

The crack of the gun butt against my temple comes from nowhere, sending me spinning, dazed, onto the concrete floor. Incredible pain daggers through my head.

'We're not in the mood to play games, Dr Southwick,' says the colonel, as he turns the gun over in his hands, almost as though he's worried he's damaged it from the force of the blow.

I'm still holding the side of my head, bracing my body for the next blow. It doesn't come. Instead, Breitmann has climbed onto the bed. He's tying some sort of material round the bare pipe that runs across the ceiling and down to the corner sink.

Specht is meanwhile getting something else from his briefcase. 'We thought you might like these souvenirs of your stay in Dresden,' he says.

They're black and white photographs. Taken – I realise with horror – by a surveillance camera in my university apartment in Leningrader Straße.

I'm lying on my back on the bed.

My hands on Lotti's head.

Hands which – in my memory – had been trying to pull her mouth away from my erect penis after I'd woken up in horror to find her in my bed.

But hands which, here in the photographs, appear to be holding her head down, encouraging her.

Breitmann has finished whatever he was doing with the material and water pipe. 'Your wife – Barbara, isn't it? – she'll be a bit taken aback by what you've been up to, old chap. Not the sort of research wives tend to approve of, is it?'

I struggle to my feet, try to lunge at him, but Specht holds me firm, pulling my arms up behind my back.

'Now, now, Dr Southwick. Don't do anything rash,' he hisses into my ear. 'Just tell us where your rewritten research paper is, and where the original documents are.'

'What documents?' I bluster.

This time it's Breitmann that answers. 'The ones given to you by Lindemann's former secretary during your cosy chat at the Lyceum Tavern last summer. They are British government property.'

I feel something pushing against my bruised temple. From the corner of my eye, I can see it's the gun.

'We want this sorted out nice and neatly, Dr Southwick,' says Specht. 'That way you can go back to Britain, your wife never needs to see those photographs, and Gordon here will make sure you get a comfortable little history professorship at some backwater university.'

'Or else what?' The challenge sounds strident. But it's not how I really feel. My legs feel weak. My heart is thumping at nineteen to the dozen. And I've got just about the worst head-ache I've ever had in my life. Not to mention that I'm struggling to stand on my bad leg.

'Climb up on the stool, please, Dr Southwick,' says Specht.

I don't move.

'Do it!' he shouts, and I hear the safety catch of the gun being released.

Gingerly I comply, not realising at first what they're planning.

Then I begin struggling as both of them try to hold me as Breitmann brings the material – which I realise is some sort of knotted bedsheet – over my head.

It's a noose.

I stop struggling, terrified, feel the piss bursting out of me. I stand stock still.

'Your last chance, Dr Southwick,' says Specht. There's an icy calmness in his tone. 'Where are they?'

I won't answer. Why should I? I know they're just trying to scare me – they wouldn't dare to actually kill me. Not in a police cell.

Then I hear Specht sigh.

And I realise he's serious.

I start to form the words, to tell them where the papers are. But my brain doesn't have enough time to order my mouth and voicebox to move.

Because Specht has just kicked the stool out from under me.

I'm hanging above the void, a terrible pressure on my windpipe.

I claw at my neck, trying to give myself space to breathe, at the same time kicking my legs frantically to find the stool or bed.

But no breaths will come.

47

LOTTI

Dresden
Early February 1982

When did I realise I'd been double-crossed? It wasn't until I heard someone hammering on my apartment door one evening.

I'd been having a bit of a snooze because I found that was one of the side effects of the cancer and the treatment they started to give me, honouring their side of the bargain. I just felt totally wiped out a lot of the time. Some days, I would feel so lethargic I'd struggle to even get out of bed. And as soon as I tried to do anything, I'd feel even more exhausted. That day, I'd come back from doing the weekly shopping, slumped down on the sofa, and fallen asleep without even putting everything away.

After a few moments, I managed to rouse myself, and opened the door.

Arnie was standing there, looking livid.

He burst past me into the flat, without waiting to be asked. Then he started ranting. 'Who put you up to it? You knew, didn't you?'

'Knew what?'

'That these documents are fakes.' He was red in the face, waving pieces of paper around in the air. 'The ones purporting to show that the Russians had warned the British and Americans NOT to attack Dresden, because of the huge numbers of refugees sheltering near the railway station.' Then he pointed his finger at my chest. I'd never seen this side of him, and I didn't like it. 'You knew, didn't you?'

'No, Arnie. I swear I didn't.'

His face was virtually purple with rage. 'I should have known it was too convenient. I meet up with someone I haven't seen for more than forty years, and then suddenly they're providing me with a lead to someone with secret documents that apparently made my thesis even stronger. Only they didn't, did they?'

I slumped down. My head in my hands. 'I honestly don't know what you're talking about.'

'The man you introduced me to was a fake, and his documents were fake. It's undermined my argument completely. I've been exposed by the university. I'm a complete laughing stock and my career is over.'

I racked my brains, trying to understand what's gone wrong. *Major* Bahlow had assured me the documents would *strengthen* Arnie's case. He claimed he had a personal interest in exposing the raids for what they were – just as I have.

'I don't know how this has happened, Arnie.' I couldn't admit to him that I agreed to work for the Stasi – that would be it. Our relationship – such as it is – would be over. 'Is there anything I can do to put things right?'

I saw in his eyes then – eyes that were red raw, glistening with tears – that he was starting to believe me. That I was an innocent dupe in the Stasi's game – I just couldn't admit to him that it was a game I'd agreed to play, in return for a salary and specialist medical treatment.

'I should just walk out of here and never see you again, Lotti. You realise you've ruined my life, don't you? I stumble across the best information of my career, documents that virtually prove the Dresden firebombings were a war crime committed by Churchill and Bomber Harris. I didn't even need these extra Russian documents.'

I wanted to tell him that he's the historian, he should have checked his facts. Why didn't he manage to find out for himself the Russian documents were fakes before he sent his research for peer review? But I knew that would just make him even more angry.

I reached out towards him. He pushed me away. 'Surely there's something I can do to try to make it up to you, Arnie?'

He slumped down next to me on the sofa. Now *he's* holding his head in his hands. Finally, he looked up and met my eyes. His were cold and steely.

'This can't be undone, Lotti. It's too late. But I want you to arrange another meeting with the man who gave us these.' He waved the documents around in the air again. 'At the very least, I want to give him a piece of my mind and try to discover his motives.'

Given the damage he's caused, I half expect my contact not to answer when I call him. But then, perhaps the man who calls himself Fyodor Chernyshevsky is just another Stasi dupe, like I am. Persuading him to meet us near the new pub in Gorbitz is easier than I expect. He doesn't seem to realise the mess he's made of another man's life.

By the time we get to Gorbitz, and are waiting outside Zum grüner Heinrich, Arnie has calmed down a little, although he barely speaks to me on the bus or train ride there. We only have to wait about five minutes until 'Chernyshevsky' turns up. More and more I'm thinking he's probably not Russian at all. After all, we East Germans all learn Russian at school. He's probably just another Stasi unofficial informer, like I am.

The man hisses at us to follow him, and leads us to an area where some of the apartment blocks haven't been completed and the street lighting hasn't yet been switched on. It will be easier to talk there, he says.

I don't like the semi-darkness, especially given the mood Arnie is in. Anything could happen.

When 'Chernyshevsky' finally gets to somewhere he feels comfortable, he turns towards Arnie.

'What was it you wanted?' he asks.

Just the fact that the question has been asked suddenly transforms Arnie into a raging madman. He's yelling at the man, beating his chest with his fists. The man can't understand what's going on. He tries to explain he was just asked to do a job for a small amount of money, that he had no idea the documents were faked. Still, Arnie berates him and has now grabbed hold of him. At first, the man backs away onto some duckboards between the newly laid concrete, but then realises he's stronger. He gets Arnie in a headlock, and starts punching him round the head. I'm worried he's going to kill him.

'Let him go,' I yell.

Then I see the man pick something up. A broken concrete block. It looks like he's going to start to use that on poor Arnie. I look round frantically for a weapon myself to try to help my friend. As the man looks on the point of smashing Arnie on the skull, I find a piece of metal pipe, grab it, and with all the force I can muster, bring it down hard on the back of his head.

The man's grip loosens, he stumbles backwards, and falls to the floor. Arnie gets up slowly, shakes himself down. Then he realises the man has fallen into the concrete. He's sinking, frantically waving his arm for help. Arnie grabs it.

'Help me pull him out, Lotti,' he cries.

But this is the man who has come between me and Arnie – the boy I fell in love with all those years ago at the top of the *Personenaufzug* in Bad Schandau. Instead of trying to help pull him out, a flash of anger comes over me and I push down on his head.

Arnie looks at me as though I'm a madwoman, yanks me away, and continues frantically trying to pull the man out. Eventually he realises he's not strong enough, that it's hopeless, and more than that – that if we stay here we're both in danger of being accused of murder.

'What the hell do you think you were doing, Lotti?' he shouts at me.

That provokes a slanging match between us. Me accusing him of never loving me. Him accusing me of betraying him and undermining his life's work.

Then suddenly we come to our senses, and realise we have to get away from here. That we're now fugitives. I reach into my coat pocket to check my purse is still there with my return train and bus tickets.

That's when I realise.

It's disappeared!

We try to look for it, but neither of us has a torch, and I realise Arnie's also lost his glasses. Then we see some people coming, and decide we have to get out of there.

I'm annoyed, though. I'd only just been paid my monthly retainer by Bahlow. I had a hundred marks in that purse.

A hundred marks I'll never see again.

48

Müller and Tilsner turned the corner into the corridor leading to Southwick's cell. Up ahead she saw two men walking quickly in the other direction. The gait and body shape of one of them looked familiar. She was racking her brain, trying to pinpoint it in her memory, when she saw a flash of the side of the man's face as he turned the far corner and disappeared from view.

It was Weiß, or Breitmann, the fake Stasi agent.

'Quick, Werner!' she shouted, as she broke into a run, desperate to get to Southwick, fearing the worst.

She turned the cell door lock and rushed in. Southwick was swinging from a makeshift noose. His lips blue, eyes bulging, tongue trapped outside his mouth in his clenched-together jaws.

Müller rushed to the body and tried to lift it up. 'Help me, Werner. Quickly!'

Tilsner dived into the cell after her and grabbed Southwick's body, lifting him up as far as possible.

'In my back pocket,' he shouted. 'There's a penknife. Use that to cut the material.'

Müller pulled the stool over, climbed onto it, then opened the penknife and began to saw at the bedsheet. After a few seconds it ripped free.

Tilsner carried the man to the bed and then began mouth-to-mouth ventilation, timing a series of blows then resting, then starting again. In between, he urged Müller to push the alarm in the corridor to summon help.

Finally, Southwick began to take a few weak breaths on his own, but they were laboured, as though he was on the edge of death.

Müller knelt down and whispered into his ear. 'What happened, Arnold?'

'T . . . t . . . t . . . two . . . men.' He barely got the words out.

'Names?' asked Müller.

The man just made a fractional shake of his head. Then he tried to speak again. 'M . . . m . . . my . . . re . . . search. Please. You must.'

'What do you mean, Arnold?'

'H . . . h . . . hid . . . den.'

'Where?'

'G . . .'

'I couldn't hear that, Arnold.'

'Gorb . . .' Each word was dying in the man's throat, as though he didn't have enough breath left in his lungs. But he was desperate to get his message across.

Müller was aware help had now arrived behind her. Medics had taken over from Tilsner. They tried to put an oxygen mask on Southwick, but he pushed it away. He still obviously needed to get his message across.

'... itz ... pub ... found ... ation ...st ... one ... be ... hind.' The man slumped back. One of the medics began chest compressions. Then he began mouth-to-mouth again.

Müller realised Tilsner was talking in a low voice to another man who'd entered ... *Bahlow! What the fuck does he want?* She beckoned Tilsner away. 'We've got to get up to Gorbitz, quickly. There's something there he wants us to find.'

Although she'd been speaking *sotto voce*, Bahlow had evidently overheard.

'I can take you up there, Comrade *Hauptmann*. Given what's just happened, there's a few things I need to explain to you.'

Müller was about to decline the offer, but Tilsner thought otherwise. 'I think he's on our side,' he whispered. 'Let's see what he has to say for himself.'

Müller was reluctant to leave Southwick until she knew whether he'd pulled through or not, but a glance at the medics gave her the answer. The one who'd been attempting a second bout of mouth-to-mouth resuscitation gave a small shake of his head. His colleague covered Southwick's lifeless body with a blanket.

49

'You do understand the danger you're putting yourselves in, don't you?' said Bahlow, as he raced through Dresden's back-streets, eyeballing Müller in the rear-view mirror of the Volvo.

'I simply want to solve this case,' replied Müller.

'I've already told you, you won't solve it. The best you can do is get the truth out there, but you won't be able to do that here in the Republic. Why do you think Southwick is dead?'

'I don't know. But I saw that fake Stasi agent – Weiß or whatever his name is – in the corridor outside Southwick's cell.'

'That figures,' said Bahlow. 'I'm going to tell you some things, and then you're going to forget you ever heard them from me. If you ever repeat them in public, linking them to me, I will deny I said them until I'm blue in the face. Is that understood?'

Müller nodded. But that didn't seem to be good enough for the Stasi major.

'I need to actually hear you say it.'

Müller sighed. 'I understand and agree with your terms. Whatever you say won't get linked back to you.'

Bahlow changed the angle of the mirror. 'Tilsner?'

'Whatever she says, I agree with.'

Müller wished it was always the case, but his answer seemed to satisfy the Stasi man.

While making sure he kept one eye on the traffic, Bahlow then began a detailed explanation of what exactly Arnold Southwick's research had involved – occasionally checking in the mirror to make sure Müller and Tilsner were listening, and understanding.

First, he revealed Southwick's personal interest in his research: the death of his baby brother in the Hull Blitz that preceded the attack on Dresden by some three or four years. Then how – as a boy – he'd taken part in a secret study into the psychological effects wrought by the Nazi bombers. Finally, the key part of the jigsaw. How, as an eminent historian later in life, he'd been presented with the evidence that Britain's wartime leaders had deliberately perverted the results of this study – which showed that carpet bombing *didn't* undermine a population's morale, and was therefore pointless – and turned it on its head to claim morale *was* destroyed. And how they then used this as justification to bomb Dresden to smithereens, unleashing a terrible, merciless firestorm on the city once known as the Florence on the Elbe.

Müller was about to ask a question, but it died in her throat as she noticed – as Bahlow held her gaze in the rear-view mirror – the moisture gathering in his eyes.

'Fearsome, massive bombing raids, barbaric bombing raids, in which I lost both my parents.' There was a pause, as Bahlow tried to compose himself, his voice choking with his own memories and bitterness. After a moment, he continued. 'To

Southwick, this was proof of a war crime – and that Winston Churchill, his chief scientific adviser, Frederick Lindemann, and the head of bomber command, Arthur Harris, were all guilty. They were all war criminals. He wanted a case brought against them – or at least against the only remaining survivor – Bomber Harris.'

'Why was that enough to get him killed?' asked Tilsner. 'The Nazis started the war, they lost, how would any war crime trial have succeeded?'

'It probably wouldn't,' conceded Bahlow. 'That's not the point. The British government didn't want their war heroes' names blackened.'

Müller was aware of her eyes widening in disbelief as Bahlow continued his account. How he himself was assigned to the case when the Republic apparently wanted Southwick's research strengthened. How he was told to use his contact, Lotti Rolf, to introduce Southwick to a Russian who would produce more secret documents – proving that Churchill ignored a request by Stalin *not* to bomb Dresden because of all the refugees there.

Tilsner gave a disbelieving laugh. But Bahlow simply acknowledged it by agreeing that it should have made him suspicious. Why would someone like *Stalin* care about something like that? Nevertheless, he explained, he had a personal interest – because of what had happened to his parents – in making Southwick's research paper as strong as possible and for the truth to be revealed about the Dresden bombings.

'The only trouble was, the Russian documents were fakes – and easily proved to be fakes.'

'I don't understand,' said Müller.

'It was a deliberate ploy by my superiors in the Ministry for State Security to wreck Southwick's research,' said Bahlow, apologetically.

He went on to explain how Britain and the Republic had come to an arrangement. How initially, the Republic saw Southwick's paper as a way to extract money from Britain in the way of reparations to help with the country's hard currency crisis. When the Stasi high-ups came to realise that wasn't going to happen, someone had the brighter idea of helping to suppress Southwick's findings – and the genuine documents about the psychological study – by providing him with more *fake* documents. These were the Soviet documents about Stalin. Bahlow claimed the aim was to destroy Southwick's entire reputation, as well as discredit his research, in exchange for a rather large sum of hard currency from Britain.

Then, as Müller stifled a gasp, Bahlow delivered his killer line – revealing who their Concrete Man was, knowledge he'd obviously had for some time, while Müller and Tilsner had been chasing their tails to try to unravel the mystery.

'The man who was killed here, in Gorbitz, was supposedly the "Russian" supplying the fake documents – although my information is that he was a fairly lowly Stasi operative suckered into doing it for a cash backhander. He's the one who lost his life – in an argument with Southwick and Lotti Rolf that appears to have gone sour.' If Müller and Tilsner now accepted Bahlow's account, it was Lotti Rolf who wielded the near fatal blow, although Bahlow's view was that she wasn't

deliberately trying to kill the man. It was more a case of protecting Southwick.

'But I was duped as well,' insisted Bahlow. 'That's when
I began helping you two. When I found out.'

'Why should we believe you?' asked Müller.

'I've already seen you looking into my eyes, Karin,' said
Bahlow, adjusting the rear-view mirror so that their eyelines
met again.

Müller could see the previous moisture had become fully
formed tears. They could be crocodile tears, of course, but she
didn't think so. If Bahlow had indeed lost both his parents in the
Dresden firebombing, and Müller had no reason to doubt that,
then of course he would have a burning desire for the truth to
come out – even after all these years.

'So what happens now?' asked Müller. She realised they'd
reached Gorbitz, and Bahlow had parked where Concrete
Man's body had been discovered, just a few days earlier at the
start of all this.

'That's up to you two,' said Bahlow. 'I saw that Southwick
tried to whisper something to you, just before he died. The Stasi
and the British know that he rewrote his research, omitting reference to the Soviet documents. They are both determined to
get hold of that and destroy it. I suspect the reason we found
him swinging there in his cell is that he wouldn't tell them
where it is. If he's told you, it's on your conscience what you
do with it. I very much hope that – somehow – it sees the light
of day. But you can be sure if my colleagues in the Ministry for
State Security or the British get hold of it first, it won't. And

if they know you've got it, I'm afraid it's your lives that will be in danger.'

Müller was tempted to wait until Bahlow had disappeared before trying to follow Southwick's whispered instructions. There was only one pub that had so far been built in Gorbitz – the ubiquitous Zum grüner Heinrich – and Müller already knew that was where the housing estate's foundation stone lay too – in the pub's wall.

In the end, it was Bahlow himself who settled the matter. He must have overheard part of what Southwick had said. 'I can help if you like. As you no doubt know, myself and some of my fellow agents posed as builders while we were staking out the murder scene at the start of all this. I've still got my hard hat and overalls in the boot. And some tools. I might be able to provide the cover you need.'

Once Bahlow had kitted himself up, they strolled towards the pub and located the foundation stone in the wall. No one seemed to be paying them a second glance, but Bahlow made play of preparing a chisel and hammer, as though he was doing something official.

Meanwhile, Müller ran her fingers round the edge of the stone, trying to find if any papers had been slipped into the cracks.

No luck.

There were no gaps. The area around stone had been freshly pointed – which seemed to imply someone had indeed recently tampered with it. Bahlow's skills as a construction worker would need to be put to the test.

'Do you think you can get it out, or at least loosen it?' she hissed into the Stasi man's ear, while Tilsner put his body in the way to try to shield what they were attempting to do from prying eyes.

'I can have a go,' replied Bahlow, as he began to chip away at the mortar.

It didn't take him more than a few minutes to loosen the stone. He gestured for Tilsner and Müller to swap places, and for Müller's deputy to help him lift it out.

Müller knew she was supposed to be keeping guard, but she couldn't help sneaking looks behind her. The two men gave one final heave and pulled the stone out. As they did so, Müller turned and moved forward.

The resulting cavity seemed empty, save for small pieces of concrete and mortar debris. Frantically, she ran her gloved hand round it – searching for something, anything.

'*Scheisse!*' Swearing was more Tilsner's forte, but she felt a horrible cloud of disappointment settle over her. But just as soon as it did, her mind started working again. The stone *had* been tampered with. *It must have been, that's why the mortar was fresh.* Without waiting to explain what she was doing to Bahlow and Tilsner, she raced towards the pub entrance. Once inside, she sought out the manageress they'd talked to about the drunk that Jäger had tried to claim was Concrete Man. She remembered the woman's apparent desire to bore them with the explanation of the pub's name.

Müller flashed her *Kripo* ID, although the woman clearly recognised her.

'The foundation stone outside. When was it laid?'

'Six months or so ago,' said the woman. 'Right at the beginning of construction.' *So the mortar shouldn't have looked as fresh and new as it did*, thought Müller. 'They didn't do a very good job, mind you, officer.'

Müller's antennae began to quiver. 'Why do you say that?'

'Well, it's already loose. We've asked the building team to fix it several times – they always seem to be too busy.'

'Where can I find the building team?'

The woman checked her watch. 'At this time, you won't. Their site hut's up at the top of the hill, where the Leutewitzer Ring bends round, but this will be their lunch—'

Müller didn't wait for the woman to finish her sentence. She ran back outside and then motioned Tilsner and Bahlow towards the Stasi officer's car.

'Are you going to tell us what's going on?' asked Tilsner.

'We need to drive to the top of the hill, as quickly as possible.'

The site hut looked shut. Müller rapped on the door.

It opened slowly, and a corpulent man who was almost a *Doppelgänger* for Bodo Achterberg appeared in front of them.

'What?' he asked sullenly.

Müller again showed her ID, but the man looked less than impressed at being disturbed – police or not.

'Has the building team done any work recently at the pub-restaurant down the hill?' she asked.

The man looked at her as though she was mad. 'How the hell would I know? I'm just the security guard.'

Müller glared at him. 'Are there log books of the work that's been undertaken? Repair requests? That sort of thing?'

'You're asking the wrong man. They're all on their breaks. You need to come back later.'

Tilsner suddenly lurched forward and grabbed the man, pinning him by the throat against the door frame. 'Do you want to be arrested and spend the night in a police cell?'

The man coughed as he fought to breathe, then rasped out a 'no'. He seemed to be frantically looking over Tilsner's shoulder. Then he saw something and slumped in relief.

'There, behind you in that mustard-coloured Trabi.' Müller turned and saw a man enjoying a quiet smoke in his car, oblivious to what was going on a few metres away. 'That's Wilhelm, the site foreman. He sometimes sits in his car to have his lunch – thank God he's still here. He'll be able to tell you all you need to know.'

Once the man called Wilhelm had been brought over to the hut, Tilsner finally released the other man, who sank heavily into the office's only chair, rubbing his throat.

Müller asked the same questions of Wilhelm that she had of his colleague a few seconds earlier.

'Yes,' he immediately said. 'It was the other day we sorted it out. The manageress had noticed the stone was loose. It wasn't a big job.'

'Did you find any documents or papers there?'

The man's thin-faced frown in the dim winter light of the hut looked almost diabolic. Then his face relaxed.

'Aha, yes. Now you mention it. One of the men said they'd found something – an old plastic bag of rubbish behind the stone. I would think one of the original crew just—'

Müller interrupted him. 'Where is it?' she shouted. At the same time, her heart sank. If they thought it was simply rubbish, then it would have been thrown away by now, surely?

The man picked a torch off the table, and took it towards the corner of the hut.

'You're in luck. We haven't emptied the bin yet.' He presented a black bag to Müller. 'It might be somewhere in there. The plastic bag was bright orange. You might manage to find it.'

Müller tipped the contents of the bag over the floor.

'I hope you're going to clear all that up again,' said the foreman.

She started pawing through the contents while Tilsner held the torch to one side, pulling back and coughing as cement dust rose from the pile.

As she scraped the debris away, she suddenly spotted a corner of orange plastic.

Shielding the contents, she pulled out a transparent plastic folder, and held it up for her and Tilsner's eyes only.

As they began to read, they realised Arnold Southwick's dying words had led them to what he wanted them to find.

The bombing of Dresden on February 13 and 14 1945 and how it can be shown to be a War Crime, with reference to the personal responsibility of Sir Winston Churchill,

Frederick Lindemann (1st Viscount Cherwell), and Sir Arthur Harris

By DR ARNOLD SOUTHWICK, Dresden University
of Technology
February 1982

Müller continued to shield the document from everyone other than Tilsner, and then flicked through it. She didn't understand all of the English – especially some of the technical and legalistic terms. But she understood enough to know that Bahlow's earlier confession in the car had been the truth.

She also didn't doubt his warnings that both the Republic and the British would go to any lengths to make sure this didn't get into the public domain. But she had been entrusted with it by an innocent, dying man. The question was, what the hell could she or Tilsner do about it now?

50

When the call from Jäger came through on Bahlow's car radio set, Müller was inclined to ignore it. But Jäger seemed somehow to know she was there, and sounded desperate.

She didn't really care if Bahlow and Tilsner overheard the conversation. But to give at least a semblance of privacy, she stepped out of the car with the handset. While she would try to do what she could to honour Arnold Southwick's last wishes, her real priority lay in getting Jannika and Johannes to safety as soon as possible, now she knew the full extent of what was going on at their special sports school. The trouble was, Jäger was intimately involved in that too – he knew everything she knew.

So when he said, '*I need to meet you, Karin,*' she knew she would.

'Where, and what's it about?'

'*I can't discuss what it's about on an open line. Just take it from me, it's in your interests.*'

'Where?' she repeated.

'*At the Basteibrücke. Do you know where that is?*'

'Yes. Near Rathen. Above the Elbe Valley. But it seems a little inconvenient. Can't we meet in Dresden?'

'*No, Karin, we can't. Where are you at the moment?*'

'In the western part of Dresden.'

'*In an hour's time, then. That should give you plenty of time. And if Southwick handed you any documents before he died, or indicated to you where they were hidden, make sure you bring them with you.*'

Instead of driving to the spa town of Rathen, and then walking, Müller approached her rendezvous with Jäger from the high sandstone plateau above the Elbe Valley. The decision meant she was soon driving through low cloud as the Wartburg climbed up towards the rear of the tourist attraction. Once she'd parked in the near-empty car park, and began walking past the hotel and restaurant – both of which looked closed for the season – to the bridge itself, she found she was trudging through an incessant fine drizzle, with visibility reduced to a hundred metres or so.

Behind the greyness, there ought to be magnificent vistas of the Elbe Valley itself, as well as the strange rock shapes for which the area – Saxon Switzerland – was famed. But in this weather, she wasn't sure she would see anything. All that was visible through the mist here were the darker, diffuse outlines of the surrounding trees.

The only sounds were her own footsteps on the track and the doleful drips of water from the tree canopy and closed buildings.

According to her map, there were just a few metres to go. And yet still she could see little or nothing.

As she got to the very edge of the high plateau, the grey veil of mist suddenly lifted. Below her, the crenelated pedestrian viaduct that was the famed Bastei Bridge, surrounded by gnarled, giant figures of rocks – hewn and weathered by nature over hundreds of thousands, perhaps millions of years.

She saw a figure at the far end of the bridge, and immediately knew it was Jäger even though his back was to her – his out-of-fashion haircut was recognisable anywhere. When he'd radioed in requesting the meeting, his voice had held an almost frightened tone. Here, he was dwarfed by nature – by the strange, almost mystical rock formations, enveloped in swirling columns of mist, and the sheer drop of hundreds of metres to the Elbe Valley below.

It took Müller a few minutes to reach him, winding down a circuitous path. Then she began the walk across the bridge itself towards the figure of the man her career had been so closely entwined with. She couldn't help feeling that career was now in its death throes – this, however it played out, felt like the final act. The location Jäger had chosen had the magnificence of an open-air theatre, and perhaps – therefore – it was an appropriate stage.

Only when she got nearer, and the man turned – hearing her footsteps, echoing against the valley walls below – did she realise what was going on.

She'd walked straight into a trap.

This wasn't Jäger. Just someone dressed exactly like him – probably wearing a wig from the Stasi's disguise box. Instinctively, she began to reach for her shoulder holster.

'Freeze!' shouted the man, drawing his own handgun. A Makarov. She was close enough to recognise it. So even though it wasn't Jäger, he almost certainly *was* a Stasi agent – one she didn't recognise. 'Put your hands above your head, Comrade Müller.'

She did as she was told, but at the same time glanced round to see if there was an escape route, back along the way she'd just come.

There wasn't. Another man was blocking the other end of the bridge. And he – too – held a raised gun.

But this was someone she *did* recognise. The English business-man from the *Interhotel* in Dresden. Brian Jones, namesake of the long-dead Rolling Stone. Only clearly he wasn't a businessman at all – and his real name probably wasn't Brian Jones.

So the trap hadn't just been laid by the Stasi. They were obviously working hand-in-hand with the British Secret Intelligence Service.

She was in its jaws – both sides determined to stop her from bringing Southwick's research to the audience it deserved.

The Stasi man spoke next. 'We need Southwick's research paper, Comrade Müller. We know you have it. It really isn't a police matter. Unless you hand it over to us, your career will be as good as over. In fact, that will probably be the least of your troubles. So could you hand it to me now, please?'

As he spoke, she saw him slip the safety catch on the Makarov.

She knew then that it was all over.

For a long time, she'd been coming to a conclusion that she could no longer work for a state which lied and cheated in this way. She knew the Republic didn't have a monopoly on lying and cheating – governments in the West no doubt acted in the same way, for different ends. The presence of 'Brian Jones' behind her was proof enough of that.

All she cared about now, all that was left, was her children and *their* future. She knew she had to survive, if only to be able to rescue them. To provide them with a better life. But how could she do that here in this rotten state, one that had promised so much, but sunk so low?

So perhaps she should have done with it. Give them their beloved research paper. Let the British hide their secrets, and let them pay the Republic for the privilege.

But then that would be betraying Rüdiger Bahlow, a man orphaned by the Anglo-American terror bombing. A Stasi agent, but – if what he said was true – one of the rare good ones.

It would be betraying Lotti Rolf, who'd only been trying to do her best in her own misguided way.

Over and above all that, it would be betraying Arnold Southwick, a man who was principled enough to die for his beliefs.

So, across the span of the bridge, she shouted a single word. 'No.'

There was a pause then. An overwhelming silence waiting for the Stasi man's gunshot. Or would it be Jones to fire first?

Then she realised they weren't shooting, but advancing towards her – one from the front, one from behind.

She made a quick calculation. Could she fire off a round before they took her down? The answer was clear. She'd be gunned down while still reaching into her shoulder holster.

They were nearly upon her, from front and back. It was almost over.

Then a shout.

'Freeze, both of you. *Kriminalpolizei!* Drop your weapons. Hands above your heads.'

Tilsner!

She tried to see where he was, but the echoes of his voice made that difficult. It sounded like there were two Tilsners, three perhaps, even four.

The Stasi officer had ducked down behind the rampart-like side of the bridge, his gun still trained on Müller, ignoring Tilsner's instruction.

Then something in his look made her turn round. Jones had crept up behind her, keeping his body below the level of the parapet side of the bridge. She started to draw her gun but he was on her before she could, and she felt the cold metal jab of a gun barrel at her temple, and her gun arm yanked up behind her back to her shoulder blades. The pain forced her to drop her own weapon.

'I've got a gun pointing at your boss's head, *Oberleutnant* Tilsner. Show yourself and drop your weapon or—'

A shot rang out.

Müller found herself thrown backwards, covered in blood and gore. Confused, at first she thought Jones had pulled the trigger, and that her own flesh and blood had splattered over her but that – miraculously – she had survived.

Then she realised the miracle was Tilsner's shooting skills.

Despite the fact that Jones had her in a stranglehold, Tilsner had blown the British agent's brains out with a single shot.

She stumbled, trying to wipe the mess away from her face and eyes.

Then another shot.

This time, it was the Stasi agent, head above the parapet, firing at Tilsner.

Then a third rang out, just a millisecond later – as though it was an echo.

She saw the Stasi man staggering backwards, clutching at his chest.

But he still had his gun in his hands.

He turned, still stumbling, and pointed it at Müller.

'Give . . . me . . . those . . . doc—'

There was no need for a fourth shot from Tilsner. The man had sunk to the floor, the life drained out of him.

Then silence. Not even the sound of birdsong. Such a stifling silence, Müller could hear her own rasping breaths, slowly settling from hyperventilation.

Then she heard footsteps, someone dragging her to her feet. For an awful moment she thought it was Jones, somehow recovered from his injuries, but as she turned, she fell into the man's arms.

It was Tilsner himself. She'd never been more pleased to see her deputy.

Slumped on the ground at one end of the bridge, in a pool of blood, his gun by his side, the Stasi agent who'd been posing as

Jäger. She turned, and just a couple of metres from her, a near identical sight. The agent known as 'Brian Jones', lying with his brains blown to bits.

She let Tilsner hug her, let him kiss her, let him almost squeeze the life out of her.

'I think I've gone too far this time,' he said. 'And we don't have Jäger to clear up the mess.'

Just then, they heard a muffled cry from a crevasse below the bridge.

'Help, help!' A man's voice.

And they knew whose voice it was.

Jäger's.

This time the real one – not the fake.

Tilsner was soon climbing over the parapet, then easing himself down onto one of the rock outcrops. Müller moved over to the side of the bridge to watch him. Jäger was there below, in some sort of small cave or crevasse in the rock, having forced the material covering his face away from his mouth. But his hands were still tied behind his back, his feet bound together.

She watched as Tilsner sawed at the bindings with his penknife, finally cutting the Stasi *Oberstleutnant* free. Once Jäger had shaken himself down, both men climbed back up to the level of the bridge, and surveyed the scene.

'I've managed to clear up the mess made by you two before, but I won't be able to do it this time,' said Jäger. 'And, however it plays out, I will no doubt be implicated too. I think they wanted rid of all of us, to be honest, that's why we were all put on this case. Although I'm sure they didn't want it to end this way.'

'So do you have any bright ideas what we do now?' asked Müller.

'We need to get away,' replied Jäger. 'And get our children away from that awful sports school.'

'And how – exactly – do you suggest we do that?' asked Müller. Stating the obvious wasn't really much of a help.

There was a moment's silence, then it was a remarkably calm-sounding Tilsner who spoke next.

'I may have a solution,' he said. 'I could see which way things were going. It's something I've been working on for a while.'

51

Just a few years earlier, this would have seemed unbelievable to Müller. Here she was, sitting in a car with Tilsner and Jäger, about to try to do one of the most dangerous things it was possible to do in the Republic. But to do it with *them*? Well, just five short years ago, when she discovered what they got up to as teenage boys during the war at Gardelegen, it would have been unthinkable. Beyond the pale. Yet here she was. Jäger – once they'd rescued him from the rock cave below the *Basteibrücke* – had convinced her this was their only option. What had surprised Müller was that Tilsner himself had already made preparations. But then again, three years ago he'd nearly done it on his own. He'd only turned back to save her. Now he'd just saved her for a second time.

'Isn't she going to smell a rat?' asked Müller, as they approached the sports school.

'Who?' said Jäger. 'The deputy director? I don't think so. I've phoned ahead, sent through the necessary authorisations outlining that we're on a joint operation in the Oberhof area. My rank and title – the ministry I work for – can still instil fear outside the organisation, Karin. Inside, well, as you know that's a different story.' The man sounded almost sad that his previous reputation *within* the Stasi had eroded so far. Eroded to such an extent that he felt this was his only remaining option.

Tilsner slapped the Wartburg's wheel. 'Come on.' He checked his watch again for the second time in the space of five minutes. 'You two need to get a move on. They'll already be waiting – ready to start things up.'

Müller knew this was it. The start of the subterfuge. The beginning of a journey where there was no turning back – whatever happened. It was all very well to risk it for herself – but she would be risking her children's lives too.

The deputy director of the school, as Jäger had intimated, was as compliant as a meek little lamb. The three children – Jäger's teenage son, a slimmed down, younger version of his father, together with Jannika and Johannes – were waiting with an overnight bag packed each.

'Once again,' said the woman, 'I must insist that all the children are returned for the start of classes tomorrow. I've agreed to let you take them out to supper as an exception – and thank you for the signed authorities, Comrade *Oberstleutnant*.' She barely acknowledged Müller – it was clear the power lay in Jäger's rank with the Stasi, something that had obviously impressed the woman.

'Aren't we going to Oma's first to pick her up?' asked Jannika, once she realised the car was heading out of Oberhof. 'This isn't the way, is it?'

'No, we're going to a special restaurant a bit further away,' said Müller.

'How much further? I'm uncomfortable sitting on you.'

With one adult and three children in the rear seats, Müller had to agree it was a squeeze. 'It won't be much longer. Try to get some sleep, otherwise you'll be tired at school tomorrow.' In the back of her mind, she wondered whether it was fair to lie to the twins in this way. But after what she and Jäger had learned, they were both desperate to get their children away from the school.

They drove for nearly a hundred kilometres, ironically virtually due east, despite their plans. As though they were going back to Dresden. But soon after Müller spotted the first signs to Ziegenrück, Tilsner turned off down a forest track. After a few metres, there was a barrier across their path. Jäger jumped out of the car. He lifted it, and then let it fall again once Tilsner was through before running to get back in to the passenger seat.

'You're sure they'll be there?' he asked Tilsner.

'Don't worry. It's all in hand.'

'Why are we driving up a forest track?' asked Jens.

His father turned to him. 'You know a lot of my work is secret. We're going on a short journey – it's a mission.'

'A mission?' the boy said, incredulously. 'I hope you're going to get me back to school on time, like you promised the deputy director. I've got time trials for my age group in the biathlon tomorrow.'

'It will all be fine,' said Jäger.

Müller didn't share his confidence. She knew what they were doing was about the riskiest thing they could do. She gave Jannika and Johannes a squeeze.

'So you promise?' insisted Jens.

'I said so, didn't I?' replied Jäger, tetchily. 'Now be quiet.'

'Are we nearly there, Mutti?' asked Johannes.

'Not long now,' said Müller. 'Just a few minutes.'

They arrived at a clearing. Tilsner killed the headlights, plunging everything into darkness. Müller had looked at the weather forecast – it was a cloudy night, but no rain predicted, but equally no moon or starlight. Blackness enveloped them.

'I don't like this, Mutti. It's frightening,' whined Jannika.

'Shush!' snapped Müller, more fiercely than she meant to.

Then they heard a match struck, and saw its flare illuminating a single figure in front of them. Then the orange glow of a lit cigarette, and a face peering at the driver's window. Tilsner wound it down.

'You took your time, didn't you? I was getting worried.' The man peered into the car. 'Jesus, how many of you are there? That's more than we agreed.'

'It is what it is,' said Tilsner. 'And it's too late to change things now.'

'Well, I suppose it's your risk.'

Müller gripped the edge of the rear seat hard. She didn't want her fears to become obvious to the children. She was going to have a hard enough job persuading them to come as it was.

For Jäger, with a wilful teenager, the task would be even more difficult.

As her eyes became accustomed to the darkness, she saw Tilsner, Jäger, and the other man hauling apparatus from the undergrowth into the clearing. The children had no idea what it was, not yet. Once the men had sorted things as they wanted them, they signalled for Müller and the children to join them.

'What's going on?' asked Jens. 'I don't like the look of this at all. I have to be back at the school first thing tomorrow.'

Müller wasn't sure if it was her place to enlighten the boy – at the same time, she didn't want him ruining everything. 'That school is a bad place, Jens. The vitamins they get you to take, the ones that are supposed to be helping you with your health and fitness, they're not. Did you not ever wonder why the Republic did so well at the last games, in the United States? The most medals of any nation, including the mighty Soviet Union. Did you not stop to think how that happened?'

'Shut up!' the boy shouted. 'You don't know what you're talking about. What the hell is going on here anyway?'

Müller grabbed Jannika and Johannes and hauled them with her, leaving the boy in the car.

'I'm frightened, Mutti,' complained Jannika.

'Me too,' whined Johannes.

She pulled them both close. Here in the Thuringian forest, the March night air was still cold. She felt them shivering and tried to stop her own trembles – even though they were nothing to do with the cold.

'We're going on a big adventure,' said Müller. 'And after that, we'll all be living together in a new house.'

'With Uncle Werner?' asked Jannika.

'I don't know about that. Perhaps. We'll see.' It was true. What would she and Tilsner do? It was the least of her worries.

Meanwhile, Jäger had started reasoning with Jens. A shouting match was ensuing, which made Müller, and no doubt Tilsner and the other man – Tilsner's fixer – nervous.

'Shh,' hissed Tilsner. 'Everyone can hear all that from miles around.'

Jäger climbed back out of the car. 'He's refusing to get out.'

'If I were you I'd tell him he'd better,' replied Tilsner. 'That car is going to be crashed off the road by Manfred here. If Jens is still inside, he'll be going over the edge with it.'

After more cajoling, Jens finally emerged with his father. But even in the darkness, Müller could tell from his body language that he still hadn't accepted what was going to happen. She couldn't worry about that. It was Jäger's problem.

Tilsner and the other man continued to fiddle with various bits of apparatus in the middle of the clearing. Finally, they indicated they were ready.

'I'm firing it up,' said Tilsner.

As he lit the flame, in the ghostly light it became clear what was going on. Müller already knew, of course.

'What is it, Mutti?' asked Johannes.

'It's a giant balloon. We're going on a balloon ride.'

'Oh wow!' exclaimed Johannes.

'I'm frightened, Mutti,' said Jannika. 'I don't want to go.'

'Shh. You'll be fine.' Müller hugged her daughter.

Gradually the balloon started to take shape as it inflated, first lying on its side on the ground, then gradually rising up, until the stay ropes holding the makeshift passenger basket became more and more taut.

Tilsner held out his hand. 'Pass me the twins.'

Johannes was no trouble, excited by the adventure. Jannika, though, was reluctant to let go of her mother until Müller promised she was getting in next. When she did, she and Tilsner looked back at Jäger.

Jens was still arguing with him.

'Are you coming or not?' shouted Tilsner. 'We'll have to release the stays.'

Jäger made to enter the basket, trying to drag Jens with him. But the boy yanked his arm away.

'Are we leaving him behind?' asked Tilsner.

Jäger looked back longingly at his son, tears in his eyes. 'Yes,' he replied, finally, clearly hoping the boy would change his mind when faced with such a stark choice.

Tilsner and the other man started to release the stay ropes. The balloon pitched left and right, as though it was going to topple. As the last rope was released, and the balloon slowly started to climb, Jäger lifted himself back out, and jumped to the ground. Müller's final view of the Stasi *Oberstleutnant* was of him clutching his son, sobbing. She dreaded to think what was going to happen to him. He'd decided to stay at the last moment, couldn't leave without his son, but how would he keep this all under wraps? Tilsner, Müller and the twins were not in a much better position – this attempt had to work. Otherwise they would either die making it, or be jailed for a very long time – and Müller would certainly have the twins taken away from her, and probably sent back to the sports school where they were filling older children like Jens with drugs.

She only hoped that Jens would recognise that, if his father was willing to drag him away from not just his sporting dreams but from his home and everything he knew, then he must have very good reason. That he was trying to save them both from a future not worth living. Could she have convinced the twins of as much, if they were Jens's age? It didn't bear thinking about.

The balloon was climbing steadily now. She wasn't sure how Tilsner was steering it – perhaps he was just trusting to the winds. They were lucky they'd picked a night when northerlies were forecast, because – although they were heading for 'the West' – the state border here with the BRD, by a quirk of geography, meant they had to travel to the south to cross it.

She felt a mixture of terror, elation, trepidation and regret. Terror that they might not survive at all, or that they might miscalculate, and land back in the Republic. Elation because – finally – she would be a free woman, and hopefully her children would grow up in a free country, able to travel where they wanted with few, if any, restrictions. Trepidation because she didn't know what they would do in the BRD, how they would survive, and whether she and Tilsner would still be a partnership, however part-time. Regret because, well, she'd shared the dream for most of her life. A dream she still believed in. A dream of a fairer, more just society, where the best health care, the best education, the best living conditions weren't just a result of how much money you earned. And now she was abandoning it, and there were no guarantees that where she was heading, life would be better.

As she thought all this, she realised the balloon had settled. Tilsner was only occasionally opening the burners to top it up with heated air to maintain their height. Finally, her heartbeat started to calm.

Jannika was still sitting, huddled, in one corner of the basket, with a blanket Müller had brought wrapped around her. But Tilsner had lifted Johannes up, so he could gaze in wonder at the scene below. They were drifting in and out of low cloud, but when it cleared the view was heart-stopping.

'Look ahead,' Tilsner pointed as he shouted. 'Those lights down there. It's the motorway crossing at Hirschberg. Those red lights are car tail lights.'

'Wow!' said Johannes. 'They look just like toys.'

'Then the row of yellowish lights facing us are the headlights of cars coming from the BRD. The line of more spaced out, whiter lights, at a ninety-degree angle to the *autobahn*, is the state border.'

Tilsner's knowledge of geography had always been pretty poor, so Müller wasn't entirely sure why she'd allowed him to become the navigator and pilot. But on this occasion, he seemed to know what he was talking about. She roused Jannika to come and take a look. The girl staggered over reluctantly, holding tight to the side rail.

'Does that mean we're going in the right direction?' Müller shouted back, knowing they were high enough up for their voices not to carry to the border guards below. She wondered if their take-off site had been discovered yet. They'd deliberately started several kilometres back from the border to try to avoid detection.

Tilsner put Johannes down for a second, got out his pocket torch, and shone it on his map. 'As far as I can work out, yes, we are. It shouldn't be too much further. But I told you before, we can't steer this thing. We're at the mercy of the wind. If it takes us off course, all we can do is go higher or lower, and hope we pick up an air current going in a slightly different direction.'

For Müller, it meant too much trusting to luck. She knew she'd put herself – and her two children – in an impossibly dangerous situation.

But she'd been desperate. To save them, and herself.

Tilsner was still having to light the burner sporadically to ensure a level flight – something he'd explained to Müller was virtually impossible. It was simply a case of knowing when to heat up the air inside the envelope of material to slowly ascend. All the time the burner was off, they were slowly descending. Already, it seemed as though the motorway crossing point was behind them.

'I'll let it descend naturally in a few minutes,' said Tilsner. 'I just want to be certain we're well into BRD territory – we probably already are.'

Müller hoped everything would hold together for the last bit of their flight. The gas tank was just a domestic propane gas bottle, turned upside down to give a better flame. The 'basket' was a large builder's pallet covered in tautened canvas to cover the gaps, and the sides were welded together handrails, stolen from somewhere or other, again covered in taut canvas-like material. The balloon itself, stitched-together material purchased by Tilsner far away near Leipzig to avoid suspicion, on behalf of a fictitious police 'sailing club'.

All of it was, no doubt, highly flammable. It was best not to think of all the things that could go wrong, and to be honest, floating relatively silently save for the rush of wind and the occasional blast of the burner, it all felt perfectly natural.

How much they were defying nature, how much they were risking, became clear in the next few seconds.

Tilsner had just opened the burner, when he let out a scream of anguish. 'Scheisse!'

Müller followed his eyeline and saw the opening of the balloon above had caught fire. Jannika and Johannes started screaming. Müller felt powerless and simply clung on to them, hoping to give them some comfort while trying to quieten them.

Turning back to the basket, Tilsner dived into the supplies bag and pulled out a handheld fire extinguisher. He broke the seal, and then aimed it at the flames.

At first, it seemed as though he couldn't get the flames to go out. Then, suddenly, he'd succeeded. But there was now a gaping hole at the side of the balloon.

'Are we falling?' screamed Müller, trying to keep the panic from her voice for the sake of the children. 'Can't you light the burner again?'

Tilsner shook his head. 'It's too dangerous with all that damaged material flapping around. It would just set light to it. We'll just have to ride it out.'

'What the fuck does that mean?' screeched Müller.

'Mutti!' yelled Jannika, more concerned that her mother had sworn, possibly not understanding the life-threatening nature of their predicament.

'Just hold on tight to the kids,' shouted Tilsner. 'We'll be descending a bit more quickly than I'd have liked, but look.' He pointed upwards to the balloon above. 'It's still holding most of the hot air, it's only the bottom that's damaged. I don't think we've got too much to worry about.'

'But have we got far enough into the BRD – are you even sure we're over the BRD?' She looked out of the basket and tried to focus on the land far below. Save for the occasional isolated light, there was nothing visible. It was all horribly dark – it looked to be a thinly populated, forested area.

'We must be,' said Tilsner in a confident voice. 'I told you, I was about to start the descent anyway. We'll just be going down a little more quickly than before.'

The children didn't seem to fully understand the conversation. To them, this was all probably like a dream. Normally, they would be safely in bed at the school – although Müller knew in a few years' time, it would be far from safe for them. She just hoped that the children's dream wasn't about to turn into a nightmare.

There was no real sense that they were descending, but Tilsner assured her they were. 'It won't be long now. When I give the word, brace yourself and the kids. Get them to hold their arms over the back of their heads, like they show you in those aircraft safety demonstrations.'

Müller sat down with the children in the basket, curling herself into a ball, and getting Johannes and Jannika to do the same. She glanced up, and saw Tilsner standing upright still, watching for where they would be landing, but unable to exert any control on their home-made flying machine.

'Right, we're landing in trees, I'm afraid,' he shouted. 'It's going to be bumpy! Brace!'

As he yelled the word, he ducked down with them. They all huddled together as they heard and felt the first crack and crash of wood splitting, then another, a third, one side of the basket splitting away so the adults and children were clinging to the remainder for dear life as they fell in jerks and judders.

Then a final thud reverberated through the whole basket, and Müller was tossed to one side.

Then silence, save for the soft sound of the remaining balloon material nestling down on top of them.

Jannika and Johannes both started yelling and crying. 'Shh,' hushed Müller. 'You're OK,' she soothed, but she didn't really know if they were.

'Is everyone all right?' asked Tilsner.

'I think so,' replied Müller, gingerly stretching herself, then getting to her feet. Up above, she could see the remains of balloon material clinging to some of the tree branches. Other boughs had been ripped off as the basket plunged to earth.

She pulled the twins to their feet. They clung to her waist. 'Are you two OK, my darlings?' she asked. But she could feel from the strength of their hugs, and the fact that they'd both stood up without problems, that they were.

Tilsner was on his feet now, too. Looking up through the trees in wonder. 'Blimey. I know I was trying to sound confident, but that was a lucky escape.'

'But we've made it,' said Müller. She hugged her deputy and sometime lover, thinking at that moment there was no one – other than her children – she would rather be with. They'd been through a lot together.

Far too much.

But they'd survived.

And now a new life beckoned them in the west. A life which – Müller knew – in many ways wouldn't necessarily be better. They had left a lot behind, and much of it she would miss. Her career as a senior policewoman – one she'd fought so hard for – was now over. There was no way the BRD would want to employ one of the Republic's cast-offs.

But one thing they had left behind, she wouldn't miss at all.

The Stasi, and all its underhand games.

The final one – co-operating with the fascists and imperialists, all for the sake of money – was too much for her to bear.

She hugged both her children tight as Tilsner started to clear away and hide the debris.

Then suddenly he stopped.

'We don't really need to do this.'

'What?'

'Hide it all away. We're not in the Republic now. We're free. We'll probably be celebrities because of our daring escape. All of this is the evidence.' He held up a piece of material – what remained of the balloon envelope – examining it as though he couldn't really believe it had worked.

Müller knew he was right. Things would be very different on this side.

Then, one little doubt entered her head.

What if Tilsner's calculations were wrong?

What if they hadn't flown far enough after all?

Suddenly, panicked, she looked left and right, expecting the Republic's border guards and dogs to pounce on them from all directions.

She realised there was nothing there. Just trees, and more trees. The trees in the west looked just the same as those in the east – that was the strange thing.

Her heartbeat settled down, and she smiled at Jannika and Johannes.

'We'd better get going then, and find western civilisation.'

One of her first jobs when they reached it would be to finally let the world have sight of Arnold Southwick's research – research which would show the terror bombings on Dresden for what they really were, and name the guilty men. It was the least she could do for the man and his memory.

Müller knew she would have regrets leaving the Republic behind. Having rediscovered her biological family – in the shape of her grandmother, Helga – she wondered if she would ever see her again. The relatives of escapers were often persecuted by the Stasi – it was a well-known fact, presumably to stop more people from trying it. She could only hope that – as a pensioner – Helga would be spared. She hoped the same for her adoptive family – Rosamund, Sara, Roland and their children. And she had never had the chance to say goodbye properly to Jonas Schmidt, who'd been with her for several years through thick and thin. She'd miss him. Even his sausage-breath and overlong explanations. Her rediscovered Father too. An army officer in the Soviet Far East. By doing what she'd done, had she wrecked any chance of ever seeing him again?

But she was thankful the other man who – by and large – had watched her back throughout would still be at her side. She grasped Tilsner's hand and squeezed it, marvelling at its solidity and power. For a man of over fifty, he was in pretty good shape. To say nothing of his balloon piloting skills.

Looking down at their joined-together hands, her eyes were drawn as always to his expensive western watch. The item that had most epitomised his divided loyalty, and his part-time affiliation to the Stasi. In the Republic, it had always looked slightly ostentatious and out of place. Here – in the BRD – it would be *de rigueur*.

She laughed to herself.

'What's wrong?' he asked.

She stopped, and turned to face him. She was tempted to caress his face, feel his whiskers. But perhaps he would find that too intimate a gesture. They still hadn't really spelled out their plans to each other – and whether their future would be together. But Müller was filled with a sudden lightness, and carefree joy. Everything would work itself out, one way or another.

She gave another little laugh.

'Nothing, Werner,' she said. 'Nothing's wrong at all.'

Epilogue

LOTTI

Sonnenstein, Pirna, East Germany
One month later

The black Volvo pulls up at the roadside just as I'm about to go into HO Gaststätte Glück Auf for the first time since all the nastiness happened. They say that timing is everything. I know who it will be even before the electric window glides down and he puts his head out.

'Jump in, Lotti, please,' he says. Ever polite, of course. Framed as a request, even though we both know it's an order.

My trip to the restaurant was partly a date – and partly a bit of solo celebration. The latest tests have shown the cancer seems to be in remission – or at least the tumours aren't growing. So perhaps all the sessions of chemotherapy have been worth it, even though I feel worse than death after each bout.

So I'm more than a little annoyed that *Major* Bahlow has seen fit to choose this moment to catch up with me. Then again, I guess I should be thankful to him. He was the one who arranged the treatment – and despite all the nastiness in Gorbitz he's kept his side of the bargain.

Of course, I was desperate when I heard about Arnold. The poor man! For a while, I felt horribly guilty, too. It was me that helped ruin his research. And it must have been the failure of that research, its undermining thanks to the false Soviet documents, which finally drove him to take his own life. I'd tried to find out what exactly happened from *Major* Bahlow – but he just parroted the official version. It's odd, really. Arnold never struck me as the suicidal type.

Once I'm in the car, the major sets off as though he's driving out towards Bad Schandau or Königstein – I hope he's not taking me back to the uranium mine. That's a part of my life I'm happy to have left behind.

'You realise I'm standing up a date by being here with you, *Major*,' I say. 'I hope it's going to be worth it.'

'I think it will be, Lotti,' he says, mysteriously.

Instead of going all the way to either Königstein or Bad Schandau, he stops the car at the nearest layby, and then turns to me.

'I'm going to tell you some things that you must never repeat, and that you never heard from me, Lotti. If you *do* ever repeat them, I'll deny it, and claim you are a fantasist. There's also the small matter of the man that was killed in Gorbitz. Now the authorities here in the Republic have probably chalked that one down to the late Dr Southwick –' as he says the name, I can't help but let out a small gasp. Poor Arnold – 'but,' he continues, 'we both know what really happened that night.'

There's a moment's silence as he allows the implications to sink in.

'Who was he?' I ask, timidly. 'I hope he didn't have family.'

'It's too late for regrets, Lotti. And no, if it's any consolation, he didn't. He was a fairly low-grade agent with the Ministry for State Security, posing as a Russian. He seemed to fool Dr Southwick, so in that respect he did his job well. His mistake was agreeing to that fateful second meeting. But I haven't brought you here to talk about that. It's history. The official version will be that he died of a heart attack or something similar, so there's no need to fret.'

'So why are we here? I haven't done anything wrong, have I?'

'Not since that night in Gorbitz, no. I want to show you something.' He delves into his briefcase, and brings out a news magazine. A *western* news magazine.

Der Spiegel.

My hands shake as I read the headline on the cover.

1945 DRESDEN BOMBINGS
Secret papers 'prove it was a war crime'

I excitedly turn the pages. There are several articles and sub-articles, photos of Winston Churchill and other wartime leaders. And a photo of Arnold, looking very dapper and professorial, poor man. Just the first few paragraphs of the main story make everything clear.

THE 'WAR CRIME' OF DRESDEN
British heroes implicated by secret papers

Previously unseen secret wartime documents suggest that the February 1945 bombing of historic Dresden and the resulting firestorm which destroyed the city and claimed the lives of more than 20,000 civilians was a premeditated act amounting to a 'war crime'. The claim comes in a paper by the late historian, Dr Arnold Southwick, who had been researching the bombings at Dresden's prestigious University of Technology.

The secret documents show how the results of a psychological study into the bombing of Hull and Birmingham were deliberately altered by Churchill's chief scientific adviser in order to justify the bombing of Dresden and other German cities – and that both Churchill and Sir Arthur 'Bomber' Harris were fully aware of this.

The Hull study – which Dr Southwick took part in as a boy, having lost his baby brother in the city's own Blitz – showed that the morale of civilians would not be crushed by heavy bombing raids. However, this study was deliberately turned on its head by Britain's wartime leaders and advisers to justify even more devastating raids on Dresden.

Dr Southwick contends this proves what many have long suspected: that the Anglo-American bombings on Dresden were a war crime.

My eyes start filling with tears as I read. I'm so proud of Arnie. So pleased that – even beyond the grave – he's managed to get his paper out into the open. That, finally, people will know the truth about the terror attacks that killed so many, and left my own face permanently scarred.

I pause a moment, and look up at *Major* Bahlow.

His own eyes are glistening. I don't really understand why – perhaps he's just pleased for me. He knows how much I suffered.

Then he seems to pull himself together.

'Anyway, Lotti. I don't want to keep you, but I thought you would appreciate that. Keep it hidden, please. It wouldn't look very good for me if people found out I'd been distributing western news magazines.'

He wipes his eyes, and starts up the car. 'You said you had a hot date back at the HO Glück Auf, didn't you? I'll take you back there now. I'm sure he'll still be waiting.'

'I'm not sure I'd say it's a *hot* date. A very lukewarm one as far as I'm concerned. It's one of the bus drivers in Sonnenstein. I think he's always had his eye on me. Mind you, he's got a bit of a roving eye, full stop.'

I don't mention it's the same driver who picked me up the night the man died in the concrete in Gorbitz.

As *Major* Bahlow says, that's best all forgotten.

Glossary

Armeegeneral	Army general
Autobahn	Motorway
Bezirk	District or region
BRD	*Bundesrepublik Deutschland* (West Germany)
DDR	*Deutsche Demokratische Republik* (East Germany)
Eingaben	Petitions. Any DDR citizen could submit these to the government
Eisbein	Salted pork knuckle
Erbsenbrei	Mushy peas
Generalmajor	Major general
Glück Auf	The traditional German miners' greeting, loosely translated as 'Good Luck!'

Ha-Neu	Nickname for the East German new town of Halle-Neustadt
Hauptmann	Captain
Hauptstadt	Capital city (in this book, East Berlin)
HO	*Handelsorganisation.* National state retail organisation administering restaurants, department stores etc.
Interhotel	East German chain of luxury hotels
Keibelstraße	Headquarters of the People's Police in East Berlin
Kinder und Jugendsportschule	Special elite sports school for children and youths
Kriminaltechniker	Forensic officer
Kripo	*Kriminalpolizei* or the *K*. The criminal investigation wing of the People's Police
Kulti	Palace of Culture
Liebling	Term of endearment, akin to 'darling'

Major	The same rank as in English, but pronounced more like *my-yor*
Makarov	Semi-automatic pistol used by the army and police in the Soviet bloc
Ministry for State Security (MfS)	The East German secret police, abbreviated to *MfS* from the German initials, and colloquially known as the Stasi – a contraction of the German name
Mit Luftpost	Airmail
Muttilein	Mother (or Mutti for short)
Normannenstraße	Stasi headquarters in East Berlin
Oberleutnant	First lieutenant
Oberst	Colonel
Oberstleutnant	Lieutenant-Colonel
Oma	Gran
Opa	Grandad

People's Police	The regular East German state police (see also *Volkspolizei*)
Personenaufzug	Passenger lift
Plattenbauten	Concrete slab apartment blocks
Polizeiruf 110	DDR police TV drama ('Police Call 110'); 110 was the equivalent of 999
Republikflüchtlinge	People who attempted to escape to the west
Sauerkraut	Fermented chopped cabbage
Scheisse	Shit
Schwebebahn	Dresden's historic suspension railway
Schwedenbecher	Swedish ice-cream sundae, a popular dessert in East Germany
Standseilbahn	Dresden's historic hill tram
Stasi	Nickname for the Ministry for State Security (*MfS*), the DDR's secret police (see above)

Unterleutnant	Sub-lieutenant
Vati	Dad
Volkspolizei	The DDR's state police (or People's Police, see above). Known as *Vopos*
Wartburg	East German car model, a step up from the Trabant
Wohnkomplexe	Housing estate
Zersetzung	Psychological manipulation technique used by the Stasi to undermine suspects

Author's Note

This novel is a work of fiction but the wartime scenes are inspired by real events.

The psychological studies carried out on children and citizens of Hull and Birmingham actually happened. They were featured in a BBC documentary on the Hull Blitz and have been the subject of research by Professor David Atkinson of the University of Hull.

According to the *Hull Daily Mail*, findings from the study remained classified until 2020. Forty leading psychologists carried out the research, and the Hull newspaper quotes Professor Atkinson as saying the results were possibly manipulated by Winston Churchill's government to justify the devastating raids on Hamburg, Dresden and other German cities.

Before his death, one of the leading scientists revealed that the study concluded that Hull wasn't going to break, and that the people were resilient, despite the ferocity of the bombings.

However, according to Professor Atkinson, once Churchill's chief scientist, Frederick Lindemann, got hold of the results, they were 'misrepresented – some say deliberately – and Churchill was told the Hull survey showed that civilians *would* break under relentless bombing, especially when they were made homeless.'

In my novel, Churchill, Lindemann and Harris are accused of committing war crimes by my fictional Hull academic, Arnold Southwick. However, I am not seeking to make that case. There are those who fervently believe the bombing of Dresden *was* indeed a war crime, but equally many who argue it was a legitimate industrial and military target, and that the attack helped to shorten the war in Europe. What is clear is that the bombing of Dresden was one of the most controversial Allied actions of the Second World War, and even Churchill himself expressed doubts after it, saying 'the destruction of Dresden remains a serious query against the conduct of Allied bombing'.

Lotti's fictional first-hand account of the bombing is an amalgamation based on some of the experiences of survivors recounted in the historian Frederick Taylor's excellent nonfiction account, *Dresden: Tuesday, 13 February, 1945*.

Much of the action in this novel centres on Gorbitz, a newbuild area in the western part of the city. Although the street and pub names are accurate, some of the blocks may not have been completed at the time my fictional events take place – I've used a little authorial licence. Similarly, I'm reliably informed that the modern part of the Polizeipräsidium was finished in 1983 and was still an uninhabitable building site in February 1982.

The suicide linked to my (fictional) sports school and the laundry woman with incriminating documents linked to East German sports doping are again based on real events – but the suicide actually happened elsewhere, and after the fall of the Wall in 1989. Jannika and Johannes were too young to have attended such a boarding school – again that is authorial licence.

Müller and Tilsner's final, desperate, act may seem too far-fetched for some. In fact, such home-made balloon escapes *did* happen: the most famous becoming a Disney film starring John Hurt. For those convinced that the ending means the series is over after six novels, well, you may be correct.

However, you might just want to check what happened when the Strelzyk family made their first escape attempt in July 1979, before successfully fleeing along with the Wetzel family in September of the same year. Would you trust Tilsner's navigational skills?

Acknowledgements

There are many people who've helped me with this series, but perhaps above all I'd like to thank those who've read and enjoyed all the novels and have written some fantastically generous reviews on places such as Amazon and Goodreads. I hope you'll be as kind to this, the sixth instalment.

Throughout the series, my BBC journalist friend and former East German citizen, Oliver Berlau, has freely given his advice and corrected many of my mistakes. Thanks so much, Oliver. For the latter books, Oliver has been joined by another former East German, the international concert pianist, Andreas Boyde. Andreas, you're a star too.

My wife Stephanie always tells me thrillers aren't really her thing, but she usually forces herself to read them and offer helpful advice. Thanks very much, Stephanie.

Particular thanks to my editor, Ben Willis, who's been fantastically supportive ever since he joined Zaffre Books. We're working on a different series next, so I can only hope that is as much fun.

And finally, special thanks to my agent Adam Gauntlett, who first spotted the potential in *Stasi Child* some six or so years ago, and has loyally stuck with me ever since. He and the team at Peters, Fraser and Dunlop have secured some great publishing deals in both the UK and foreign territories. Long may it continue, even if the 'Stasi Series' has reached its end.

Notice I said 'if'.